Averton

Terry Pellman

www.ingramcontent.com/pod-product-compliance
Lightning Source LLC
Chambersburg PA
CBHW070914180626
46817CB00003B/1049

This novel is an edited version of the book by the same name published in 2009 by Authorhouse.

Averton

by

Terry Pellman

At 1:30 A.M., a motorcycle pulled up slowly in front of a Manchester Valley Power substation, located on a rural road just outside of Averton, Ohio. The headlight and taillight were covered by sections of a plastic trash bag secured by duct tape. The passenger slid off the back and ran down into the ditch, lying tight against the ground, while the driver moved the bike a hundred feet down the road and pulled behind a roadside maple tree. Its June foliage provided cover from the minimal reflection of the pale blue crescent moon, itself partially concealed by the clouds containing what had been a potential rainstorm that passed over the yearning dry soil below.

The driver killed the engine and turned off the gas line, then lowered the bike gently to the ground and lay on the parched soil behind the craggy trunk of the tree. There was no traffic and the only sound to be heard was a thumping heart, felt in a tight throat.

The passenger had already clipped the barbed wire strands at the top of the security fence and gone over the side, landing with a soft "crunch" in the pea gravel that covered the entire area inside the enclosure. He unzipped a backpack and took out a dozen small packages. He then unwrapped the first dough-like block of C-4 explosive, the size of a television remote control. He attached the aluminum detonator, and connected it to the battery-operated timer.

The timer was set, and then the device was attached to the first tower leg. Looking around for a couple of seconds, he went on to the next, working at a feverish pace until all twelve explosive charges were in place.

Reversing his prior actions, he climbed over the fence once again and ran in the direction of his companion who had already returned the motorcycle to the pavement. As soon as he had mounted, the motorcycle sputtered away. It traveled in darkness until it was four hundred yards from the substation and around the corner of the nearby intersection with another empty road.

Fifty feet beyond the crossroad, the bike stopped again. The passenger looked at his watch while breathing rapidly from the climbing and apprehension at the realization that his watch read 1:59.

The illuminated digital display changed and the driver watched with teeth clenched in anticipation. Finally, there was a flash of light and thunderous roar of an explosion. A few seconds later, there was another, followed by the rest, no more than a few seconds apart.

The riders were bathed in heat and light. The motorcycle moved once again, dangerously fast for the lack of a headlight or light from the moon. The driver accelerated through the dancing shadows, holding onto the grips with all possible strength. However, the front tire hit a rock in the road, and in reacting, the driver under steered in a curve. The riders were cast into a ditch, while the bike stayed along the edge of the pavement.

The passenger got up slowly, in pain from many parts of his body. As he rose, he shook his fist and swore. Looking off two miles into the distance, he saw two sets of flashing blue and red lights rushing toward the sights of the explosions and resulting fires.

The driver loosened the strap of the helmet and the hair that had been tucked up into the helmet fell down around her neck as she removed it. She attempted to stand straight but found it painful to stretch to her full height of just barely over five feet.

The passenger, seeing that his companion was also reeling in pain, limped over to help her. She was still having difficulty standing, so he set the bike upright and then was relieved to find that it still ran after only one downward thrust on the kick-starter. Changing roles, the woman in the ditch became the passenger. Once again, the ride in the darkness commenced.

Near the city limits of Averton, the plastic that had shielded the headlights was ripped away. The pair motored quietly into an older residential section of the unlighted town, to a pitch-black alley behind where the slightly injured rider lived in a second-floor apartment. She strapped her helmet to the seat and then limped to the house as her companion rode away. Slowly and painfully, she climbed the dark indoor stairway to her apartment. She pulled a solitary key from her pocket and then entered the room as quietly as possible.

~~~

The fire and law enforcement personnel of Averton and Manchester County struggled to cope with the explosion and fire at the power station and resulting electrical outage for fifty square miles. Meanwhile, a muscular figure operated in the total darkness around the National Guard armory that divides the east edge of the business district from one of the worn and tired neighborhoods. Working quickly and unnoticed, he placed numerous bundles of dynamite around the foundation of the aged concrete and brick structure. A fuse was then leisurely run to the bundles and twisted together.

There was no apparent need for concern of discovery or to use any type of remote device. In the thirty-minute process, only two cars moved down this particular street of the darkened town of twenty thousand at such an hour on a Monday morning. Those who had heard the distant explosions had assumed it to be some type of accident and those who had come outside had gone back inside their homes.

The job nearly finished, there was only one more task. He looked for the non-existent traffic or observer, and then strolled casually to the van parked arrogantly near the main door to the building. He opened the rear cargo door, then with a straining tug pulled a body bag from the van and allowed it to fall to the ground with a thud. He rolled the bag and its occupant to the front steps, next to one of the dynamite charges.

A simple book match lit the end of the main fuse. He closed the van doors, then got in and calmly drove away.

Three blocks away, parked on the crest of a steep grade, he got out of the van and replaced the license plates. Back inside the van, he lit a cigarette and watched impassively at first as the armory exploded. He saw the building ripped into fragments from the several rapid blasts, then leaned forward in stunned amazement as sheets of fire and concrete projectiles obliterated the two homes bordering it as well.

The damage was enhanced by the explosion of a heating oil tank behind one of the garages. Then, burning debris that had landed on a troop transport behind the armory and set it on fire caused the flaming vehicle to erupt and explode when the inferno reached the gas tank.

The man who had set all this in motion watched intently, satisfied with his work. He let out a low whistle, shaking his head as he stubbed out the cigarette and drove away.

~~~

For several blocks in every direction around the armory, residents with racing hearts, confused in half-sleep, fumbled through the darkness. Some had been initially awakened by the destruction of the distant power station but most were now greeted by the glow of fires and shattered windows that had followed the shaking of their dwellings.

Suddenly the street in front of the armory heaved upward in flames as a natural gas main erupted, leveling one-half of a house across the way in a fiery collapse. Seconds later a woman in her early sixties ran from the ruins screaming, her pajamas in flames as she collapsed and sank into the boiling asphalt of the melting street.

Some near the blast were beginning to run outside to use garden hoses to attempt to contain the fires. Others concentrated on the many fires now feeding on the dry grass of the yards in which flaming debris had landed.

One man in his thirties, not realizing that his own house had been damaged, threw on his robe and ran down his stairs and out onto his front lawn. Looking around at the surreal spectacle of scattered brilliant fires, he turned to go back inside. He then saw that the top half of a power pole in an alley had fallen into his upstairs, the crossbeam having crashed through a window in his daughter's room.

Unable to breath, but running nonetheless, he bounded up the stairs and flung open the door to where he hoped to find the five-year old unharmed. However, as he scraped away the shards of glass from the face of the unconscious child, he was given sufficient light from the nearby flames to see that the beam has pinned her to her bed. He could hear no cries above the surrounding shouting and sirens.

Screaming his wife's name, he once again half-ran, half-fell down the stairs past his bewildered spouse. In a panic, she chased after him begging him to tell her what had happened. Bounding down the unlighted steps to his basement, he groped in darkness for the chainsaw he had used the previous day at his father's farm and rushed back upstairs to cut the beam. The saw did not start until the third try. The sobbing gasping man cut by the flickering light until he could shove the heavy pieces from on top of the girl.

The mother dove to the edge of the bed and placed her face next to that of the child. Soon she was laughing and crying hysterically as she could feel the welcome, soft breath against her own cheek.

<center>~~~</center>

Those injured themselves, or with loved ones bleeding or unconscious, tried to call for help. For their efforts they were rewarded either with dead lines damaged by the blasts or constant busy signals and overloaded cell phone circuits. Some attempted to find their way to their cars, but others jammed the streets in similar dilemmas as well as emergency vehicles rushing to the area.

This night would be filled with wailing, shrieking sirens and calls for help. The darkness was driven away by the pulsing colored lights on top of police cars, fire vehicles and ambulances. Through the night, the urgency gave way to the slow mournful pace of rescue vehicles removing the remains of several victims beyond treatment, beyond recognition.

In the shadows in her apartment, the still-trembling cyclist opened the medicine cabinet in the cramped bathroom and fumbled with the bottle of aspirin tablets. She placed six on her tongue before filling a paper cup with water and washing them down all at once.

She took a hand mirror from its place on a hook on the bathroom wall, and then shuffled into the one room that serves as the bedroom, living room and kitchen. Hands shaking, she fumbled for a flashlight in the drawer of her nightstand. Standing next to the narrow bed, she forced off her tennis shoes and raised each foot to pull off her socks.

She unsnapped the button to her torn jeans and unzipped them. Gingerly, she pulled the jeans downward and grimaced until they reached her ankles so that she could step out of them. Next, she took hold of a ragged edge of her torn nylon briefs and yanked the fabric away from the raw wound, nearly the size of the palm of her hand. In frustration and pain, she ripped away the remnants and tossed them to the floor.

She lay on the bed on her stomach, the flashlight in one hand, the mirror in the other. Moaning in pain and exhaustion and fatigued from tensing her body, she was relieved that the adventure was over. She let out a deep breath and looked backward to where the beam of the flashlight was now aimed at her backside. With the mirror, she was able to survey the extent of the damage, which extended down to the upper thigh of her right leg.

The rough surface of the edge of the road had not only ripped away her clothing but also the outer layers of her skin. She was relieved to see that though the sore patch may be ugly and full of fire there would be no need to see a doctor and rehearse a false story as to how she was injured.

She got up wearily from the bed, finished undressing and then walked back into the darkened bathroom. As she turned on the shower, she was grateful that the town's water supply was still working. She adjusted it until it was lukewarm and stepped into the stream, squinting her eyes as the water rushed over the stinging patch. It burned even more as she carefully soaped the wound to remove the remaining particles of dirt and asphalt.

Fumbling for a towel, she patted herself dry and then reached again inside the medicine cabinet, impatiently searching for a bottle of iodine. Standing on her tiptoes, she found the bottle and stepped back into the tub.

She knelt in the tub, leaning over the side. She shuddered as her lower abdomen pressed down upon the cool enamel. Suddenly shivering so that she almost dropped the full bottle, she unscrewed the top and poured the stinging orange medication over the wound. Tears streamed down her face as she laughed softly, but her silence was maintained.

CHAPTER 2

Kelly Hastings stood at the desk in his home office and looked out at the gathering in his back yard. It was a reminder of days when things were still normal, but the assembly of friends at his home was little more than a summer ritual for a Sunday afternoon, a vain attempt to grasp a carefree moment.

The Chief Detective for the Averton Police Department was weary from several twenty-hour days. They had been long and painful days of work leading nowhere but to frustration and confusion.

Spread out on the desk before him were materials for the final class he was soon to take to finish his PH.D. Next to those papers were his notes for a lecture he had been preparing for the class on rural crime he taught at the local college. However, classes had been suspended indefinitely, and regardless, Kelly was no longer available to his additional role as a college instructor.

He turned his gaze to the diploma on his wall, a Master's Degree in Criminal Justice from Ohio State. Nothing in any of his classes had prepared him for the crimes he was now confronting.

He crossed his arms on his chest, arms that strained at the sleeves of his tee shirt, a chest that rippled from endless hours in the gym over many years. Only 5' 7'', the slightly balding man still struck a powerful pose. However, at age fifty-two, his conditioning notwithstanding, his stamina was being tested.

Not only was his physical endurance being strained. He picked up the container of Xanax tablets, holding them in appreciation, yet frustrated at their presence in his home.

He chastised himself for succumbing to the fright. But each time he recalled the charred tiny hand in his own, and the elderly woman's head beside her body, separated by the blade of window glass that had decapitated her, Kelly had begun to shake and find it difficult to breath.

He sighed and began a slow walk down the stairs and to the back door. He stepped out upon the large patio and greeted his guests already being entertained by his wife Mollie.

Franklin Norwood shouted an acknowledgement to the host and slowly carried his glass of lemonade to a folding chair beneath a tree. More than twenty years older than the other men, he presented an imposing presence even among those who knew him with affection and friendship. Well over six feet tall, still slender and rock-hard at seventy-five, the silver-haired retired foundry owner could hold his own with his younger friends on the tennis court or the jogging path.

Another neighbor, Carl Brooks, had already positioned a chair out of range of the smoke that would soon emanate from the charcoal grill on the patio several feet away. He was a full professor at the college where he and Kelly had met at Kelly's first faculty meeting, and the two became casual friends.

In his role as host of the Sunday afternoon cookout, Kelly tended to the grill full of steaks rescued from a thawing freezer after the power station had been destroyed, his mind and heart not at all with the endeavor. He watched the steaks with disinterest, placing the turning fork on the picnic table, and then leaning back against a tree with closed eyes.

Noting Kelly's demeanor, Franklin leaned forward and broke what had been several minutes of silence disturbed only by occasional shouts and clamors from the Brooks children inside the Hastings home. "How's Molly doing, Kelly? I know the funeral was rough. It'd be bad enough to have one of your little students die getting hit by a car or dying from some disease, but......this." Franklin shook his head and leaned back in the chair.

Kelly slammed the turning fork on the picnic table next to the sizzling grill, then walked over by his friends and once again leaned against the tree. "She goes by what's left of the girl's house every day. She hasn't slept much since last Monday. She says that when she does nod off she sees the girl running on the playground.'

"Four of the teachers in her building had one of those kids in a class. It's like….I don't know….it's like I almost forgot that there were two more killed who weren't even school age. I'm just glad to get part of a day away from it all. I've gotten sick of smelling that odor a burned house….a burned body…. leaves behind."

Carl Brooks shrugged. "Patrice started to come apart at Wally March's service yesterday. When the firing squad shot off the salute and that bugler played 'Taps', she lost it. She couldn't help but still care.'

"She talked to Wally's widow, and she told Patrice how she worried about him when she found out he'd gone into Baghdad during the war. When he got back with that Bronze Star on his chest, he went into the Guard. He found a job, never missed a beat. Then the other night he just never came home from work.'

"She said that for the past couple of years, since he became company commander, she'd gotten used to him stopping by at the armory to check the doors or something. When the officer took her to where they'd found his car and she saw the bloodstains on the seat…well that had to be pretty tough."

Kelly slapped Carl on the shoulder before walking to the patio to turn the steaks once more. "I forgot that she used to date him."

Carl nodded. "A long time ago, but it still got to her real bad."

Kelly stared at the ground for a moment. "That's part of life in a small town. We're never that far separated from each other. I'd talk to him when we'd happen to run into each other. I did know him from the YMCA, but not real well. Nice guy, though. Ironic….how I'd hear rumors that he was having nightmares about seeing those burned bodies in the desert. Then….this happens to him."

Franklin stood up and stretched, his back resting against the trunk of the tree. "I know you really can't tell us anything, Kelly. But the whole town's gonna pop if somebody doesn't explain something. There've been too many funerals this week for folks to stay rational. I don't know how long this town can handle all the news vans and reporters."

The older man took a sip of lemonade and peered quizzically at Kelly. "I heard that what they found of Wally indicated that he was dead before the explosion."

Kelly nodded and then began turning the steaks with little care. The gathering had not been arranged with an expectation of enjoyment, but from a need to be with others at a time of crisis and fear. "No secret to that anymore. I'm sure it's on TV as we speak. But it's the body bag that has everyone wondering. Every damned network called the department several times this week asking if we knew any more about the fragments from it. They ask us if we know why he was put in a military-issue body bag. It just makes the whole thing more bizarre….nothing makes any sense'

"The Chief stuck me on the phone last night. I know people just want to help, but everyone has a theory. The e-mail is astounding…all the text and Twitter messages. I've heard about all the wild stuff on the internet. Now I get calls telling me it was this or that terrorist group or some kind of homegrown anti-government extremists. Then I got calls telling me it was a group of anti-military anarchists."

Franklin sat down again and ran his hand through his hair. "Is this where we're going to be left hanging? A whole town…..Hell, a whole country left wondering why? Why us? Some small, unremarkable town…..if we're not safe here….".

Kelly took the steaks off the grill and then tossed the serving plate to the table. "I suppose anything I say is safe enough. Everything's wild speculation and every possible angle's been on CNN and Fox News. We hardly have room to park our cruisers with all the media vans surrounding the station."

He sat down at the table with a weary sigh and began rubbing his eyes. "We've got so many investigators, we're tripping over each other. The Chief's working to get things under his control…that's a story in itself. It's our town, but the state police are hinting they'll want jurisdiction because the Governor commands the National Guard. The feds say that ATF should have the lead because of the use of plastic explosives and dynamite. Homeland Security says it's their case because of the possibility of organized terrorism.'

"I don't know…it'll be on the news before the day is over, but the networks have been getting some calls with a common theme. The calls are anonymous, of course, but they say that some anarchist terror group picked out Averton at random just to prove that no place is safe from them. You know, the point is that there was no point to it. Everyplace and anyplace is vulnerable.'

"We even had reports that this is an extremist paramilitary group wanting to show how ineffective the government is in protecting the citizens. Some say that extremists promoting state sovereignty are at fault."

Franklin nodded his agreement. "After 9-11, we knew we were in for some more trouble. And we have had some nasty jihadist attacks. But even when those were followed by the car bombings in the big cities, I know that most of us thought that if we stayed around home we were safe. Now we have some other bunch trying to rattle our nerves."

Carl shook his head. "What paramilitary group was mentioned?"

Kelly shrugged. "Just that it was a militia group….we got two anonymous calls at the department last night accusing them. Couldn't get much out of them. One started to say something about how the country was in peril of turning Socialist. The caller said that the Congress was plotting to disarm the citizens, turn America over to the United Nations, and that would be the beginning of a one-world government. They never stay on long enough for us to get a trace, or else they call on one of those disposable cell phones." Kelly looked around while his face flushed. "I guess I'm talking too much, but almost all of this is on the internet."

Carl moaned. "It would be hell if this was a domestic bunch."

Franklin shook his head. "I'm guessing they are domestic. But why would that be worse, 'Professor Carl'? You're the head of the college history department. What's your take?"

Carl knelt down in the grass and sipped at his lemonade. "All that has held this country together for all these generations is the agreement that the Constitution rules. Our country has never had a coup. When Nixon left office things could have gotten ugly. But we handled it peacefully.'

"All we have is a collective agreement that one document has designed our government and sets the boundaries. When you think about it, just how fragile it all is, it could keep you awake at night."

Franklin pulled a chair closer to the other men. "If you listen to some people, they'll have you believe the country's just fine, on the right track. Quite frankly, I'm surprised the nation's held up as long as it has. As you say, Carl, it's held together by something precious but fragile."

The older man went on. "Think about it. We get complacent as long as we don't feel that our individual lives are being disturbed. What worries me is that I'm afraid things are going to deteriorate even more. We're way too naïve about those who would sacrifice out sovereignty for their vision of the whole world sitting around a campfire together."

Kelly shrugged. "I don't know, Frank. After the week I just put in, I may seem like the last to disagree. But bad as it, at least for Averton, it's one incident. That's why everyone is so horrified. If it was more commonplace here, we'd be more numb to it."

Franklin took another sip of lemonade and then pointed directly at Kelly. "This type of attack, on Averton of all places, if this is some anarchist bunch, this is just some warm-up. I tell you, son, I've seen this crap coming for a long time."

"Just a minute', Carl interjected. "Wouldn't someone want credit for this? No one has claimed responsibility."

The elderly man's face grew tight as he continued. "You would think so....but it's been happening all around the world, if we would just open our eyes.'

"Our President may be with the common man but the Congress has lost touch with the fears of the people. They're more worried about offending someone than protecting us. They're bankrupting us, and they treat the states like mere political subdivisions of the federal government instead of being the entities that give the federal government its power."

Carl walked over and placed his hand on Franklin's shoulder. "My dear old reactionary friend."

Franklin laughed, then gazed downward as a serious look came over his face. "There are a lot of people who feel that they can vote for whoever they want, and the judicial system will just overrule them. At least we get to elect the Congress."

Carl looked up and smiled. "Ah, but the Congress votes according to emotion and what will keep them in office. Then, the courts decide what is constitutional. Remember that 'fragile document' we were just talking about?"

Franklin leaned down and good-naturedly shook his finger at Carl "And those liberal judges are out of control. They're appointed for life and they have their own agendas."

"Ahaaaa.", Carl waived away the comment. "Judges have always had a variety of interpretations."

Franklin grew animated in his gestures. "Carl....I think Marlboro is as honest a President as any. He has integrity. But three months into his term, he gets to appoint two Supreme Court Justices. Nobody knows how they really feel about the Second Amendment. So the run on gun shops started right away because people are afraid they won't be allowed to own guns. Then, this happens and now the fear is going to spiral out of control. I'll tell you fellows…something is upside down when the people fear the government, rather than it being the other way around."

Carl laughed. "Frank….Frank. You're buying trouble we don't have."

Franklin threw up his hands. "I listen to the talk radio shows. I listen to the short-wave firebrands and I read a lot of web sites. There are those talking about the concept of succession or some revised confederation….leaving the liberals on the East Coast and West Coast to go their own ways. I don't agree with that type of talk, but I can understand it. They feel betrayed."

Carl nearly choked on his drink. "Betrayed by whom?"

Franklin hesitated before speaking. "Let's…let's just say that a lot of people see the America they've always known and loved being trashed….trashed by the media….trashed by liberal politicians. Let's face it….our culture is dominated by the media and news establishments on both coasts. Somewhere in the middle, folks want to see things run with common sense. You preserve your values…keep the nation safe. That's not asking for much.'

"When people see a lack of commitment to their protection…when resources go toward the environmentalists' fad of the week, when hard-earned money is taken to cover the butts of the irresponsible…people become unhappy."

Carl put his arm around Franklin's shoulder. "You right-wing son of a bitch….."

Franklin laughed. "Take a hard look Carl. As a history professor, don't you find it ironic that our nation was founded along the eastern seaboard, but now that part of the country has little in common with the principles that characterized the original Colonies?"

Carl began shaking his head. "Frank, it's not practical any more to see the country as a bunch of independent provinces."

Franklin began shaking his finger at the Carl. "Not independent…but sovereign."

Kelly began laughing. "I should arrest both of you for disturbing the peace."

The men's attention was diverted to the parade of wives and Brooks children emerging from the house, carrying side dishes, plates and silverware. The mood of the women was somber, perhaps more so than that of their mates. As they sat around the table in the webbed folding chairs, the adults remained nearly silent. The common thought was that no gathering in the brutalized town would be joyous again for a very long time. The deaths of three entire families and the abduction and murder of a local hero had combined with vast property destruction and the unwanted glare of national attention.

"I can still remember", Franklin continued when all the men had again gathered under the tree, "When I bought the foundry here twenty-five years ago. This was such a secluded safe place. Now, seeing this place on the news networks around the clock…wow. I look back and remember thinking I might have been crazy. But Katie and I came to love the place after just a few weeks."

Franklin gave a heavy sigh. "Everyone I've talked to the past few days says the same thing. It's almost impossible to concentrate, to take care of what needs to be done. I didn't tell you guys, did I, that I bought the book store?"

Kelly glanced over. "The Bitterroot? I was afraid we'd lost our only book store forever."

Franklin nodded. "You bet. And don't worry Kelly. I'll make sure you have all the science fiction to pick from you could ever want. Katie talked me into this little project. She wants to run it, but we have someone to help her out. And there's something else." Franklin rose and leaned against the tree once again. "I bought the old Heritage Lodge and all that wooded land across the road from it."

Kelly and Carl looked at each other in amazement. Kelly stood up and placed his hand on Franklin's forehead. "No fever.

What's making you spend all this money? Burning a hole in your pocket since you retired?"

Franklin laughed heartily. "We're going to renovate the lodge and move there. The builders are going to start next week." The older man seemed to gaze into the distance while smiling. "I've had my eye on the place for years. When the church put it up for sale, I had the first offer in place."

Kelly shook his head. "Aside from living there, what are you going to do with it?"

"Well, it has that big meeting room and that oversize kitchen, and it sets on five acres. Sure, it will be our home but we can have groups hold meetings there. Across the road are two hundred acres. I'm going to renovate that old abandoned house and barn, triple the size of the pond and clear out an area so groups can set up tents for campouts. What can't I do with it? We'll still have plenty of privacy, even with the development that'll come along now that the lodge has been annexed into the city.'

"The best part is the land across the road is outside the city limits, so I'm thinking about putting in a rifle range and teaching marksmanship to kids. It can also be an outdoor learning lab. It can provide great field trips for schools. We can have a nature center there." Franklin reached for a leaf, cradled it in his fingers and examined it.

"It's mainly the kids I'm thinking about for now. A lot of them lost friends this last week. Having a place to observe wildlife and take a hike through the woods or catch a fish can bring back a lot of smiles. I wrapped up the deal the day before….it happened. Maybe now I can feel excited about something. I got the keys the day we signed the papers. Now it's ours. What the hell…we've got no one to leave our money to. Let's all just enjoy it."

~~~

The gathering broke up and the Hastings home became quiet and eerie when the Norwoods and the Brooks family had departed. Kelly sat restlessly in a recliner, in front of, but not watching the television. He was in front of, but not absorbing an old black and white movie just to see something other than the news or to leave his mind wandering. Nonetheless, his hands grasped at the chair's arms as he relived the past several days over and over again. He wanted to sleep but constantly strained to wonder why it had happened.

The craving for a beer was nearly maddening. He knew that he was not supposed to drink while taking the Xanax but he was finding the prospect of a more pronounced sedation an inviting thought.

He rose from the chair and walked back outside in the dimming light. Looking around, he scanned the neighborhood wondering what his neighbors were feeling at the moment. His own neighborhood had been left untouched physically by the violence, but a pall had been cast upon the innocent residents.

The night of the bombings, he had rested peacefully in bed. Earlier on that day he had overseen a rare weekend raid of an even rarer Averton crack house. He settled in that night reading a history of Averton and Manchester County that related how the town had begun as a settlement, a sleepy river trading post. The noise of explosions had roused him from his sleep that night. In the darkened house, he had no idea that the peaceful image of Averton was gone for eternity.

~~~

Molly sat alone in the kitchen. The cup of coffee she was sipping was perhaps the last thing she needed in her already tense state. She had hated to see the Norwoods walk home and dreaded their move to the lodge, although it was only two miles away.

In spite of the differences in their ages, Katherine Norwood had become her best friend after having met at a dinner to recognize those, who like Katherine, volunteered as tutors at the local school system. The two would visit more days than not, and the friendship grew deeper as time went on.

Mollie loved to hear Katherine talk of her childhood in Pennsylvania, her life in Philadelphia, and how she had been apprehensive of remarrying after being widowed. Still, she had told of marrying a seemingly confirmed bachelor who soon surprised her by announcing that he would like to move away from the big city and buy his own business and felt that they should make a visit.

As for Franklin, he had become like an uncle to Kelly, but Katherine had taken the place of Molly's own mother who had died long ago. At fifty-one, Molly Hastings had gone through many changes, but the warm friendship provided an essential continuity.

~~~

At midnight, three blocks away, Franklin and Katherine Norwood settled into their bed. The petite seventy-three year old woman with snow-white hair leaned back on her pillow and then noticed that her husband was unusually agitated. She reached out for his hand. "Worrying won't make things change one way or another. Nothing in our lives ever goes quite as planned."

He propped up his pillows and sat upright. "Do you think you'll ever convince me of that?"

Katherine shook her head and laughed. "Not after all these years, not really." She looked over at him again, reached up, and brushed a lock of hair from his brow. "Molly told me more about those concerns of hers today. She's becoming more worried."

"About which thing in particular?"

"The same thing. She's growing more and more worried that she doesn't live up to Kelly's expectations…..romantically, let's say. She says she knows that Kelly enjoyed…. well, she referred to '….that wild, kinky ex-wife of his'. I told her they've only been married for three years, and that some things take time. Marriages later in life are just different. But she's afraid of their marriage eventually falling apart."

"I need to understand exactly why she's that pessimistic."

"Kelly never expresses any dissatisfaction. She claims it's her intuition. She's aware of how obvious he is when he notices a nice-looking woman. She also knows all too well that he did stray from his ex."

Franklin nodded. "I take it she does know that the marriage was already on the rocks….that she was already cheating on Kelly? Not that it justified…..".

"She understands that. It's part of a combination of things that make her feel uneasy. In her rational moments, she knows that Kelly loves only her. And she's deeply in love with him. But she also knows that female flesh is his weakness. He's been quite candid with her about his past behavior going all the way back to high school.'

"Mollie says that when they were dating, Kelly confided that he did see another woman before his divorce was even filed, but never before the marriage was all but over. Then she laughed and told me that Kelly has an incredible libido, and she's having a great time, but she wants to be his only outlet."

Franklin rubbed his chin as he considered his wife's words. "So that vulnerability you suspected is definitely still there."

"Yes. I just thought you should know what she said on the phone this evening."

Franklin rearranged the pillows to lie down. "Yes, it's important to know how they're doing."

Katherine ran her fingertips over her husband's cheek. "Frank, you're concerned about them aren't you?"

He reached for her hand and kissed it, then placed his forearm over his eyes. "Yes, I am. We both know they're like family to us now."

~~~

At 6:00 a.m. on Monday morning, Kelly Hastings sat down in the conference room in the police department next to the Chief. He nodded to the Major from the Ohio State Highway Patrol, but did not recognize the husky gray-haired man sitting to his left.

The Chief looked over some papers in silence and then began to speak. He looked at Kelly and gestured toward the stranger. "Kelly, this is agent Calvin Meyers, FBI. Kelly, you're going to continue to be the designated lead man for our department for the long-term. Agent Meyers here is going to take over coordination for everything to and from the Feds from here on out including Homeland Security. Anything the Bureau or ATF can help us with goes through him." The Chief motioned to the State Patrol officer. "Any vehicle checks you need, anything the state can help with, you call the Major. He's heading back to Columbus."

The Major allowed himself a grim smile. "No offense, Chief, but I'm ready to say goodbye to that old cot you found for me."

The Chief then began a recap of what little evidence had been gathered. He talked swiftly without looking up and avoided any acknowledgements of disagreements with his view of how things were progressing. One thing that Kelly had learned about his boss over the years, was that it was best to argue with him in a more private setting.

It was with respect and affection that Kelly watched his mentor summarize the chaos around them. Chester Todd was of slight build, with a flat-top hair style above large black-rimmed eyeglasses. But all who worked for him knew his resolve.

After an hour of general acknowledgement of the lack of leads, the Chief and the bleary-eyed patrol officer left the room chatting about the lack of sleep. Kelly now sat alone with Meyers who produced a file folder from his briefcase.

"Well, Hastings, I guess your Chief's being realistic. Here's a report from the labs. This is a photo of one of the remnants of the body bag. So much of everything got trampled over or soaked from the fire hoses that we don't have much. But since the wind was calm things settled down fairly close to the blast.'

"This is a photo of the best piece of the bag we have. This fragment was found just across the street, on the porch of the house facing the front door of the armory. Did you see the Captain's remains before they were removed?"

Kelly bit his lip and nodded.

"Remember how his feet were shielded from the blast by the concrete corner of the steps? Well, this fragment is the same material that covered his feet, but that was melted and fused to his shoes by the heat."

Meyers took out another sheet of paper. "This is a lab report that says the body bag's composition and condition indicates that it'd been stored away for a long time, maybe thirty years or so. This is the material the bags were made of that were used in Vietnam.'

"In addition, the dynamite used to blow the place was also aged and the analysis says that it wasn't stored very safely. Whoever handled it was using some very unstable stuff."

Kelly leaned back and reached to the floor for his own briefcase. He laid it on the table and removed a legal pad. "One of the calls I took the night before last made that second reference to this anarchist group called the Fourth World and bragged that some of the 'supplies' had been provided by the U.S. government, courtesy of Fort Campbell. It was clearly implied that there had been a theft at the base years ago."

Meyers Sighed. "Anonymous calls, and they're all we have to go on. Odds are this Fourth World group doesn't even exist in any formal terms, if at all. We don't have anything on them in our databases. You know that there are a lot of groups out there but they may only consist of a few people if not one or two. Most radical groups just want to hear themselves talk. Such extreme action is rare."

Kelly considered the thought. "Why Averton? There's nothing special or strategic in the town. No defense plants, not even any tourist attractions."

Meyers looked down at his file. "Why not? During World War Two the Germans bombed Coventry just to show that no city in England was safe. It wasn't a military action. It was terrorism. Look at 9-11. We're about the same age, Hastings. I've seen some strange motives over the years."

"But wouldn't the impact be greater in a large city?"

"Not really. If this is an Islamic terror group, they've been pounding the big cities with those car bombs. This is the type of place people live to feel safe. They may move here to feel secure. I'm from a small town myself."

Kelly shook his head. "Sorry. It makes no sense for some extremist group of any stripe to bomb this town. There's nothing unique about Averton....unless that's the point."

"I would agree. We're not dealing with logic Hastings. These are people who just don't think the same way the rest of our minds function. It's not like the ordinary criminal mind. Extremists feel that they can help their cause in the long run. Anything is justified if fifty years from now the world is going to be running their way. Sometimes they're almost like cult members. Perhaps someone has talked them into believing by sheer strength of personality."

Kelly shook his head. "I do understand that a lot of things happen for the sake of political ideology. Still, I remember a seminar at the F.B.I. Academy. The instructor said that he couldn't help but wonder if some movements don't simply attract people who are prone to mayhem."

Meyers glanced at Kelly. "Whatever the case, just think. Nothing was stolen, at least that we know of. They put out the power, then blow the armory. They brutally murder a part-time commander and in the process, they kill four adults and several kids. Just to make a point."

Kelly watched as Meyers stood and stretched. Kelly also rose and began to walk with him to the lobby, the F.B.I. man towering over him in height.

Meyers gestured toward the media vans parked across the street. "How long did it take you to get tired of that?"

Kelly laughed. "It took about two hours".

Meyers patted him on the back as he walked away. "They're part of your life now."

~~~

Kelly leaned back in his desk chair and stared at the phone in front of him. Glancing again at his watch, he knew that he might as well stay seated and wait to be connected to the expected conference call.

He was to speak with some other city officials needing to make contact in spite of their constant and frantic visitors. Most of the news correspondents and their crews were now familiar with him, so traveling to a meeting would simply make him part of a parade.

The phone finally buzzed and he was greeted by the voice of Marie Mentano, one of the city council members, then by Albert Hall from the Chamber of Commerce.

"The Chief said I can speak for him. What's up?"

Marie began. "This. This is what's up. Nothing is normal. The mayor is hiding from reporters. I've been going out for him because they don't know me as well. The mayor can't get anything done. He can't think straight because if he doesn't have a camera on him it's someone on the phone with a problem. The whole town, the whole county's paranoid."

Hall took up the litany. "The public's afraid to go out. They even think the shopping center's a target for a bombing. We had two small manufacturers thinking about relocating here. Some that are already here have had orders slow down. My neighbor's trucking company lost a two hundred thousand-dollar contract this week. If this were New York, the rest of the town could go on. Here, the only thing the town's going to be known for will be these explosions. The place is gonna die."

Marie Mentano stood up and tossed up her hands in frustration, even though she was alone. "As you know, the schools had to cancel the last week of classes.....parents are hiding their kids. I can't tell you how many have sent them away to stay with relatives. Now there are all those extra guns out there."

Kelly nodded his head, looking down. "We've heard. Every gun shop from Cincinnati to Cleveland has just about sold out. But you can't blame them. They're scared. They've had days of sirens and nights of flashing lights to keep them awake. That's not to mention the days without electricity and all the food spoilage."

The councilwoman sighed. "At least some are wanting to get more aggressive on the positive side. Tell your boss, Kelly. I've heard about a meeting being called at the Community Arts Hall for tomorrow night. The details leave a lot to be desired because it sounds rather disorganized. It's something about some people getting together to make a list of information they want from your department, the F.B.I, and so forth. I hear there's going to be a list of demands for improving the security of the community. The city manager has been taking calls from the networks, but he was in the dark."

Kelly lowered his head and moaned. "What the hell does this mean?"

Marie continued. "That's the point, Kelly. None of this could have been anticipated. Everything just leaves us guessing. We've been sitting here for a while making a list of people we think we can count on and some we think may not be rational. We thought it might be a good idea for us to encourage some particular people to be there, maybe some voices of reason, some calming influences. I'm concerned about the temptations a scared citizen may face with a group of microphones thrust under his nose. Any suggestions?"

Kelly thought for a moment. "I suppose the school superintendent should be there. So much of the anxiety revolves around the fact that those kids were killed."

"I agree", Marie interjected. "Albert will go. I'll be there. At least three clergymen have promised to attend. Kelly, use your judgment. If you can think of anyone else go ahead and talk to them."

~~~

Kelly spent the rest of the morning and part of the afternoon reading the autopsy report on Wally March that was waiting on his desk upon his return to the office. Several times, he had to stop and walk around the department to alleviate the queasiness from reading the words and gazing at the photos. Although he had seen the remains that night, there was something about reading the cold clinical report that made his stomach churn. There was a lingering taste in his mouth, the haunting odor of burned human flesh still in his every breath.

He reviewed the notes from interviews with neighbors who lived near the armory and rural residents nearest the power station. Unable to sit still any longer, he drove to the site of the armory explosion, parked, and walked toward the rubble. Bits of charred wood crunched beneath his feet as he walked through the cordoned-off area. The same sickening smells began to make his feel like retching, along with the memories and the pictures he had reviewed earlier.

Possibilities began to flood his mind and he began to chastise himself for falling into the same trap as all the other investigative agencies. The brazenness of the act, the absence of care for the innocents nearby had seized upon his energy. Until that day all their attention had been devoted to getting the town back in order.

Was the whole thing an elaborate grotesque cover-up of something simple? Kelly returned to his car and began to make notes on a pad. Was this nothing more than a simple murder? Was Wally March's death the whole story, and the power stations destruction, the armory bombing and the phone calls about extremists some method of screwing up everyone's thinking? The autopsy report said that March had been garroted, strangled horribly but quickly by a thin cable or wire, forcing him to choke up the blood found in the car.

Was Wally March the target of revenge for his actions in Iraq? Was he messing around with someone else's wife or girlfriend? He could consider that someone did not want March to come home at all.

What if the war hero was involved in something illegal? He did have a brother in a state penitentiary for dealing crack in the town. Was he carrying on the business? Was it some disgruntled employee of the power company or someone who felt cheated or abused in the Guard outfit? The F.B.I had five agents following up on those possibilities.

Does someone hate the town? Was someone in one of the houses the real target? Someone tired of paying child support?

What if Meyers was wrong? Is there something missing from someone affected by the power outage? Was there anything of value taken from the armory before it was blown? Is there someone missing? He would need to check for any missing person reports. When he had been hired as a rookie patrol cop the current Chief, then his shift supervisor, had told him to "Never ignore the obvious, but don't depend on it either".

~~~

Shortly after midnight, Kelly picked up Calvin Meyers at the police department and drove out to the remains of the substation. Kelly parked along the road and then they began walking along the ditch. "I thought you'd be back home in Cincinnati by this hour."

Meyers shrugged. "I wanted to see this area at night again. The news crews are more scarce this time of day." Meyers looked around and then laughed. "No one within an eighth of a mile, but we're only a quarter-mile mile from town. Perfect."

Kelly pointed down the road. "We have a plaster cast of those bike tracks from the ditch and down behind that tree. The ground's been so dry it didn't sink in much so there wasn't a very deep impression. It looks like standard treads, probably from a 400-650 cc bike. Only hundreds of those around here. There was also some scorched grass, we figure from a hot exhaust pipe. When the power generator trucks rolled in, that may have damaged some evidence."

Kelly pointed to the south. "We figure that would be the logical escape route, away from Averton, out into the country. Maybe to Dayton, then most likely out of state."

Meyers stopped walking. "Why not Averton? Why the bigger towns? Is that what you want to believe?"

Kelly shook his head. "No. I'd feel a lot more in control if I thought it was somebody local. If it were just the armory I'd think somebody could have stolen some old dynamite from a farm shed. It used to be pretty popular for removing tree stumps from fields. It still wouldn't explain why, though. But people around here don't typically handle plastic explosives and electronic detonators."

Meyers waved toward the destroyed terminal. It was bathed in the glare of floodlights illuminating the generator trucks and temporary power cables. The work crews were in the process of re-connecting the city and the facility was patrolled around-the-clock by six sheriff's deputies. "I'm just trying to provoke you into solving this. We don't have any original thoughts as to what this was all about and we don't know if it's over. The two blasts were so damned different…..one high-tech, the other with all the subtlety of a sledgehammer.'

"The Bureau doesn't have a single idea. The ATF tells me the explosive did not contain any taggants to identify it. Besides, those are being counterfeited anyway. We've interviewed eighty Guard members and forty power company employees. Nothing there. Half the Feds are chasing this right-wing crap around, the rest the anarchist and Islamic terror angles. At least we can say we're looking into something specific, even if we don't know if this militia group even exists. There are all kinds of militia outfits and they can be as different as night and day. They make great whipping boys for the media. Talking about them does take some heat off of us with the media and the agents don't go so crazy following a weak lead, compared to no lead at all."

"What if no specific militia comes forth? Maybe somebody planned to send us in all different directions."

"Within a couple of days, something should rise to the top. Maybe we'll get someone willing to talk. The chance is always there that some imposter will become the 'militia'. All we need to throw us way off track is some loser trying to feel important.'

"It could be somebody's lost in the seventies', Meyers continued. "You were right, Hastings. At least from the body bag and dynamite I'd say that we've pulled something out of the past. If this is somebody local, since the armory was hit, I'd look toward somebody who got passed over for a promotion. Maybe somebody got pissed off about Iraq or even Vietnam and something just now set him off. Try looking around for somebody who lost someone in a war. I don't know."

~~~

It was nearly two o'clock when Kelly silently unlocked the kitchen door to his house, then went into the bathroom. His eyes ached as they strained to adjust to the light, made more difficult as they temporally dimmed from the insufficient power. He splashed cold water over his face, soaking the edges of the remaining brown hair as well as his sport coat and slacks. Back out into the dark of the shadowy kitchen, he tossed the jacket over a chair, then unbuckled the strap to the shoulder holster and carried it to the closet outside the bedroom.

Back in the kitchen, he moved around cartons and bowls until he found a lone can of beer. He calculated the time since his last dose of Xanax, then decided that if the mixture would make him sleep more soundly, all the better. He walked into the living room, kicked off his shoes and collapsed onto the couch.

He sat in the dark, not wishing for a light or sound to waken his wife. He hoped that she was resting rather than being haunted by the faces of children she had seen each day at the elementary school where she had served as a principal for twenty years.

He rose wearily and walked slowly to the bedroom door. He opened it carefully, and then peered in. He was relieved to see that she was on her stomach, motionless, her usual position during sound sleep.

Finding himself relaxing at the sight of Molly's respite from reality, Kelly decided that he could probably slip into bed without rousing her. But when he had finally slipped under the sheets carefully and quietly he did not lie down. He propped his pillows against the headboard and simply gazed at the slumbering figure next to him. He nearly reached out to place his hand on her bare shoulder and stroke it, but caught himself in time.

Kelly closed his eyes and smiled to himself in the darkness. He felt at peace knowing that Mollie was simply beside him.

It had not always been so. Married at thirty, divorced at forty-eight, he had taken a sabbatical from actively seeking a mate when the Chief assigned him to attend a community meeting on drug awareness. He was part of the panel and took a turn speaking about the effects of drug trafficking on children in the city.

During the forum, his attention was diverted at times and he struggled to maintain his concentration on the topic. Kelly found that he was repeatedly and discreetly gazing at an attractive middle-aged woman sitting in the front row in a black dress.

As the meeting ended, he realized that he had seen her picture in the newspaper on occasion and recalled that she had been the recipient of a national award regarding reading programs. Still he could not remember her name. He felt the urge to simply walk up and introduce himself, but was uncharacteristically intimidated by the thought. However, luck was with him when he saw an attorney he knew go up to her and begin chatting.

Kelly took a deep breath and strode to where the women were standing. When the attorney saw him approaching, she reached out her hand.

"Kelly….it's been a while."

Kelly nodded, still shaking her hand. "Caroline….haven't seen you since you got that forgery arrest we worked so hard on thrown out of court."

The attorney shook her head and grinned. "I'm good." She turned toward the other woman. "Kelly….do you know Mollie Casland?"

Kelly took her hand. "I've seen your picture…..school activities……that award."

Mollie nodded. "Yes….you were that police officer, right…..you traded yourself for that little girl whose father was holding her hostage last summer? I'm so glad you didn't get hurt…that no one got hurt."

Kelly shrugged. "It was close. Custody fights, loaded guns and tear gas make for an interesting afternoon."

Caroline elbowed Mollie. "I know you remember that newspaper photo of this guy walking to the house in his boxer shorts with his hands up."

Kelly gave an exaggerated sigh in mock indignation. "That bastard demanded that. He just didn't seem to trust me that I wasn't armed."

Caroline turned to Mollie. "But that was a great picture, wasn't it?"

Kelly looked at the blushing woman, and was enchanted by her dancing eyes. She finally nodded. "Yes, it was a nice picture."

Kelly struggled to make small talk about the meeting they had just finished, then asked Mollie questions about the reading program she had initiated, making sure to compliment her.

When the conversation broke up Kelly could not get those eyes out of his mind. A week later, he garnered the courage to call her and ask her to go to dinner.

Over dinner, Mollie told of her own divorce from a husband of twenty years who had been found by his employer to be embezzling funds. He had not had charges filed against him but Mollie could not remain in such a marriage. At forty-seven, she had dealt with the delicate matter of someone in her position in the community facing a marital break-up.

Kelly and Mollie decided to be cautious and celibate, as she was too visible to be otherwise. They set out on a courtship of a year and then had a small wedding of close friends and their sparse family members.

Kelly had never been able to father children. Mollie had two daughters, and pictures of them and her grandchildren were a welcome addition to the home they had chosen together. When he and Mollie went to the Bahamas for their honeymoon it was Kelly who most enjoyed picking out gifts for his step-grandchildren, and Mollie was moved at how he cried the first time one of them called him "Grandpa" when they phoned home from the cruise ship.

Kelly loved his new life. He attended school functions and helped decorate the school gym for parties.

At home, he felt at ease when looking at Mollie curled up with a book in her overstuffed chair. Her reading glasses would be perched halfway down her nose and her salt-and-pepper hair would tickle the nape of her neck, bringing about the inevitable shake of her head and the repositioning of the glasses.

There were certain things that Kelly now counted on to be the same each day, to carry him through the fear and horror. Those things in their relationship that concerned her would be addressed another day.

~~~

It was one minute past seven A.M. when Kelly turned on the small television mounted to the underside of the kitchen cabinets and sat down to eat a bowl of cereal. Though he should have been used to the scene it was still jarring to look upon the screen to find a view of some image from Averton behind the tall woman speaking into an unseen microphone. Behind her, cars maneuvered around the traffic circle in the middle of the town:

"It has been eight days now since the citizens of this small Ohio city were brought into the limelight of worldwide attention. The unexplained acts of terror bombings that blacked out most of the area for nearly three days resulted in the deaths of six children and four adults in three homes close to the National Guard armory. In addition, there is the mysterious murder of the commanding officer of the Guard unit. The commander's body appears to have been placed upon the steps of the armory before it was reduced to rubble by the massive explosion."

The scene changed to films of the armory, then to stretchers with covered bodies being taken from the still smoldering houses. "The funerals are over now. The residents of Averton and Manchester County have replaced spoiled food, and those occasional appliances and such that were damaged when the power substation was blown up. Other neighbors of the armory have replaced or boarded up most of the hundreds of windows that were shattered and the cuts are healing. But life here is far from normal. Local residents tell me that shoppers move more quickly in and out of stores and that people feel nervous when stopped in traffic near any government offices or public utility buildings. One local clergyman told me that the bombings have had some confusing results in his church. He said that at Sunday's services he saw some parishioners for the first time in years, while others who had attended faithfully did not show up. It seems that the fear is widespread that any type of assemblies will invite attack.'

"Averton police chief Chester Todd will say only that all possible leads are being pursued and when I spoke last evening to Calvin Meyers from the Cincinnati field office of the F.B.I., he would state only that more than one group was being investigated. Federal sources speaking under the condition of anonymity state that a possible militia group and a formerly unknown anarchist organization called 'The Fourth World' are subjects of concern.'

"Another unnamed source within the FBI in Washington did confirm to me that a para-military group referring to itself as a militia has been linked to these acts. It should be noted that nearly every militia group in the U.S. has issued statements condemning the Averton attacks and disavowing any involvement.'

"The source did stress, however, that this group is linked to the attacks only by some anonymous telephone calls. There have been no statements issued by anyone claiming to speak for this alleged militia or any other group.'

"Among most news agencies it is the consensus that the FBI is following these leads simply out of lack of having any other course to pursue. Those in and around the federal law enforcement agencies, including the Justice Department, say that high level officials, also speaking under the condition of anonymity, stop just short of admitting to being lost in this case. Though the events took place a mere eight days ago, there is fear that the crimes may never be solved. And local residents who were at first dismayed by the media attention now express concerns that if these riddles are not quickly answered, the attention of federal law enforcement, as well as the concern of the nation will move on to the next incident somewhere else.'

"Gone is the irony of Ohio National Guard units from around the state who brought in power generators and trucks full of food. Those Guard units ceased round-the-clock patrols of city streets just this morning. Gone too are the police officers from neighboring towns and counties who helped to maintain order.'

"The curfew remains and the state of emergency is said to be indefinite. However, with each day Averton is left more and more on its own. This is Cynthia Yardley, reporting from Averton, Ohio."

Kelly shook his head, then picked up the remote control and changed to another of the morning new programs. There he saw a vaguely familiar man gesturing in an animated fashion:

"What we have, Carol, is that one of the predictable results of the last Congressional election. The voters believed that by turning to the right, their homes and families would be safer. It's an old canard of the conservatives that they can bring down crime. But we have the most conservative Congress in a long time and no one feels sage today."

His interviewer shifted uncomfortably in her chair: "Congressman, are you blaming this tragedy...."

Before she could finish the question, the guest interrupted: "This militia group supposedly wants an even more extremist and intolerant America. Their friends captured Congress, now the right-wing militias, the NRA and their buddies aren't satisfied."

"Isn't that a rather sweeping condemnation of people who have not even been previously mentioned in this situation?"

"The FBI is getting phone calls about how much this was a protest against the country being too 'liberal'. The truth is that is this country goes any further to the right we can break out the Swastika armbands again."

The anchorwoman nodded toward the Congressman. "That's all the time we have and we want to thank Representative Lloyd Simon for being on our program. Tomorrow morning the Speaker of the U.S. House of representatives will be here to offer perhaps a different view of the role of conservatism in our national consciousness."

Kelly turned off the television and as he walked outside to his car, the words of Cynthia Yardley haunted him. On the way to the station, he pondered whether a reduction in media attention might be just what he and other investigators needed. It was difficult to think straight, knowing that each day the Chief and Federal cops were being asked for the latest results. Perhaps seeing the story move from the front pages of national magazines to a section of photographs in "Life" would not be all bad.

When he walked into his office, he found a sleepy Calvin Meyers waiting for him. Before the two could even exchange greetings, Chief Chester Todd walked in and sat down.

Chester drummed his fingers on the desk as if he were waiting for someone else to arrive, "Kelly, I've decided we're not gonna get anywhere unless we concentrate on March's murder. Maybe it'll lead us to everything else. So…just make that your case to solve. Find out who murdered the local hero. Try to forget the bombs, the kids, the blackout. You've done a couple of homicides. I know it sounds difficult but treat it as just a murder. Solve that and maybe everything else will fall into place."

Kelly turned to Meyers. "What're you going to be doing?"

Meyers yawned and stretched. "I'm flying to Chicago. We have an expert on terrorism who works out of there. He would've been here, but he's been in the hospital. Nothing against the folks we have here from the Bureau already, but Willard's the best. He can't get out of bed but his opinions are worth the trip. Alcohol, Tobacco, and Firearms is trying to track down the stuff used to blow the power substation. They're left with testing residue.'

"They're looking at who's under watch for importing explosives and where it's come up missing from domestic handlers. You said it the other day Hastings. These aren't common goods."

Kelly nodded. "And the militia…and the states' rights guys?"

Meyers laughed. "Yeah, we have some people checking that out. Last word I got last night, there's still no verification of those guys. There's no name of an organization so we can't even find references to them on any internet blogs except those generated by the recent events. We need something about their origin, if there is one."

"What about that reference to the 'Fourth World'?"

"Same story. Nothing we can find on the internet, let alone any of our own files or database. Just a couple of clowns on YouTube making fun of us wearing 'Fourth World' tee-shirts."

Kelly looked to the floor. "We're starting from scratch, all the way around?"

Meyers got up from his chair and grabbed his briefcase. "Yes we are. After Oklahoma City, they caught McVeigh in that routine traffic stop. Didn't even realize what they had at first. No such luck for us. Good luck on finding March's killer. I'll be in touch." Meyers waved and walked out.

Kelly turned toward his boss. "Do I have everything?"

Todd pointed toward a stack of papers on the desk. "Photos of the car he was presumably murdered in....the DNA tests are still pending. There's a transcript of a taped interview with his widow.....Kelly, I know it's a real grind."

"We've lost a lot of time."

"I know." Todd stood up and leaned against the wall. "All the man-hours directing traffic....tracking down rumors. I can't even guess how many panic calls we sent 'em out on. Teenagers breaking curfew get turned into terrorists by frightened people."

Todd walked toward the door. "Don't forget the meeting tonight. I want you there. Community Arts Center at 7:00."

~~~

Kelly drove to the abandoned warehouse behind which Wally March's bloodstained car had been found. News from the coroner was that according to the manner in which the blood had settled in the legs and feet, March had been killed at least six hours prior to the explosion. Further, due to the absence of any signs of the presence of insects normally found when a death takes place outdoors in warm weather it would be assumed that the body had been left in the car or placed in the body bag immediately after the murder.

There had been too much damage to the upper parts of the body to determine how much of a struggle there had been. Even the damage to the tissue on the throat from being garroted was barely discernible after the burns and effects of flying concrete fragments.

Kelly stood inside the yellow-taped perimeter where a routine police patrol had found the car just a few minutes before the first explosion. There was nothing of value being kept inside the building and the owner, as evidenced by the beer cans, liquor bottles and condoms strewn about had never closed off the driveway to it.

He took a file from the front seat of his car and read the report on the car being found, which noted there were no working lights around the building. Walking toward the two light poles, he could see that the bulbs had been shot out. The report noted, however, that this was the normal condition of the property.

Still, there were homes within two hundred yards of the warehouse and perhaps it would have been possible for someone to see if the body was taken from the car at this location. There were no fingerprints other than those of Wally March and his wife to be found but this could have meant that someone else drove the car there wearing gloves just to throw off the investigation. Whether the murder had taken place there, or the car taken there later, whoever had committed this act had done so in a brazen reckless manner.

Kelly sat down in his car and looked over the notes from that night. The explosion that knocked out the power had taken place at two in the morning and the armory had gone up an hour later. Wally March was assumed to have been dead since eight o'clock that evening. That meant that the murder had taken place in the daylight. He stopped reading, considering the brashness of someone perhaps dragging a body out of a car at such a visible location as this.

He cursed the fatigue that was clouding his thought processes, causing him to re-think the most basic elements of the case. He looked back through the reports but could find nothing to verify that a sample of blood on the pavement next to the car had been found to be March's. Nor had it matched any known criminal's DNA in the Federal database. The environment around the warehouse would not rule out blood being present from some previous altercation.

He called the department on his radio and requested that records be checked to determine whether the blood comparison had been double-checked. He waited for a couple of minutes, then the dispatcher read the lab report to him, which indicated that it was March's blood outside the car.

He pondered how anyone would feel safe to commit a murder in such a location, let alone drag the body out of a car when it was still light. Yet, it seemed characteristic of other occurrences that night. It seemed to parallel the insolence of the armory bombing, compared to the apparent stealth and concealment used in the destruction of the power substation. He would need to re-interview those who lived nearest the warehouse, a task that should have been completed in the days before. However, the scope and trauma of the events had blown away all standard police practices and plunged the entire department into chaos.

He drove back to the main part of town, but instead of heading to his office, turned into the neighborhood in which he lived, then onto the street where Franklin and Katherine Norwood's home was located. That street served as an unofficial border with one of the more exclusive areas of the town. He began to scold himself for making a personal visit to deal with something which could have been handled by phone but wished for another reprieve from the media and their inquiries.

He pulled up in front of the large brick house where the familiar figure of his friend sat in the shade of a tree. "I thought you guys hit the donut shops when you goofed off during the day. It's not even lunch yet." Franklin pulled up another lawn chair for Kelly, who sat down and took a deep breath.

"Believe it or not, I'm working right now. I wondered if you'd go to the meeting tonight."

"If you mean the one at the Arts Center, I'm already planning to be there. Albert Hall called me. He seemed pretty worked up. I'll do what I can, Kelly. I do know who some of the hotheads are. Matter of fact, a couple used to work at the foundry. I think I can help."

"It's not that we don't want people involved."

Franklin placed his hand on the younger man's knee. "You just want the energy directed in a constructive manner?"

"You've got it. Any ideas?"

"I suppose the most important thing is for everyone to feel more secure, whether they really are or not. Maybe if they feel that they have some control over the situation, that the loonies don't have free rein in their lives.....at least, not yet. Kelly, you and I know that no ordinary neighborhood watchdog program could have done a damned thing to prevent what happened. Folks will take this type of action seriously for a while until they want to play cards or watch a movie instead. Then someone will get their home robbed and it's on again.'

"Maybe the worst that can happen is maybe they will actually catch some small-time mischief in progress. Maybe they will stop something in its planning stages and feel less impotent."

The older man looked at Kelly. "You're finding it hard to be optimistic about anything right now, aren't you?"

The detective looked at the ground and laughed. "I've never felt so drained in my life. I keep telling myself that somewhere out there's a weekend off, a couple of days in my hammock with a book and a beer." Kelly rose and stretched, then began walking slowly toward his car.

Franklin slapped him on the back. "Katie's going to have The Bitterroot open in a few days. When you get that weekend off stop in and pick out a book, on the house."

Kelly got in and started the car. "She's moving that fast?"

Franklin leaned closer, and then spoke in a lower voice. "Just in time, I'd say. All this stuff's gotten on her nerves, real, real bad. She needs this to take her mind off of it. Besides, her niece is going to do a lot of the work, considering Katie's age and her arthritis. They're both looking forward to it."

"Her niece? From back East, I suppose?"

Franklin shook his head. "Pennsylvania, originally. Been in Boston since she got out of college. Not Katie's niece by blood. Actually, she's Harold's niece, but even after he died and she married me she kept in close touch with Harold's family. I think it helped both of us make the adjustment, especially moving here. Anyway, the investment company Laura worked for cut back. But she's single….made a lot of money. She got some pretty serious walking money and she says she could use some time away from the big cities.'

"Katherine told her about the book store and Laura asked if she needed some help. Katherine jumped at the idea of having her here. She actually moved here last month. She has her own place temporarily. She could pay cash for any house in Averton, but she wants to move into that little loft over the store. She fancies herself to be an artist, and I suppose she couldn't find a better atmosphere. Plus, it'll help us keep an eye on her. She's forty, a real looker I might add. Never married, and for someone who was such a tiger in the business world, she's a shy one when it comes to men."

Kelly laughed. "She sounds intriguing".

"She's been rather stressed out. Her job was tough, then there was getting let go. This way, Katherine won't have to worry so much about her and maybe Laura can figure out what she wants to do with the rest of her life."

Kelly nodded, and then put the car in gear. "Tell your wife I wish her luck. I can't wait to browse." He pulled away and headed for the station.

~~~

What Kelly first noticed upon entering the Community Arts Center was that the gray haze of cigarette smoke was unlike any he had encountered in years. The "No Smoking" sign was being ignored, as were the violations. This signaled to Kelly instantly the level of tension in the room. There were forty or so people in the hall ten minutes prior to when the meeting was scheduled to begin, and he took a seat in the last row of metal folding chairs lined up on the concrete floor.

Over the course of the next several minutes, he counted fifty more filing in. He attempted to be nonchalant in the process of counting, though he realized that most in attendance by now knew who he was.

The walls of the chamber were ringed with the media and uniformed police, and Kelly observed a couple of mild confrontations between those who wanted the meeting more private and those who felt obligated to tape it.

Kelly got up for a moment, walked to the door, and scanned the scene. Reporters standing with microphones in front of camera operators outnumbered his department's officers.

Just as Kelly returned to his seat, a nervous-looking man in a white shirt stood up in front of the room to face the crowd. Kelly recognized him as Paul Woodruff, the owner of an auto dealership on the edge of Averton and president of the Rotary Club. The man was holding a legal pad and pen and made notes as he scanned the crowd. Finally he raised his hands to signal that the meeting was about to begin, then seemed to shuffle his feet impatiently as some in the crowd continued to converse.

He raised his hands. "Attention......attention, please. Some of you've asked me to get this meeting started. I don't know the proper procedures for such a thing as this, but maybe I could make a list of what you want the law to do and we can decide where to go from here."

A middle-aged woman Kelly did not know stood up immediately. "I want to know why we're days past everything that happened and nobody's been arrested. After 9-11 and the bombings in New York and Washington, doesn't the government try to track people who might do something like this?" Her voice quivered as she shouted her question.

Woodruff put up his hands. "I know that Averton is on television around the clock, but maybe we can get a local update each evening on the radio, now that the station got its power back yesterday."

The woman remained standing, and shouted even louder this time, tears streaming down her face. "I lost a dear college classmate in the Trade Center on 9-11. The other night I lost my youngest sister and two little nieces and a nephew."

Three others began to speak at once before an elderly man stood up and shouted above all the others. "Everyone I talk to wants to just keep the town sealed off for a long time. Just like they're doing now….don't let anyone in who doesn't live here or have legitimate business. I know trucks have to go in and out and people have to work in other towns. But we need some more time to just feel like we're keeping out anyone who might try to do more damage."

There was another barrage of voices in varying states of distress and urgency. Paul Woodruff attempted to write down comments as they were shouted. But as the minutes wore on the tone grew more exasperated and strident. Shouting became interspersed with the vain attempts of some present to calm the edginess and anger so evident.

Kelly glanced to his right, his attention caught by the sight of Franklin Norwood rising from his chair. As his friend and neighbor began walking along the ends of the chair rows, the group quieted out of anticipation and curiosity.

Seeing someone else coming to the forefront, Paul Woodruff heaved a sigh of relief. He stood aside for Franklin, who clasped his hands together and took a deep breath before speaking. "I'm Franklin Norwood. I know a lot of you, but for those of you I've never had the pleasure of meeting, a couple of years ago I took a long-overdue retirement from running Averton Castings."

Franklin looked out over the gathering with a somber look, and then forced a meek smile. "I meant to retire to some nature hiking and oil painting. But I came here a stranger twenty-five years ago and I was never treated any differently than if I'd been born in Averton. What I'm getting at is that I've got the spare time to help out. Maybe I can repay the kindness I've been shown over the years.'

"Since I heard about this meeting, I've done a lot of thinking. I've wondered what I could do any differently than our law enforcement has already done. The answer I keep arriving at is that all I can do is support them. There are a lot of us who can keep alert for the suspicious, the out-of-place. We know our neighborhoods. We know whose car should be parked on our streets and who on the block or down the street works nights instead of days.'

"Maybe this isn't enough, and if it isn't, I understand. We're all fearful right now. But I'll be glad to talk to the police and sheriff. They have to deal with the Feds. But a lot of you have hobby radios and other gadgets I don't understand. Perhaps we can divide the town up into sectors and help patrol."

Franklin hesitated as if he had to force his words. "I'm afraid too. The truth is, no local police could have anticipated what happened to us. And folks……in my opinion, aside from helping them keep watch I don't think there's anything else we can do. Personally, I'm of the belief that what happened here is part of a much larger picture. No one would terrorize Averton without it being part of a grander scheme. God knows, since 9-11, and the subsequent attacks there are wide-ranging possibilities out there.'

"But it's not that Averton, Ohio is under siege. Rather, it's our whole society that's in danger of being shredded. Those of us who live here can do what's reasonable to protect ourselves. Each community that takes care of itself, well, that leaves the rest of the country free to concentrate somewhere else."

Voices, mostly hushed, rumbled through the room. Franklin extended his arms to the crowd. "If any of you can give any alternatives to what the police are doing, or of you have any ideas better than mine, I'll just go home and be quiet."

Paul Woodruff stepped over beside Franklin. "Is there any serious disagreement with Mr. Norwood taking these steps?" In contrast to the earlier mood of the group, there was mainly only quiet shaking of heads. Then, without any formal adjournment, Paul Woodruff walked away and Franklin headed slowly to the back of the room. The rest began to leave or stood around to talk in small clusters.

Those from the media were swarming around Franklin, taping his answers to questions, basking in his folksy demeanor. Next, they were taking turns escorting him away for individual interviews.

When Franklin finally walked out the door, his name was called from the parking lot. Looking around, he saw Kelly gesturing to him and walked over to where the younger man was sitting in his car. "A lot of us owe you one, Frank. The more you talked the more reality sank in."

Franklin shook his head back and forth. "I don't know, son. I didn't know some of the people in there or how capable they may be of keeping themselves focused. Between you and me, I kind of hedged my real feelings in there tonight. How about if we get together sometime in the next few days? I have to talk to you about some of this."

It was after ten o'clock before Kelly was able to leave the station after writing up a report to the Chief on the meeting at the Legion hall. He resisted the urge to look at his mail slot or to check his e-mail, for he was fatigued beyond what his active curiosity would normally compel him to do.

It took him only ten minutes to reach his home from the station and in spite of some of the concerns building within its confines, it was a welcome sight on this night. He parked in the driveway, and after turning off the engine, paused for a few seconds before getting out and walking to the door that opened into the kitchen. It was unlocked, for he was never able to convince Mollie to make it a habit to secure the home when he was away, even with the events of the past several days.

The house was dark but for a table lamp in the living room, next to where Mollie lay on the couch in her nightgown and robe. She was asleep and a book rested next to her nose ready to fall off the edge of the cushion. Kelly picked up the book and set it on the table. He carefully removed her reading glasses and placed them next to the book. When he began to reach for the lamp switch, his wife opened her eyes and stretched.

She glanced up and smiled at him. "You live around here stranger?" She sat up and patted the cushion beside her.

Kelly more fell than sat down beside her. He began running his fingers through her hair. "How are you? I guess we haven't seen much of each other the past few days."

Mollie put her arms around Kelly. "It's like you're away somewhere. I miss you. I've been worried about you. I don't know who you're dealing with." She drew her arms away and then ran her hands over his cheeks while gazing into his eyes.

"I don't know who I'm dealing with, either." Kelly leaned back, put his arms around her and drew her close. "You sleeping any better?"

Mollie rested her head on his shoulder and then shook it back and forth. "Last night was okay. The night before was bad. I kept dreaming about the kids. There were those others, but for some reason I kept seeing that little Samantha, then I'd wake up. I keep thinking about those big brown eyes, so full of wonder." Kelly felt her begin to shudder and then heard her begin to cry. He held her more tightly but she began sobbing loudly.
"Oh…..Kelly…..she was only eight……just eight…and the others…..Oh, Kelly. I'm a grandmother…..those were someone else's grandchildren."

Mollie put her arms around his neck once again and continued to weep. Kelly pressed the side of her head against his own. He felt a sense of abject hopelessness, as his own face became wet from her tears, holding her as she heaved convulsively.

Silently he damned himself for thinking only of his own troubles. He knew that his wife was mourning, mourning the loss of someone else's children.

Tears welled in Kelly's eyes too, for he remembered the past August day when school had begun. Mollie was reading the newspaper when she dropped it and began to laugh. "Oh, Kelly, there's this new little girl at the school. Her name is Samantha and she's the sweetest thing. I've got to tell you what she said when she walked into the building for the first time....".

Kelly could not recall the first thing about what Samantha had said that day. It was sufficient to simply remember that Mollie loved that little girl. That was all he cared to remember. He had kept from Mollie the detail that he had helped a fireman pull the charred body of Samantha from the wreckage of her home two hours after the house had exploded in fire, though he did not know her identity at the time. Her own mother, also killed in the fire, would not have been able to identify her. It was not until he and the Chief were briefed by the fire inspector the next day that he even knew it was a little girl they had recovered.

Mollie had quieted now, still trembling and crying softly. Kelly ran his fingers through the shoulder-length salt and pepper hair, and felt himself holding her more tightly. "I'm sorry", he whispered. "I'm sorry I've left you alone so often. I love you very, very much."

She drew away slowly, and then put her face close to his. "I know that. And I'm crazy in love with you. I just wish things were..... you know....just right."

"Don't start thinking things are worse than they really are. Okay? A lot of us are rattled right now."

"For a detective you sometimes have a hard time sounding convincing."

Kelly placed his own hands around hers. "There's a big difference between real problems and things not being perfect. Besides, I don't see any real problems."

Mollie leaned her head against his chest. "I may have to keep reminding myself that you said that, especially when you're not around."

Kelly sighed. "That probably won't change for a while. When this is all past us I want for us to go away for a while. I need a change of scenery….the first chance we get."

~~~

Kelly rose at 6:00 the next morning and was fumbling with the coffee maker at the kitchen counter when he stopped and turned on the small television mounted beneath the cupboard. He was greeted and startled by the coverage of the town meeting, centered upon comments by Franklin.

A reporter from NBC held a microphone in front of the familiar face. "No, I feel that the people of Averton are reacting quite logically to such an unthinkable tragedy. And if I can do my share to help reassure them that everything is being done to protect them, it's the least I can do.'

"We don't want to overreact at all. Still, the happenings here have been extraordinary, so we have to be creative. Perhaps we can do more to protect ourselves."

Kelly smiled and shook his head. He suspected that he would soon be called upon to attend a few more meetings and lecture residents on the dangers of finding enemies in the bushes.

Suddenly he saw Franklin's face again but realized that now the picture was live, although the backdrop was the site of destroyed armory. He stood motionless as the Today Show host interviewed his friend.

"Mr. Norwood, it's evident that the people of Averton are looking to you for some leadership. Does that say something about the local law enforcement and city fathers?"

Franklin laughed and made a waving gesture. "Of course not. As a matter of fact, our police force is excellent, as is the city's leadership in general. You just have to understand, Averton is a small town. We are certainly not used to being attacked, nor are we accustomed to all of this attention."

The host paused for a moment, while a five-second clip from the town meeting was replayed. "Mr. Norwood, after the meeting last night some have likened you to Averton's version of John Wayne riding to the rescue. How do you react to that characterization?"

Franklin laughed heartily and appeared to blush through the make-up. "No.....please, let's not go there. I'm retired. I have more time than others may have, that's all. I may try to establish some form of citizen patrol, perhaps in the form of an enhanced community watch program. We just have to make sure we stay out of the way of the police and sheriff's folks. Nothing more elaborate than the conditions call for."

The co-host came onto the screen, removed her glasses and smiled. "Mr. Norwood.....after the clips from the town meeting were shown on the evening news yesterday, we got some e-mails about you, mainly from women. One described you as 'sexy, in a folksy kind of way'. Do you have any response to that?"

Franklin shook his head. "I'm an old man. Let's not get silly. But I must say, my wife is taping this and I just may have to play it for her from time to time."

The co-hosts laughed and thanked Franklin for appearing, before going on to another story. Kelly shook his head, smiling as he poured his coffee, anxious to see Mollie and tell her what had happened.

CHAPTER 3

Two weeks after the explosions and deaths, Averton was a town without a sense of balance. People would meet each other on the street and converse but what was noticeably absent was laughter. There was a sense that to laugh was to show disrespect, to exhibit a lack of sensitivity to the dead and a way of life that was gone. Averton is a small place, yet large enough that you never knew when the stranger next to you on a street corner or in a checkout line was a close friend or relative of a victim.

There was hollowness in the sunken eyes of the now insomniac populace. Local businesses suffered from a lack of patronage from outside Manchester County while residents escaped to nearby towns for the smallest of reasons to spend some time in places assumed to be safe and removed. However, doctors, pharmacies and liquor stores could hardly keep up with the demand for their services.

Calvin Meyers drove along the state highway between Cincinnati and Averton enjoying the green early-morning landscape. He had called Kelly Hastings three times during the past week to exchange what was very little information that each could give the other, but it was time for a face-to-face meeting.

As he pulled into the town at eight o'clock, it occurred to him that the place seemed to be the way it was before. On the few occasions on which he had driven through the town he had never seen the streets crowded. He did not mind being in a place where you could find a place to park and be in and out of the city limits within a few minutes.

He waited in the police department lobby for a moment, until Kelly ushered him in and the two walked to Kelly's office. Meyers sat down and began to speak

"I called you on Tuesday but you were out. I ended up talking to the Chief. Now, if I understand this right, he's going to retire in two years. You going to try and move up?"

Kelly waived away the suggestion. "I'm already eligible to retire. I have to decide if I want the extra headaches. I almost forgot that break-ins didn't stop just because of these bombings. The assaults still happen and folks still try to walk out of markets with a free pack of smokes. And, in the meantime I don't have the first clue as to who killed Wally March."

Kelly halted and nodded toward the door. "I want to bring in Marcia Young. She's my second-in-command among the detectives and she also serves as a shift supervisor during the day." Kelly picked up his phone and a few seconds later a tall slim blonde woman joined them. Marcia shook hands with Meyers and took a seat at the corner of the desk.

Kelly moved a stack of files toward Meyers. "Naturally, I'm working mainly on this case. I've re-interviewed every neighbor I could find around the armory. Some still haven't come back and we need to talk to them.'

"As for the warehouse where we found the car, three neighbors said they saw vehicles around there in the evening. They tend to keep an eye on the warehouse because of crap that happens there. But all they had was a blue sedan, a small red coupe, and an old green station wagon. Nothing more, except one of them saw a husky guy walking along the road near dark."

"Much of a description on him?"

"Not as much as I'd like. A passing jogger called us a few days ago and said there was a guy, maybe in his late sixties, five-nine or ten, real burly, wearing sunglasses. We don't have hair color because this guy was wearing a cap. Not enough for a sketch artist to work with. What have you got?"

Meyers laughed. "The ATF says that the C – 4 explosive was nothing special. It's domestic. The detonators were typical."

"Made in America?"

"Yes, but made in America in somebody's normal everyday house or apartment. Maybe not just anybody's, but someone who has a hobby shop or small lab could have come up with something."

Marcia seemed stunned. "The feds have to look for some hobbyist? There's nothing to trace?"

Meyers shifted in his chair. "Three years ago, outside of Pittsburgh, some plastic was stolen from a secured vault at a demolition company. The same general type was used to blow your substation. But, get this – the demolition company had three different brands in that vault and some of each was taken. The records were deficient, so the theft was never solved. Somebody thought ahead."

Kelly folded his hands on top of the files in front of him. "I've gone through our own local paper…..nothing. I've talked to retired cops, former prosecutors and judges. I tell you, this has been a dull town. I can't find anyone who has a grudge this major against the town in general. No one's been shafted by March or the local unit, at least enough to stand out as a suspect."

"Any other physical evidence?"

Kelly shook his head. "That night everything got so chaotic a lot of the normal care that would have been taken got pushed aside. We sent some stuff away to the labs, even in the last couple days, things that were collected from inside and outside the car."

"Like what?"

"Nothing much inside the car except for a crushed pine needle and a few grains of real fine dark brown sand. There were some grains on the pavement outside the car, too.'

"We also sent away some carpet fibers. Mind you, Marcia here took those samples after officers had walked around and they could have been there for months. Things could have been transferred from the pavement to the inside of the car. For that matter, kids play there. Some hang out there to smoke dope."

There was a knock on the door and a uniformed officer leaned in. "Excuse me, Captain. There's someone out here we think you ought to talk to."

"About the big case?"

The officer nodded. "She saw something."

Kelly got up and pulled another chair up. "Bring her in."

Meyers was moving his chair aside to make room for the visitor when the door opened again. A short overweight young woman pushing a stroller containing a sleeping baby was brought in. Kelly gestured to the vacant chair and she sat down without saying a word.

"I'm Captain Hastings. This is Lieutenant Young, and this is agent Meyers from the FBI. Could I have your name?"

The young woman stared unemotionally at the pad upon which Kelly took notes. "Marilyn Brenner."

"Where do you live?"

"301 West. I live in the yellow house across the street from the armory. The duplex next to the house that burned down….?"

Kelly nodded. "We didn't know where you'd gone. None of your neighbors did either."

The woman shrugged, and looked down to check her baby. "I found your note attached to my door. I didn't want anyone to know where I was. I've been trying to keep away from my husband. Plus, there was glass everywhere."

"Is that what you wanted to tell us about? Something to do with your husband?"

"No….well, I saw a van at the armory that night. Sammy woke me up. He was crying and I was going in to give him a bottle. I must have slept through the power station getting blown. That was the first I knew the power was off. His bottle was cold and he didn't like the cold milk, so I had a hard time feeding him."

"What time was this?"

"Well, it had to be past 2:00 in the morning, if that's when we lost power. I don't have a watch. The clocks were already stopped…..I'm not sure what time it was. I just know that sometime later, all hell broke loose across the street. Sammy was screaming, and I just bundled him up and ran a few blocks away to a friend's house."

"Is there some reason you waited this long to tell us about the van?"

The woman took a deep breath. "I thought it was my husband. He has a dark-colored van. That's all I know, is that it's dark blue, or black or something. My sister told me about it. He bought it after we split up a few months ago."

Kelly leaned back in his chair. "Why did you think it was him? What would he be doing there in the middle of the night?"

"He's done it before. We've broken up a couple of other times. He's sat down the street and watched the house. He's even set out in front. I guess he'd like to know if I was seeing anyone else. That's why at first I thought it might have been him sitting at the armory." She leaned toward the desk, and he voice lowered. "He's beat the crap out of me, lots of time. I didn't really want to talk to you guys."

"Did you ever call us for help?"

"I was afraid to. That'd only make it worse."

"What's his name?"

"Tommy. Tommy Brenner."

"About thirty, short, wiry guy?"

"That's Tommy."

Kelly nodded. "I know him. I've talked to him a few times, different things. I don't remember you, or coming to that address."

"We were on and off, like I told you. We moved around a lot. We've been on welfare a lot. I am now."

Kelly leaned back and nodded. "Tommy's been arrested a few times. I've picked him up for petty larceny if I remember right. Maybe some disorderly conduct?"

"That's Tommy, all right."

"You said that you weren't that familiar with his van."

She squirmed in her chair, and her face flushed. "I don't think it was him I saw that night. At least, my sister says so."

"How did she know?"

The young woman tilted her head and looked at Kelly as if she were annoyed. "She says she slept with him that night. That's happened before, too. She likes to rub my nose in it."

"You're sure he was with your sister that night?"

"That's what she said."

"What can you tell me about the van at the armory?"

"Just a plain, regular van. I thought it was him because it was a dark color. The power was out though."

"I know it was dark out there. But the license plates….did you see them?"

"I looked because I thought that's how maybe I could find out if it was Tommy. But there weren't any."

"Do you remember anything else about the van? Old, new, the type of wheels? Do you know what type of van it was?"

She shook her head. "I can't tell one from another. It just looked like a…regular van."

"Did it have a lot of windows?"

"Uh-uh. It was like a delivery truck kind of van. No windows."

"What about people? Did you see anyone nearby?"

"No. The baby had me busy. I'd just look out every once in a while to see if it was still there. It scared me that I didn't see anybody, 'cause I thought Tommy might be outside my place."

"Is he living with your sister now, or does he have another place?"

"Tommy's livin' in the back part of that carpet shop on South Main. It has a little apartment, a one-room place. He knows how to lay carpet and he's working off his rent, and picking up a little spare money."

"How could he buy a van?"

The woman shrugged. "It could be really old for all I know."

Kelly leaned forward over the desk. "I know your sister said he was with her. But, this is very important. We'll want to talk to him."

She shook her head vigorously. "He'll know I've talked about him. He'll come looking for me."

"Can you go anywhere for a couple of days?"

She stood up quickly and then angrily turned the stroller toward the door. "I suppose I'll have to."

Kelly stepped quickly in front of her. "What address will you be at? We may need to ask you some more questions. And….I'll see to it that our cars cruise by there."

The young woman sighed while looking at the floor. "881 Columbia. I'll be with my mother."

Kelly picked up the phone, and called the shift supervisor, who arrived in the office within seconds. "Have Mrs. Brenner here fill out a statement about the van she saw the night of the bombing."

Before Kelly could thank her, she was out the door so he immediately pulled out the phone book while Meyers watched with amusement. "How well do you know this Tommy?"

Kelly pushed buttons as he replied. "A real loser. We need to follow up on this, but I think it's a dead-end…...Mary? Kelly Hastings here. Tell the judge we need a search warrant for….let's see……902 South Main, rear. Occupant is one Thomas or Tommy Brenner. Oh, we also have to search any vehicles on the premises. How quick? I'll be there."

Kelly hung up. "Want to go along? We can have the warrant in a half-hour."

Meyers nodded. "I doubt that this is your guy. But, in case it is, I want to be there. You were going to tell me more about this guy?"

"Small-time stuff. A little drug involvement, we think. He's a real hot-head, pretty unpredictable. I even pulled him over for a speeding ticket years ago and he started to take a swing at me.'

"He's a loner too. I've never known him to work with anyone else on his petty crimes. He probably was screwing his sister-in-law." Kelly got back on the phone and told the Chief what had developed and then asked for two uniformed officers to go with him and Meyers when he took the warrants to the carpet shop.

~~~

In the back of Morrison's Fine Floors on South Main Street in the downtown section of Averton, Thomas Henry Brenner filled a small pipe with hashish. He sprinkled the PCP powder on it, before lighting the mixture and passing it on to his companion. Cynthia Hammonds bore a close resemblance to her sister, Tommy's wife.

He was giddy from possession of the large sum of money before him on his narrow sofa bed. In anticipation of the feeling of exhilaration to soon come from his newly designated favorite drug, his "angel dust", he fondled the wads of bills in a worn shaving kit resting on his lap.

It was the revenue from the completion of a delivery of cocaine and a half-dozen handguns. He had three hours before he was to meet the true owners of the money, and receive his small portion for having made a substantial delivery, the fourth such he had made to establish his reliability.

Tommy knew that he planned to meet no one. He would shortly head for the interstate highway and begin a trek to Los Angeles. He would drop in on an unsuspecting cousin who would be asked to take him and Cynthia discreetly into Mexico. There, Tommy Brenner would realize his deepest ambition, looking forward to three or four years of life with no job or obligations.

The impulse came to him during the night and for several hours, he had been discounting the thought that this exchange was being monitored to test his loyalty and ability to resist temptation.

Just in case, he reached again into the battered overnight bag resting on the sofa next to him and felt the gun. He rubbed his fingers over the .45 caliber pistol along with three additional filled clips.

As he checked and re-checked his belongings, he realized that he was working more slowly. The sensations from the drugs were making him lose track of time. One more time he felt to insure the gun and clips were just below the zipper of the bag where he could retrieve them quickly.

Cynthia sat next to him inhaling hashish and PCP, taking turns with Tommy. He also gorged himself with the remaining food from the tiny refrigerator that had been furnished with the apartment.

Impulsively deciding it was time to leave, Tommy sprung up from the sofa. Just as he reached down to pick up his gear, he chanced to see moving feet in the grass through his one small window. Dropping the bags upon the sofa, he pulled back a zipper and grabbed the pistol. With his hands shaking, he flipped the safety off.

Even hearing the knock on the door and the voice stating that he was from the police, confusion set in. Tommy Brenner knew not who was at the door, but only that he was being beset upon by someone out to destroy him. He heard himself yelling as Cynthia ducked down below the window but it was as if he was listening to someone else. His own voice was divorced from him with a will of its own, making sounds unguided by his thoughts.

Kelly, Meyers, and the other officers were befuddled by the incoherent screamed oaths and ramblings coming from the other side of the door. They had decided to call in a S.W.A.T. team and cordon off part of the block against the yet unevaluated, unseen threat when Tommy began firing wildly through the closed and locked door. The crazed man began turning and firing at nothing, six shots hitting nothing but walls and furniture, the seventh blowing out a window and hitting the sidewalk next to where an officer stood. The eighth exploded into Cynthia's spine.

While the police withdrew from beside the building to take cover behind their cars, another officer ushered out the two remaining carpet store staff. Within minutes, much of the town's police department was involved in sealing off the block and evacuating surrounding businesses and homes.

Within twenty minutes from the time the shots had been fired specially trained officers with protective jackets and rifles arrived in a large tactical van. They took up positions near and on top of the surrounding buildings and began adjusting their rifle scopes. The one with the best view of the apartment's lone window was ready with both a rifle and a tear gas launcher.

Inside, Tommy Brenner could hear, but not understand, the sounds from the loudspeaker outside. The voice was imploring him to surrender but he was in a rage of revenge to punish whoever had killed Cynthia.

He sat squatting on the creaking floor, rocking back and forth on his heels. He pressed his hands over his ears as he tried to force himself to remember what to do when he had fired all the bullets from the clip.

The frustration spiraled and the confusion deepened his rage. The drugs teased him with delusions of invincibility. When the loudspeaker once again called to him, he leaped upon the sofa and jumped headlong through the window.

A dozen startled police and deputies surrounded him. Still, he rolled and stood up, his empty pistol waiving at everyone and no one. He charged at the first officer he could focus upon and was cut down by a trio of bullets.

~~~

For an hour after Brenner died, the police were engaged in stringing yellow barrier tape to keep away observers and the media while photographs of the bodies and the scene in general were taken. Kelly and other officers combed through Tommy Brenner's apartment and van looking for other clues and evidence to go along with the money found in the luggage. News crews converged on the scene, anticipating that any violence could be at least temporarily tied to the bombings.

Nauseated by the sight of the splinters of vertebrae and pool of blood and spinal fluid on the floor next to the dead woman, Kelly stepped outside to take a breath of fresh air. Soon he spotted a cruiser pulling up and saw that the passenger in the back seat was the same woman to whom he had spoken earlier that day. Upon reaching the car, he opened the door and out stepped Marilyn Brenner.

"Mrs. Brenner.....I know that you and Tommy had problems, and that your sister.....I just want to say how sorry I am." She nodded as she scanned the scene.

"Mrs. Brenner, I need to know something. Where would your husband get a large sum of money?"

She shook her head and stared blankly at the building still containing the bodies. "I don't know. He always hustled for change."

"Was Tommy ever in the military?"

Again, she shook her head back and forth.

"To your knowledge did he ever work in a job where he'd learn to use explosives?"

She stared up at Kelly. "All Tommy ever learned to do was make a woman wish she'd never met him. Can I go now?"

Kelly nodded and then opened the car door for her. "Again, Mrs. Brenner, I'm sorry."

The police department of the City of Averton had not held press conferences on a regular basis before the night of the bombings. The only room in the building sufficient for the purpose was the expansive room where the City Council met. Here it was that at 2:00 in the afternoon Kelly Hastings stood next to Chester Todd in front of the warm glaring lights accompanying the television crews. They looked out over a swarm of microphones and listened to unintelligible words echoing throughout the room as technicians mumbled into the receivers.

Kelly had only a couple of minutes with the Chief before the conference and he winced at the thought that everyone, including the Chief, may make assumptions he did not share. Standing straight but uncomfortably in front of the audience Kelly tried to memorize his superior's statement as he heard it for the first time.

"This morning our department received information that a dark-colored van was seen at the Averton armory of the Ohio National Guard shortly before it was destroyed in the explosion that resulted in the deaths of several children and adults in nearby homes as well as the mutilation of the body of the Guard unit's already deceased commanding officer, Captain Walter March.'

"Further, it became known to us that an individual who had lived on that street and may have had reason to return from time to time owned a vehicle of the same general description. Not wishing to fail to explore whether there was a connection, combined with the fact that this individual had a history of sporadic criminal activity, it was decided to interview him.'

"After obtaining a search warrant officers of the Department accompanied by an agent of the Federal Bureau of Investigation attempted to search the premises of one Thomas Henry Brenner at 902 South Main Street in Averton. Upon arrival of the officers Mr. Brenner refused to comply with our orders made over a loudspeaker to open the door and allow us to search his residence and vehicle.'

"Without provocation Mr. Brenner fired several shots through the door in the direction of the officers present. No one was known to be injured at that time.'

"An internal team of officers trained in siege and hostage situations was deployed and other precautions taken to protect the citizenry. Not a single shot had yet been fired by officers of this department or those of the Manchester County Sheriff's Department who had arrived at the scene to back up the city officers.'

"During another attempt to call Mr. Brenner out he suddenly exited the apartment through a closed window. He charged the police barricade pointing a pistol directly at one of the officers. Mr. Brenner was shot three times and was pronounced dead at the scene,'

"Inside the apartment we found the body of Cynthia Hammonds, the sister of Mr. Brenner's estranged wife. Indications are that she died from a single bullet wound to the spinal column. Further, there is evidence that Mr. Brenner was preparing to travel and one hundred twenty thousand dollars in cash was found on his possession. In addition, we found three loaded clips that fit the .45 caliber handgun he was carrying as well as small quantities of what is suspected to be hashish, PCP and cocaine. All assumed drugs found were in quantities that would be considered to be for personal consumption. I'm willing to take questions at this point."

There was an uproar of simultaneous questions and the Chief pointed to a young woman from CNN. "Chief, is it your opinion that Mr. Brenner is the likely suspect in the armory bombing or the murder of Captain March?"

Chester cleared his throat. "There are several factors which lend itself to that possibility, although there is no way at this time we can confirm that the van found at his residence is the same one seen at the armory that night. We were told that there was a 'dark-colored van without windows, like a delivery truck'. The one found at his residence was a 1984 dark-blue Dodge cargo van with windows in the back doors but none along either side of the cargo area.'

"Secondly, Mr. Brenner was known to have a very sporadic and marginal employment history. The fact that we found such money in his possession would indicate that he had been paid to perform some unusual and risky task.'

"Last of all, Mr. Brenner had a history of aggressive behavior and certainly showed callous disregard for the lives and safety of others by shooting his sister-in-law and firing several shots in the direction of officers this morning. So I would say that the possibility that Mr. Brenner is a piece of our puzzle would be a possibility."

Again, there was a chaotic shouting of questions and the Chief pointed to a reporter from the local newspaper. "Chief, will you now be focusing on how Brenner could be linked to the bombing of the power substation?"

"Certainly. Of course the big question for this whole series of incidents remains to be the motive or the intended results." The Chief pointed to a Columbus CBS affiliate reporter.

"Chief Todd, is it possible that Thomas Brenner is solely responsible for the murder of Captain March, and both bombings?"

Kelly tensed up. He feared that the Chief could not resist the temptation.

Chester paused and remained silent for a moment. "I would have to say that given the fact that the two locations are only a few miles apart, yes it is theoretically possible that he did it all. However, we found motorcycle tracks neat the Manchester Valley Power substation, rather than tracks made by the type of vehicle seen near the armory. That would mean that the motorcycle tracks were just a coincidence and that the van or some other vehicle was allowed to sit in the roadway while the substation was sabotaged, since the driveway there is gated off at the road. It's more likely that Mr. Brenner, if involved at all, was only one of the players in this story.'

"In addition, to have pulled off both bombings would have required Mr. Brenner to have possessed a great deal of quickness and agility."

Without being called upon the same reporter shouted above what had become the loudest clamor yet. "Chief, are you saying that with the death of Brenner, the murder of Captain March has been solved, if nothing else?"

Kelly glanced over, only to see the Chief smiling faintly. "I cannot make such a sweeping generalization. We need to have more time to evaluate that possibility."

The Chief pointed to a reporter he recognized from NBC. "Chief, is it true that Brenner charged the police but never fired a shot in the process?"

"Yes, that's true. For some reason his gun was not loaded. An empty clip was found in the gun and full ones in the apartment. Only Brenner or Cynthia Hammonds could explain his actions this morning. Certainly though, the officers present at the scene had already been fired upon and could not have known that the gun was not loaded."

"A follow-up, Chief. I know the answer died with him but does it make any sense to you that someone would charge a police barricade with an empty gun?"

The Chief only shrugged with his arms outstretched. "We are waiting for some lab tests to come back. Those may not provide us with any answers."

Another reported shouted out. "Chief….will the officers who fired at Brenner be put on automatic leave?"

The Chief waved to the still clamoring reporters. "No…can't spare any officers now……I have to go."

~~~

In the early evening Chester Todd left the station and headed for his new Oldsmobile parked in his reserved space just outside the rear door. It had been at least two years since he had been to the home of his favorite detective. That time his wife Sarah, who died of lung cancer just a month later, was with him.

Just several months before he himself had been promoted to Captain and continued his own rise through the ranks of the Department Chester Todd had taken an immediate liking to the newest rookie officer. He thought back and laughed when recalling the broad-shouldered shaggy-haired applicant who had come to the station to inquire about taking the test for one of three vacant patrol officer positions.

He had watched Kelly Hastings fill out his body in frequent sessions in the department's exercise room until he began winning lifting competitions within the department. Most of all he had seen and nurtured the evolution of a mind full of questions and concern, concern that the job be done with as little fanfare and disruption to the lives of citizens as possible. When the previous Chief of Detectives left to open a private security firm in Cleveland Chester was more than willing to encourage Kelly to apply for the position.

For Chester Todd, it was ironic that Kelly Hastings would now watch as he battled to hold on to his own stamina. Unknown to his protégé, the Chief was now fighting a malignancy. It had been a week since Chester had escaped the madness of the bombings' aftermath for a couple of hours to have the tests done. They confirmed the doctor's conclusions that the liver had been ravaged by a hopeless tumor. Only sixty-two, Chester Todd had already begun the downward slide in weight and endurance and he was unsure whether those around him had taken much notice. He doubted that he would tell Kelly on this day. He knew that he had been invited to dinner to discuss serious matters, but in a relaxed atmosphere.

As he sat in the kitchen of the Hastings home engulfed in aroma and memories, he sipped coffee while Kelly and Mollie conversed with him while preparing his favorite meal of spareribs and sauerkraut. He envied them. He envied them their health and he envied them for having each other.

After the hosts had cleared the table Mollie left the two men alone in the kitchen. Kelly excused himself for a minute and returned with his briefcase. He took out a legal pad, the top page of which was covered with writing.

"I don't think Tommy Brenner blew the armory. I don't think he killed Wally March, either."

Chester leaned back and placed his index finger over his lips, a gesture Kelly knew to mean that he was ready to listen intently. "Okay. Tell me what happened today."

"We caught him in the middle of something. Maybe his wife knew more than she let on. Regardless, I can't imagine anyone who knew this guy would turn over anything so serious to him."

Chester nodded. "Why would anyone trust him with that much money?"

Kelly pondered the question. "There's a big difference between being linked to a murder rap and losing some cash. Even if it's drug money, it's rarely traceable. This was one erratic low-life punk. Besides, we haven't seen PCP in this town for some time. He was working with someone from out of town, probably out of Dayton. He used to hang out there when things got tough and tight for him here. Plus, if he'd done such nasty stuff, would he be hanging around here?"

Chester considered the question. "And, why wouldn't he have gotten rid of the cash by now?"

Kelly slapped his hand to the table. "Exactly."

Chester stared at his coffee cup. "Problem is, I think we need to work for a while on the assumption that he is our man." He saw a frown develop on Kelly's face. "Look, Kelly…..prove I'm wrong on this by trying to prove I'm right."

He saw Kelly begin to laugh, as they relived the type of exchange they had known over the years. "Do whatever you can to find any links this guy could possibly have to anyone with a motive. Check out any interactions he may have had with March even if it's a playground fight in elementary school. Check out the wives. See if these guys ever worked together. Was Brenner ever in the Guard?"

Kelly shook his head. "That's the thing. I pulled his file today. He was always impulsive. He'd get in a fight, but not if you'd tell him to meet somewhere. At least, that's what I'm being told.'

"I saw that Mike Stepple busted him a month ago for an open container. Mike told me that he went to high school with Brenner and that the guy couldn't think past today. He'd get wrapped up in something he thought would make him hot stuff then back out. He talked a lot but he was always somebody's bootlicker."

Chester shook his head. "He seemed pretty bold today."

"Angel dust, Chester. It wasn't him. It was the drugs. It fits. Any other time, he was a gutless wonder. Just wait until the lab comes back with something."

Chester shook his head. "It could explain the jump through the window. It won't explain away the van, the money or the fact that he was getting ready to take off."

"I know that."

The Chief folded his hands on the table. "Give this a chance, Kelly. I've talked to people today who just seemed so relieved because they thought we'd found at least one of the bad guys. Maybe we haven't. But if people are feeling a little more secure let's not take that away from them until we can prove conclusively that it's not the case. If some time goes by, then we have to tell them Brenner wasn't part of the bombings, then they'll handle it better than if we spring it on them now. Remember, the last thing we want to happen is to discount Brenner then have to reverse ourselves again."

"What're you saying?"

"What I'm saying is, all we can offer the folks right now is a little calm, even if it's shaky."

"Not much, is it?"

"Uh-uh. I do meet with the Sheriff and Franklin Norwood in a few days about this citizen watchdog plan. I don't think Mike has any more enthusiasm for this than I do. He's afraid they'll just get in the way. I feel the same."

"If Frank hadn't spoken up, who knows what kind of half-baked schemes we'd be trying to call off?"

The Chief waved his hands. "Don't get me wrong. I know your friend did us all a favor. My guess is he'll try to set up something symbolic then after a while let it dry up and blow away. Mike and I just know we'll be asked to get involved more than we can really afford to."

"Want me to talk to him?"

"Please do. While you're at it ask him something else. The lab called today. We may have something to check out. That sand we found inside and outside of Wally March's car? It's foundry sand. It's what goes inside the hollow parts of the castings then gets shaken and knocked out when the metal cools. Ask Franklin if he knows of any other uses for it. And ask him about the guys who work there."

Kelly leaned across the table. "Tommy Brenner hasn't been working there, Chief."

Chester seemed to be staring into the wall. "It was probably already on the pavement and got picked up on a shoe." He rubbed his forehead and seemed to tremble. "We need to re-examine the Armory site to see if there's any more there."

Kelly leaned back and sighed. "Pretty rough. You know, after all the walking around, the hoses, all the particles of brick and concrete."

"Kelly, nothing's gonna come easy from here on out."

Kelly leaned forward. "We still haven't established whether someone can tell us if Brenner was somewhere else that night. We just started digging into that."

"I know that. And if someone can claim he couldn't have been out in the middle of that night….." The Chief stopped talking suddenly and began to get up slowly. "I'm really beat, Kelly. Thanks for having me over."

The two policemen walked into the living room where Mollie was sitting and reading a book. Chester reached down and patted Mollie on the shoulder. "Great dinner, you two. I don't know which of you is the better cook."

Mollie got up and walked with the Chief to the door. "Don't be such a stranger. Promise?"

Chester nodded, then walked out to his car in a light rain as Kelly and Mollie stood under the awning on the front porch and watched him drive away. Mollie shook her head. "He's not feeling well?"

Kelly seemed to be staring into the night. "He went pale in the kitchen. I guess it's fatigue, but he's not that old. Maybe just the stress….."

Mollie leaned her head against her husband's shoulder. "Have to go away this evening?"

Kelly nodded. "I really need to follow up on something." He put his arm around her. "But I'm staying home this evening."

Kelly opened the door and they stepped inside. He glanced at his watch. "Seven. This is a short day, compared to how it's been."

Mollie pointed toward the living room. "Go have a seat. I'm going to get a couple of beers."

Kelly sank into the cushion on the sofa and gratefully accepted the chilled can from Mollie, who sat down next to him. He took a sip, then set the can on the end table.

Mollie began to speak, halted, stammered, and then began again. "I just love you so much. I'm sorry about how I've acting."

Kelly turned slightly sideways. "You mean about our love-making?"

Mollie laughed nervously. "Yeah."

Kelly sighed. "You've spoken in half-sentences…you've hinted at things. You leave me confused. Please…..talk."

Mollie took a deep breath. "I can't get past that…..I never get all….."

Kelly sighed. "It bothers you that you don't…….."

"Yeah. I keep thinking I'm doing something wrong…not doing something."

Mollie put her hands on her knees. "You know I've been checked out. It just doesn't happen for me anymore. I'm sorry. When we got married, I just thought it would happen."

Kelly placed his hand on her knee. "When we were dating, you told me all about it. You always make way too much of it."

"But I never feel horny. I mean, you know that I do feel anticipation…I always feel ready…..I think about it and look forward to it."

She leaned over and pressed her forehead against Kelly's. "It feels great. I enjoy it. I mean I….really…..really enjoy it."

Kelly took a deep breath. "Maybe I'm not very good."

Mollie snuggled against him and giggled. "That's certainly not it. I think you're quite talented."

Kelly laughed. "Maybe I'm getting old."

Mollie squeezed his knee. "When the lights go out you get younger."

Kelly put his arm around her and gave her a hug. "I know it bothers you that you don't get all crazy…a lot more than it bothers me. It's not at all unusual, you know."

"But…it does bother you."

Kelly sighed. "Mollie…..I only wish you got more pleasure, and yeh…..it gives a guy a big thrill to have a woman go off like a rocket. But you should relax about it."

Mollie paused. "Sometimes I feel like I'm always comparing myself to that super-orgasmic wife you had."

Kelly grunted in frustration. "Mollie….I've never talked to you about that. She's the one that…ahhhh. Damned life in a small town. Why can't that former sister-in-law of mine keep her mouth shut about Deb's bragging?"

Mollie let out a deep breath. "Deb tells Connie, and Connie tells me….all the details."

Kelly sat upright in mock terror. "Not all the details…..".

"Yes, all the details, even about that nickname you gave that birthmark on her abdomen."

Kelly began to sink theatrically into the couch. "Not…'the compass'."

"Yes, 'the compass'."

Both began to laugh before Mollie grew serious once more. "She talks a lot. I've heard all about how she'd really work you over …."

Kelly interrupted her. "Please. Let's stop this. Deb is my past."

Mollie leaned forward. "But there are things she did that I can't get into."

Kelly shook his head. "I couldn't live with her anymore. I'm glad I ended up meeting you. I would never trade you for her."

"Even if she was better in bed."

Kelly knew that his exasperation was visible. He turned her to face his squarely. "All I know is that I'd rather be in bed with you."

Now Kelly went silent for a moment. "Maybe I need to ask the question. Do you really enjoy having sex with me?"

Mollie crawled onto his lap and leaned back on the arm of the sofa. "Listen, big guy. I need for you to understand. You excite me. I enjoy our lovemaking. Our honeymoon was the best week of my life. Remember? You were there."

Kelly laughed. "Yeh. You about wore me out. You always give me a workout. You seem to have these…..oh…special……moves."

Mollie giggled. "I never told you this….but I remember seeing your eyes light up when I showed you that old gymnastics trophy from college."

Kelly nodded. "Yes, you do have moves….and I must agree you show enthusiasm."

"Exactly. I love to start it. You need to understand. I love the touching. I love the sensations. It all feels great to me. I need all of that regardless of the absence of any spasms and moans you may be watching and listening for."

Kelly smiled and kissed her. "Sometimes I think you start it just make me feel good, to relax me. You know, mercy sex."

Mollie put her arms around his neck. "What's wrong with a little mercy sex?"

Kelly began to stammer. "I just mean…..Oh, Mollie. It always feels great to me, too, whatever the reason".

Mollie ran her hand along his cheek. "I hope you always feel that way, even as we get older."

"I always will."

"But I'm nearly fifty-one. I'm getting more wrinkles in my face."

Kelly sighed. "I'm fifty-two and I'm growing bald."

Mollie patted herself on the hip. "My butt's getting bigger."

"I like it that way. I love to caress it."

"The veins are starting to show all over my legs."

"I love your legs. They bring you to me."

Mollie sat upright on his lap and kissed him, then stood up. "Go ahead and finish your beer. I feel like getting out of these jeans and taking a nice shower."

After the conversation just ended, Kelly wondered if she was giving him a signal. Any doubt was erased as she looked back over her shoulder at him while treating him to a series of exaggerated wiggles.

No sooner had she left the room, the phone rang. It was the shift supervisor from the Department relating that a network reporter was demanding to know department protocol regarding the use of deadly force against someone found to have an unloaded weapon.

Kelly listened patiently as the officer read to him the lengthy and nettlesome inquiry. He interrupted the caller on several occasions to object to no one in particular. Some of the passages in the letter he considered to be more accusation than question.

After nearly twenty minutes, Kelly finally hung up the phone. As he sat drumming his fingers on the end table in frustration he saw the lights dim slowly. The next thing he saw was Mollie sitting down on his lap clad in a short nightshirt.

She placed her head against his chest and sighed. "Bad phone call?"

Kelly let out a deep breath. "Uh-hum. Just a little nuisance."

Mollie slid off his lap and sat next to him, then unbuttoned his shirt and began running her fingers across his chest. "This is a good time for some of that mercy sex." Kelly kissed her then scooped her up in his arms and carried her into the bedroom.

~~~

It was an hour later that Mollie saw Kelly's eyes open. He smiled and began feathering kisses over her neck and breasts.

Mollie scooted against him and placed her head on his chest. "My, my, Detective. We haven't done the doggy thing for a long time. I don't know whether I should go chase a car or wag my tail."

Kelly laughed and patted Mollie on the bottom. "It was that tail-wagging you did in the living room that gave me the inspiration."

Mollie tugged at his ear. "Good dog. Want to get a shower together?"

Without another word, they walked into the bathroom and set about soaping and scrubbing each other. Just as they had stepped out and begun toweling themselves off the phone rang again. Kelly hurried into the bedroom wrapped in his towel to answer the call.

Mollie followed, clad in her robe, and then opened a drawer to retrieve her pajamas. She listened sympathetically while Kelly dealt with yet another media inquiry. He was sitting with his back to her, slumped over. When he hung up the phone, he moaned and remained sitting on the edge of the bed.

Mollie looked at the panties and pajamas she held then dropped them to the floor, followed by her robe. She lay down on the bed, reached for Kelly's arm and tugged him back down beside her. She then grabbed his towel and flung it away. Next, she crawled on top of him, reached over to the nightstand and dealt the phone a crashing fall to the floor.

~~~

It was just before nine o'clock, and the rain had turned to a light drizzle when Chester Todd pulled into a parking lot in front of the pharmacy in the shopping center on the edge of Averton. He waited near the counter as his prescription was being filled, then walked slowly to the checkout. As he approached, he saw a familiar figure in front of him.

"Franklin, what's new?"

The large man turned around. "Why, what's the Chief up to?"

Franklin waited until Chester was finished paying then opened the door for him as the two men walked out into the light rain.

"Anything new on the investigation?"

Chester shook his head. "Not a lot. Doesn't Kelly keep you posted?"

"He may be a good friend but he's pretty tight-lipped. You have a good man there."

The Chief nodded. "The best. Say...he didn't happen to talk to you this evening, did he?"

"Nope. Katherine tried to call Mollie to chat but their line was busy. Why?"

Chester looked around. "Then let me ask you something. That sand you use in the foundry...any other uses for it?"

Franklin looked at him with his head cocked to the side. "Not that I know of. Why?"

"Kelly's supposed to talk to you about this. You need to keep this quiet Frank. We found some grains of foundry sand in and around Wally March's car. Just a trace."

"You don't think someone from the foundry did it, do you? I thought that Brenner guy did it."

The Chief shrugged. "You know how cops are. We like to check everything out."

Franklin leaned close to the Chief. "I'll try to think of anything that might mean something. Most of the fellows there are just lunch bucket types, pretty good people. Who all knows about this sand?"

"The patrol cop who found it and the lab guys. But aside from me and Kelly, no one else knows about it. We need to keep it quiet until we find out if it means anything."

Franklin nodded. "With something of this scale I'd hate to see anything leak out that could hurt your case."

Chester began to walk slowly to his car and stretched his arms out. "What case we do have…." Chester clutched his side, bumped against his car and slid to the wet pavement. Just as Franklin rushed to him, the pharmacist came outside after locking the door. Franklin called to him and he took out his cell phone to call an ambulance.

Franklin followed the ambulance to the hospital and then waited in the emergency room lobby. After an hour, a nurse came to tell him that Chester was being admitted for observation but that he was asking to speak to him.

Franklin took the elevator to the second floor room where the Chief had been taken and found the pale weakened man in a private room. In spite of the intravenous tube in his wrist, Chester waived to him as soon as he entered the room and motioned for him to come near.

"Thanks for waiting around for me, Frank."

"What's wrong? Do they know?"

"I know you don't know me real well, Frank. But under the circumstances I'm gonna tell you something nobody outside this building knows. I'm dying. The liver's about gone. That's why I got so weak and tired tonight. They say I'll just be in here a couple of days. Then I 'm going to go back out and go to work. I have nothing left."

Franklin shook his head. "Nothing they can do…..?"

Chester grunted. "I waited too long. I had myself convinced that there was nothing wrong."

"Did you have anyone call Kelly?"

The Chief waived away the suggestion. "I'll have them call the station after you leave. The shift supervisor can leave a message for him. He can come around tomorrow and I can tell him. He's a good second-in-command. I'm hoping he'll be the new Chief. Problem is….he can retire now."

Chester's face went dark. "I thought I could hold out just a little longer. I really don't have anything else to live for."

Franklin did not notice the nurse standing behind him. "Mr. Todd, you may not feel that way after you get some rest." She looked down at Franklin. "I'm afraid I'll have to chase you out now."

Chester looked up at Franklin. "Thanks again. Remember don't bother Kelly tonight. He'll have his hands full when he has to fill in for me."

Franklin nodded and then walked out of the room. He went back outside into the rain that had once again turned into a heavy shower. He argued with himself for a moment, but then resolved to follow the Chief's wishes and not call Kelly.

~~~

Kelly awoke the next morning just before the clock was to wake him. He could not recall that Mollie had any reason on this day to rise early so he showered and shaved quickly and then dressed in the dark to not wake her.

Even after finishing breakfast, he found her still asleep. He walked silently to the side of the bed and gazed at her. He felt a maddening mixture of love for her, and anxiety over the comments she had made the previous evening.

Her doubts and insecurities were haunting. He also wondered if he had inadvertently conveyed more dissatisfaction than he felt or if his own appetites seemed to make him vulnerable to straying.

However, his mind was rested and his body sated. He looked down at the person who had offered him comfort and outstretched arms, who had just sheltered him for hours with her words and body from a hostile and trying world. He felt tears well up in his eyes and the sensation made him uncomfortable.

He left the house and as soon as he arrived at the Department a group of officers asking what he knew of the Chief's condition met him. He left immediately for the hospital and after having to show his badge to be admitted so early in the morning he walked in to find Chester Todd just waking up. The Chief was fiddling uncomfortably with the tube stuck in his arm.

Kelly pulled a chair up next to the bed. "What are you doing in here? Was our cooking that bad?"

Chester shook his head but managed a quiet laugh. "A couple of months ago I found out I have a tumor on my liver….branching out to everything around it. The son-of-a-bitch is way past the surgery stage. I have just a little time left. I'll have to step down. I….I was hoping to do that in my own good time….".

Kelly sat stunned, a chill throughout his body. "I'm sorry. Anything special I can do?"

Chester sank deeper into his pillows. "Just run the place for a while. I'm

sorry…..I know you're already horribly overworked." Chester seemed to wince from pain. "I'm sorry. I'm really tired. I can't stay awake. They gave me some stuff for pain….the pain just got bad the past couple of days. Before that I just felt sort of weak all the time." Chester's eyes went closed then blinked open again. "Talk to your buddy about that sand."

Kelly watched as his boss of many years drifted off to sleep then got up and began to walk toward the elevator. He began to feel queasy and went to the stairwell instead. As soon as he came to the ground level, he began walking rapidly to the lobby, feeling as though he could not breathe.

He exited through the main door of the hospital and walked slowly to his car. He felt as if everything around him was spinning and he had to steady himself against the fender of his car.

Once inside he opened the glove box and fumbled for a pack of opened and stale cigarettes. The bombings had not caused him to pull one from the pack. The words of Chester Todd, and before that, thinking of Mollie had overwhelmed his willpower.

~~~

Katherine Norwood pulled her car into the Hastings' driveway. Mollie, still eating a piece of toast, locked the front door and got into the car.

"I tell you, Katie, I have mixed emotions about going on this ride with you. I really hate to see you move out of the neighborhood."

The older woman reached over and patted her on the leg. I know. But we'll only be a few miles away. We can still visit a lot. For you and Kelly it can be a refuge. Anyway, I want you to see what we plan to do with the lodge."

Mollie sighed in resignation. "I suppose Frank's all excited, too."

Katherine shrugged. "As much as anyone can be, in light of all that's happened. It's all he can think about….all he talks about."

Mollie looked out the window as the countryside sped by. "It'll take a long time for us to get over what happened to those families."

Katherine's voice turned sharp. "There was no sense in those innocent people dying. Franklin says so too. He's very upset."

"It's not like he could have helped what happened, any more than the rest of us."

"I know. But someone just didn't care very much, did they?"

The two women rode in silence for a minute before Katherine spoke again. "How are things with you and Kelly?"

Mollie felt her face getting warm. Katherine looked over and noticed the redness of her friend's face.

Mollie looked over and smiled. "This morning I would say things are fine."

Katherine laughed. "I see that blush on your face."

Mollie shook her head. "Yeah......it was a great evening. We needed that."

Katherine shook her finger at Mollie. "Keep things in their proper perspective, child. Doesn't a good night give you more confidence?" She turned into the driveway of the camp, pulled up next to the lodge and turned off the engine.

Mollie seemed lost in thought. "It should."

Katherine shook her head. "Mollie, you're fifty. You're a successful school administrator. You have nothing to prove to anyone, not even Kelly.'

"You are who you are, and you're the way you are. Your husband is a lucky man, Mollie. Both of you need to accept you the way you are."

~~~

Kelly drove toward the foundry, calling in along the way to tell the dispatcher of his next stop. After parking, he opened his briefcase and took out a file photograph of Tommy Brenner. He tucked it into his sport coat and left his car.

He walked into the foundry office, showed his badge to the receptionist and asked to speak to whoever was in charge of pouring castings. She told him to talk to Louie Welch, and then escorted him to a metal door. When Kelly opened it, he was greeted by an acrid odor, a wave of heat and the sound of motors and air hammers.

He descended a long flight of steps down into the foundry and tapped a man on the shoulder, asking for further guidance. Without speaking, the man motioned for Kelly to follow and escorted him through the wilting heat and clattering sounds.

Once he was in front of a large open door, he was pointed toward a barrel-chested man holding a clipboard and shouting at the driver of a forklift. The face of the young driver was red as he nodded in response to the barrage of instructions and obscenities.

Kelly strolled into the welcome fresh air and approached Welch, who was still swearing to himself as the object of his wrath drove away. He simply held up his badge and Welch let out a grunt of acknowledgement but remained silent until Kelly produced a photo.

"Have you seen this man around the foundry?"

Welch looked at it for a moment and then nodded his head. "Looks familiar."

"Where have you seen him?"

Welch shrugged. "Aside from the newspaper? Look over here."

Welch gestured to the expansive paved area in which they stood, full of large crates, coils of copper and piles of scrap metal. He walked out into the middle and Kelly followed him.

Welch pointed to an open gate in the high chain-linked fence that surrounded the area. "We get guys walking through here all the time. Kids, too. Seems like every day somebody with no business in here cuts through. Too lazy to walk around the block, I guess. Sonsabitches would steal us blind if we let 'em."

"See that other gate over there? You go through there and you end up on the other side of the block. We leave 'em unlocked during the day to save us time. Hell of a lot cooler than going through the plant."

Kelly pointed at the photo. "You've seen this guy walk through?"

"Yeh, yeh. I've chased him out of here a few times."

"Remember the last time?"

"I remember seeing his picture in the paper after you guys put him down, and I thought how I'd just chased him out the day before."

Kelly poked at the pavement with the toe of his shoe. "You get a lot of this sand out here?"

Welch looked at him blankly and pointed over his shoulder toward the foundry. "Damned place is full of this crap. Gets in your eyes, gets in your lunch. I piss the stuff."

Kelly nodded and smiled at the foreman then handed him his card. "Thanks, Mr. Welch. Call me if you think of anything else." Welch turned away without saying a word, then aimed an obscenity-laced harangue toward a young man pushing a two-wheel cart.

It was nearing lunch time when Kelly was interrupted from signing stacks of forms. A call came from a nurse at the hospital that Chester Todd was asking to see him.

Kelly rarely used his siren and lights but did so on the way to the hospital. Upon arrival at Chester's room, he was relieved to see his mentor sitting up nibbling on a small meal.

Brushing off his hands with a flourish, Chester motioned for Kelly to sit in the chair next to his bed. Kelly was left to shake his head.

"Just a few hours ago you seemed so weak."

Chester motioned to the IV stand. "I guess I haven't been taking care of myself. The doctor was in, said I was sort of starving myself. You know, not much appetite.'

"This stuff they're giving me seems to pep me up a little. Still........Kelly, the doc says I have a few months at most. And I want to work until the day I can't go in at all.'

"This morning the mayor and city manager were in to see me. I told them both, if you want to be Chief, you should have it. All off the record of course, but they agreed. There's no one better on the force. Even if you'll just do it for a couple of years....let the town settle back in to some type of normal existence."

Kelly shifted uncomfortably in his chair. "Well....".

Chester managed a grin. "A little while ago your buddy Frank Norwood was here. I made him promise to talk you into it."

Kelly smiled and nodded. "Frank can be a convincing man...but I think that may be stretching it."

Chester leaned back into his pillow and sighed. "Please...think about it."

~~~

At 7:30 the next morning, Detective Marcia Young pulled into the parking area behind the flooring shop where Tommy Brenner had lived and died. A patrol officer stood by as she ducked beneath the yellow tape cordoning off the area then unlocked the door and set down a briefcase.

The officer watched as she knelt beside the case, took out a pair of sterile surgical gloves and then took out a compact battery-powered vacuum. She began vacuuming the floor of the tiny apartment, using a scalpel and tweezers to remove any small masses clinging to the vinyl flooring. After an hour on the floor, she moved to the cramped bathroom and went through the same routine.

Stepping outside when finished, the other officer looked at her inquisitively. "What are we looking for?"

Marcia wiped perspiration from her brow. "Pine needles.....sand......carpet fibers."

The officer nodded toward the building. "Carpet fibers? He lives in the back of a carpet store."

Marcia nodded and stepped toward her car. "Humor me. And don't let anyone cross this yellow tape. Some dogs are coming in a few minutes to sniff for explosives residue."

~~~

It was the middle of the afternoon when Kelly ventured once again to the hospital housing his mentor and friend. Arriving at Chester's room, he was at first concerned that the bed was empty. Then he looked down the hallway to see a fragile but steady figure in a robe coming his way.

He waived a file folder toward the older man. "Up to signing some papers?"

The Chief grunted and smiled thinly then guided his IV stand to his bedside. He swung his legs over the side, waving away any assistance from Kelly. He took the folder and a pen from Kelly and signed the forms without reading them.

"They say I can go home tomorrow. A nurse is gonna' stop by once a day and my brother Joe's boy is gonna' hang around some. Whenever I feel like it I can go to the office for a few hours."

Chester nodded toward the bedside table. "Thank Mollie for the flowers."

Kelly feigned a hurt look. "How do you know I didn't order them?"

Chester laughed. "Yeah, right." He looked at Kelly and his expression changed.

"Don't feel bad for me. I've had a good life. It just wasn't meant to be real long. I know I was never meant to live alone, either. Carla being gone….it sort of makes this easier. You know what I mean?"

Kelly looked down at the floor. "I hate to hear you sounding so defeated, that's all."

Chester shook his head. "It's acceptance Kelly. There's a big difference. What's this 'defeated' stuff? It's not like I'm falling short of some goal I set. Hell, it's way out of my hands. Now it's

Friday. When you wrap up today try and not go in over the weekend."

"Sure there isn't something I can do?"

Chester began rubbing his side. "Yeh, but you can't do it here. Go on now."

Kelly walked toward the door then turned and looked back at the figure in the bed. But Chester had turned his face toward the window and held his gaze there.

~~~

Kelly looked expectantly at his door when he heard Marcia Young telling his departing secretary to have a good weekend. Before her knuckles could rap the door, he flung it open.

His hopes were dashed when Marcia shook her head and frowned while sitting down in front of his desk. She took a legal pad from her briefcase and waited for the dejected Kelly to sit down.

Marcia tossed the pad onto the desk unceremoniously. "We took out a drug courier. That's all, I think."

Kelly looked at the floor. "Let's hear it."

Marcia sighed. "No pine needles. No sand, aside from normal pavement grit. Of course, there were carpet fibers but it was all the household variety. None was automotive except for a few that matched the carpet in his van."

Kelly leaned forward in his chair and began rubbing his temples. "Nothing to tie him to the March murder. Nothing to tie him to the bombing except that he drove an older van."

Kelly bit his lip. "The explosives dogs......?"

Marcia shook her head. "Nothing...no reaction."

"So Brenner......".

Marcia leaned forward. "Brenner was a piece of scum. He was running drugs. He fired toward our officers."

"And Cynthia Hammond......?"

"Was in the wrong place, at the wrong time, with the wrong guy. Her sister's husband, for crying out loud."

Kelly shook his head and rose slowly from his chair. "I'll tell Chester sometime over the weekend."

Without saying a word, Marcia turned and left the room. Kelly walked out into the hall, waved to the dispatcher and exited through the front door and into the bright June sun.

It was 5:30 when Kelly and Mollie strolled through their neighborhood toward the home of Franklin and Katherine Norwood. He could not remember the last time he had the luxury of walking slowly.

Suddenly he realized that Mollie was waving her hand in front of his face. "Hello, where are you?"

Kelly laughed, and put his arm around her. "I suppose I'm back at the Department...I'm in Chester's hospital room." He hesitated for a moment. "Chester would like to me to be the Chief when he has to step down...or dies. He's sort of greasing the skids with the city fathers, too."

Mollie stopped. "How do you feel about that?"

Kelly shrugged his shoulders. "Ten years ago I would have jumped at it. Now I can walk away today with my pension if I want. I can be a security consultant or just do more teaching....some writing like I've always wanted to do. I could move through my Ph.D. program so much faster.'

"Just think. No more victims with those pleading looks.....no more supervision." He patted the Glock pistol beneath his sport coat. "No more wondering if I can make it to retirement without shooting someone. And I came close yesterday. The others were just quicker and in better position."

Mollie patted his arm. "But if they ask you.....?"

Kelly laughed and began walking slowly again. "If they ask....I suppose I'll say yes. Chester wants me to say yes."

Kelly pointed to the Norwood home, now just thirty yards away. "What's this little gathering about?"

Mollie smiled. "Stress relief. Grilled food and beer. Just what we all need."

As they neared the house, they could see the curl of smoke from the back. There they found Franklin busy impaling chunks of meat and vegetables on metal rods.

Seeing his friends approaching, Franklin smiled and waved one of the kabobs at them. "I hope you kids are feeling carnivorous."

Kelly walked closer and stared at the meat. "That's not regular beef, is it?"

Franklin smiled widely. "Moose meat kabobs. Remember that hunting trip I took to Maine last year? I bet you two have never had moose."

Mollie shook her head. "Not unless we've had it here. Let's see, you've fed us venison, caribou, elk…".

Franklin began to chuckle. "And rattler."

Mollie turned suddenly toward Katherine, who just folder her arms and nodded.

Franklin walked toward her. "Remember that chicken salad last fall that you liked so well? You started on that sandwich before I had a chance to tell you it was snake."

Mollie grimaced and sat down in a folding chair.

Franklin shook his head. "I had promised Katie I'd never tell you." He glanced at his wife. "I think we'd better change the subject. I'm glad this stuff cooks quickly. It's almost done."

Franklin turned to Kelly. "I understand you met my old foreman Louie Welch?"

"Yeah. I did."

Franklin moved closer and spoke quietly. "Louie's a little rough around the edges. But he worked hard for me and I respect him. We stay in touch. Anyway, he called me this morning. He just got word his older brother in Alaska's getting a divorce. It hit Louie hard so I invited him to be here."

Franklin had just finished speaking when the subject of their discussion came around the corner of the house. Franklin introduced him to Mollie and he shook hands with Kelly, adding a grunt of recognition.

~~~

Through most of the meal, they made small talk. There were some teasing references to Franklin's interviews on national television and how the reporters had returned for more chats with the man who had become Averton's father figure. Kelly had found a brief respite from his job until Franklin finished eating and leaned back in his chair.

"I heard that your boss went home today."

"Yeh. I'll stop by and see him again tomorrow evening. He doesn't like people around when he's sick. Even when it was something mild, he was that way. His wife told me he'd about chase her out of the house if he had to stay home and that didn't happen very often. I'll leave him be until he gets settled in."

Franklin nodded. "I felt sorry for him the other night Kelly. He was really down. The nurse and I heard him say that he didn't have anything to live for."

Kelly sighed. "Being widowed has been really tough on him. I know he was looking forward to them traveling when he retired. He isn't the type to talk a lot about personal things but he does mention that fairly often."

Franklin moved his empty plate aside. "Any luck with anything?"

Kelly shrugged. "Still trying to nail down the final proof that Brenner guy killed March."

Franklin appeared to be surprised. "I thought that was settled."

Kelly shook his head. "If Brenner was alive we could never convict him on what we have. Everything's circumstantial. A van roughly similar to his, a lot of money and a gun, one that wasn't even involved in the murder."

Katherine broke in. "Maybe that stuff is circumstantial to the police. For everyone I talk to, it's good enough."

Franklin put his hand on Kelly's shoulder. "I know your point Kelly. You're a professional. But, under the circumstances, can't you give yourself a break? It was Brenner that killed March. We all assume that. How many hours can you work in a week? I'm telling you, son, the whole town believes it was him. Chalk one up on your side."

The silent Welch finally spoke. "I just know when I had to chase him out of our shipping yard, I could see it in his face......the piece of crap was no good."

Kelly leaned forward. "Please fellows, take this the way I intend it. First of all, if I can't gather the type of evidence to prove the case in court, I don't know if the next steps are the right steps. Second, think about what you're saying. Everyone believes he was guilty even if no one knows a motive. Brenner wasn't much but he still has relatives here and other places. Some kids are going to grow up as Tommy Brenner's children. It's important for them. It's important for everyone he's related to and everyone he was friends with, no matter what or who they are."

Welch took a drink from his bottle of beer. "Yeh.....I suppose it means something to remember your old man as a drug dealer rather than a murderer."

Franklin sighed loudly. "I think this Brenner guy was a hired fellow....hired by somebody.....actually, some group. I still think he blew the armory.....killed March, too."

Just as the gathering went silent, they heard a car engine rev then a door close nearby. Franklin started laughing. "She always has to goose that BMW before she shuts it down."

A moment later, a stunning and petite woman with shoulder-length red hair strode into the yard. She wore a short blue flowered sundress, one that scooped low in the front, and when she walked over to kiss Katherine it was revealed that the back was cut away halfway to her waist.

Katherine rose and then introduced her to Molly. Next, she walked the younger woman to where the men were sitting, and introduced her to Louie Welch, who simply remained seated and shook her hand. Franklin received a hug before Katherine guided her to where Kelly now stood.

"Kelly…this is Laura Bond…..my niece by marriage. I mean…..my first marriage….". Katherine put her arm around the redheaded beauty and laughed. "She's my niece."

Kelly took her hand lightly. "I've heard of you of course. Frank and Katie are certainly happy to have you in Averton."

Laura nodded. "Not as happy as I am to be here. After the rat-race I left behind….well, the thought of coming here and working in a book store…..it seems too good to be true."

Kelly found himself nearly stuttering. "If…if I can be of any help, let me know."

"I will." She smiled to Kelly over her shoulder as she and Katherine walked back to where Mollie sat.

Kelly tried to hide his distraction as he casually conversed with the other men but found himself watching the enchanting woman listening to Mollie's every word with rapt attention as they occasionally glanced in his direction.

Franklin suddenly stood up and walked to where Laura sat. Speaking loudly so that all would hear, he proclaimed, "Laura has a talent. She does impressions."

Laura turned and feigned outrage. "Uncle Frank…..".

Katherine waved away the words of her husband. "Not now, Frank."

Franklin stood. "Come on Laura. Do Bette Davis."

Laura put her hands over her face and began to laugh. However, just as she rose again, Kelly's pager beeped. He leaped to his feet, took several steps away from the others, and punched a speed dial number on his Blackberry. As she watched her husband's expression Mollie's own face went ashen. There was a special gravity in his look. The rest could not hear what he was saying but after a few minutes, he returned and did not sit down.

He looked toward Mollie and shook his head. "A squad car is coming to pick me up" His voice grew louder so that all could hear. "There was a truck bomb in Ithaca, New York…the Cornell campus. It went off on the street between a classroom building and a co-ed dorm….lots of casualties. And another went off in Southington, Connecticut. It was sitting in a narrow alley between two factories."

The pager toned again and he once again distanced himself from the rest as he called his office. He listened intently, ignoring the police cruiser now parked along the street. Finished speaking, he snapped the phone closed and took a step toward the street before turning around again.

"Small town…..Florence, Arizona. Their water plant blew up along with their electrical plant….." Kelly began rubbing his forehead. "Corcoran, California….Amtrak station blew up. There were some people in the terminal….lots of track ruined, too."

Kelly saw Katherine rising slowly, a look of anger on her face. She turned toward Franklin, tears welling in her eyes.

"This…… isn't necessary. Why do so many people have to be killed?"

Franklin walked to her side and put his arm around her. "Katie…..you're getting too upset by all this."

Kelly walked slowly at first toward the waiting car. He looked around at the group and shrugged his shoulders.

"I've got to go. Sorry." He fixed his gaze for a moment on Mollie then turned and waved to the others before breaking out in a jog as the others walked inside the house to turn on the television.

Laura Bond grabbed her purse and pulled out her car keys. "I have a friend teaching at Cornell…". She ran around the house and to her car.

The scene inside the Averton Police Department was a buzz of activity as was every other in the United States at the moment.

However, in Averton, it took on a heightened sense of urgency and before he had arrived, Kelly had ordered all off-duty officers to report. Within minutes, every available officer was cruising the city, paying special attention to stores, churches or any other building that could hold large numbers of people.

Kelly strolled to the break room, where the television was turned to a news channel. He watched one station for a few seconds, and then would switch to another. The results of the bombings were predicable.

The Secretary of Defense announced a higher alert for the military while half the states had put their National Guards on standby. News pundits interviewed retired military commanders about the possibility of martial law and former mayors and governors weighed in with their advice.

Reporters stood in front of mall entrances from which shoppers and store employees were being evacuated. Video footage showed increased security personnel around the country guarding buildings, tunnels and bridges.

As for Averton, it was as if the people had returned to the feelings they had known seventeen days before. Stores emptied and even the typically minimal traffic in the downtown was cut in half. Inside the homes of Averton guns were loaded, hands wrung handkerchiefs and nervous fingertips ran across knuckles as hands folded in prayer.

~~~

As the gathering at the Norwood home remained riveted to the scenes on the television, they did not notice the white *Newsnet* van pull up in front of the house. Cynthia Yardley departed the vehicle then looked in the side-view mirror and examined the raven hair to insure it was in place. She nodded at her own image and then motioned for the camera operator to follow her to the house.

Having the iconic Franklin Norwood all to herself was some consolation for being the only news network reporter left to stay behind in the small town as her colleagues went off to chase the newest upheavals around the country and the world. Two of her keenest rivals within her own network happened to be in New York today and were quickly on the scene in Ithaca, a turn of fortune that grated on her.

When Franklin answered the doorbell, the look on his face was one of amusement. He stepped out onto the porch and placed his hand on the shoulder of the correspondent.

"Ms. Yardley.....I thought you'd be covering the latest carnage."

"I am. I'd like to get some comments from you."

Franklin nodded. "Okay. I hope this is okay out here....we have some company."

The reporter attempted to move and see around Franklin. "Maybe they would like to give some comments....as Averton residents seeing this happen in other places."

As she took a step toward the house, Franklin suddenly stepped in front of her, so quickly it startled her and made the camera operator take a fast step toward him.

Franklin held up his hands and smiled apologetically. "Please, no....I just have to trust that this would in no way be mentioned. My wife....Katie.....all of these incidents has affected her greatly. She's in the house and very upset. She can't sleep. I do what I can to keep her away from all this. I hope you understand."

The reporter took a position next to Franklin and waited as the camera operator counted down with his fingers. She held her microphone up and began the interview.

"Mr. Norwood, what is your reaction to the breaking news of attacks on other American communities?"

Franklin took a deep breath and looked thoughtfully at the camera. "I know how the folks in these other towns feel and I'm sure the thoughts and prayers of all of us in Averton go out to them. I'd say now that someone has thrown down the gauntlet to the American people."

The reporter tilted her head as if confused. "Could you explain what you mean by that?"

Franklin remained silent for a moment, and then began gesturing with his hands. "Obviously, some organized group has set out to unravel our feelings of security and safety. This is different from 9-11. As horrible as that was, as immense as the damage and loss of life I find the attack on Averton and all these towns today to be more ominous.'

"You see, the 9-11 targets were symbolic of American power and influence. The same with the later car bombings in New York and Washington. The seeming randomness of these attacks can only be for the purpose of telling Americans that no one is safe and no one can protect them."

Cynthia Yardley was nearly giddy with her fortune. All the other networks were probably taking turns filming the same scenes.

"Mr. Norwood, we saw the people of Averton turn to you for leadership. What can you suggest to anyone concerned for the safety of their own communities?"

Franklin nodded. "I say this with great reluctance. But even the finest police force such as ours right here can only do so much. I believe it's time for citizens to organize and protect themselves, of course within the laws of their communities."

The reporter could barely contain her gratitude for good luck. "Are you suggesting that Americans form local defense groups, even armed? Even militias?"

Franklin laughed. "Please, let's be clear about this. A lot can be accomplished by simply organized vigilance, keeping an eye out, let's say. But each community should decide for themselves what level of increased protection is needed. And, of course, each individual must make decisions about how to protect yourself or your home and family."

~~~

Kelly could only remain in his office for a few minutes at a time. As the evening wore on toward midnight, he made more trips to the break room television than he could count.

Gazing once again at the set, he did not at first notice the contingent standing in the hallway, visible through the glass wall. There stood Mollie, her eyes red, her expression distressed, next to the shift supervisor.

They entered the room, where Kelly stood alone next to a table. Mollie turned to the other officer and placed her hand on his arm. "Thanks for calling me, Mike." The officer nodded and walked slowly away, his own face contorted in pain.

Mollie ran quickly to her husband, put her head on his shoulder, and began crying. Slowly, she pulled away and looked up at Kelly's face. "It's Chester."

Kelly shook his head, his eyes closed tightly.

Mollie wiped tears from her face. "His nephew brought him home this afternoon, then tonight he found him hanging in his garage."

Kelly nearly collapsed, but managed to lower himself into a chair. He glanced up and saw Mike Halbertson still standing by.

The officer walked in slowly, his hands in his pockets. "Sorry, Captain. I hope it's okay that I called….".

Kelly stood and nodded. "Thanks Mike. I'm glad you called her."

The officer turned to walk away but Kelly called after him. "Mike….what do we know?"

The rattled policeman took a deep breath. "The 911 call came about 10:30. First impression is that he'd been dead for about a half-hour. The nephew works in the evening, so he'd stop in around eleven to see if the Chief was in bed or needed anything. He's all broke up, finding him like that."

Kelly looked down and rubbed his eyes. "Has he….been removed yet?"

Mollie looked at the other officer and shook her head. "No Kelly, not this one. Tomorrow will be hard enough. Let your officers handle this."

For a moment, Kelly was unable to speak. Finally, he stood in silence as Mollie fished her car keys from her pocket and gently took hold of Kelly's arm to guide him out of the station and to her car.

In silence on the drive home, Kelly still did not say a word as he unlocked the door to their home. He walked through the dark house and opened a cupboard in the kitchen to find aspirin for the throbbing headache that had beset him.

A few minutes later, Mollie looked for her husband, only to find him lying on the bed in their dark bedroom.

"Are you okay?"

"I don't know", Kelly replied with a gravelly voice. "What else can happen?" He raised his head and propped up the pillows.

"I can't stand it that I'm this way. I never thought that I'd break down like this. It's not just Chester....it's all those others. What am I up against? All around the country…".

Mollie lay down next to him. "I hated to see that much death. But now it's going to be more of a national case. There won't be so much pressure on you now."

Kelly shook his head slowly. "But it started here. We can't get away from that. It started here. That means even more pressure on me."

Mollie patted his arm. "I know. I was lying to make you feel better."

There was silence for a minute, before Mollie spoke. "I left the Norwoods a little after you got called away. Katie was so upset she had to go to bed. I thought Franklin seemed a little cross with her. Normally, he's a big teddy bear when it comes to Katie."

Kelly moaned. "It's the stress....the damned stress. Right now, it seems more than I can handle. But guys see a lot worse than this in war. Why can't I handle it?"

Mollie pushed herself up on her elbows. "Are you serious? For weeks, you've had very little sleep. How many cops have to deal with what you've faced? A lesser man would have buckled under it all. And you just lost your mentor….your friend."

~~~

It was six o'clock the next morning when Marcia Young knocked on the door of the Hastings home, bringing Mollie to answer in her nightgown. "Kelly's still asleep. Have a seat."

Marcia sat down on the sofa and waited nervously while Mollie entered the bedroom quietly and sat down next to Kelly. She shook him gently, and then he woke with a start. He looked at her with an expression that made her feel that he was pleading to hear something.

She leaned down and kissed him, then simply whispered, "It really happened." She watched as her husband seemed to sink lower into the bed, and then gestured toward the door.

"Marcia's here. You ready to talk to her?"

Without saying a word, Kelly got up slowly and walked out of the room in the rumpled clothes he had on when he went to sleep. His legs were rubbery and he sat down heavily on the sofa next to Marcia.

The detective took a deep breath and looked down at the floor. "The coroner says that the medics were right about the time of death. His body temp was still at 90, so he wasn't gone long at all before his nephew found him.'

"The nephew stopped by late afternoon and everything seemed alright, except that he said Chester was kind of cranky."

Marcia managed a thin smile. "He said he didn't think that much about it because Chester was always cranky.'

"There wasn't a note. It looks like he made a quick decision….he was hanging in the garage. He'd tied a yellow nylon rope around a crossbeam. There was a stool lying on the floor. Apparently he'd stood on it and kicked it out from under himself."

Kelly put his palms together, pointed upward. "Does the coroner say whether he went fast?"

"Kelly…..".

"Tell me, Marcia."

"He….he strangled to death. He didn't snap his spinal cord."

Kelly sighed heavily and covered his face with his hands for a moment. "I suppose I shouldn't be surprised. He was so depressed….he was talking like his life was over."

Marci nodded. "That's what we're all hearing, in bits and pieces. Oh….one more thing. He had a picture of him and his wife on a workbench in front of him."

Kelly let out a deep breath. "Nothing suspicious?"

Marcia shook her head. "We checked the stool, the rope, the picture. No prints but his. The coroner can't find any bruises on the arms, nothing that would indicate being held. Looks like a pure suicide."

Marcia stared at her now silent boss. "Kelly….Captain. Okay if I call the Sheriff….ask him to notify the surrounding agencies so they can start planning for the service?"

Kelly nodded. "We need to think about this too….considering everything maybe we should keep most of the force on duty and on patrol during the funeral.'

"The chief dying may generate more fear, so even if the Sheriff can have some patrol cars on the streets that day it would allow more of our force to attend.'

"There's always some possibility of a copy-cat incident with the idea of striking while the force is distracted."

Kelly rubbed his temples. "There could be a lot of rumors….wild speculation. Tell all the officers that it's okay to tell anyone they talk to that Chester was terminal….and depressed."

Kelly could not remember the last time the entire force had been assembled on a Saturday morning. Three officers were on patrol, but the roll call room could barely hold the gathering. As the officers filed in, he tried to listen carefully to the hushed comments in order to analyze their moods. He waited until everyone was seated, then scanned the room for a moment before sitting on a table in the front of the room.

"Let's have a moment of silence in honor of the Chief." He closed his eyes and counted silently to thirty, listening as feet shuffled and throats cleared to prevent shows of emotion. Finally, he looked up.

"As bad as we all feel, I know Chester would want us to go ahead. I hope none of you is offended by my holding this meeting. You're not an easy group to get together. I especially appreciate you guys who came in off the night shift.'

"I won't keep you long. The city manager called me last night to tell me I'm acting Chief until a permanent replacement is named. I'm designating Marcia to be the acting Chief Detective. When I'm not here, she's in charge, then the shift supervisors. That's your chain of command."

Kelly purposely avoided scanning the expressions on their faces. "Marcia will be giving out instructions for two projects. First of all, we're going to re-interview everyone who has as much as waved to Wally March before his death. Relatives, friends….key in that brother of his, the one we busted for possession. See if Wally may not have been the hero we thought. See if there's a motive for something illegal he may have been doing.'

"I know that the whole country's in a buzz this morning about the other attacks. But until we're convinced that the attacks are linked we're going to concentrate on what happened here as if nothing else had taken place.'

"The word we have so far is that the collective death toll from yesterday is close to four-hundred, most at Cornell. The blast there left a huge crater in the street. The timing caught the neighboring buildings full and the street packed with pedestrians.

That was a fertilizer bomb like the one at Oklahoma City. All the other attacks involved plastic.'

"One common trait with yesterday's attacks and ours is that all the cities are small and none are situated along interstate highways.'

"For now, we need to check out every major local blasting or demolition job over the last few years. Check with gravel quarries, anybody clearing land.....find out who does dynamite, authorized or otherwise.'

"Now, I need to know what your questions are so far."

"Chief?" A voice came from the back of the room, and Kelly felt a chill at the reference.

"Yeah, Mark?"

"What about the substation? Anything new?"

Kelly heaved a sigh. "The A.T.F.'s working on that because of the nature of the explosives. Even though the substation's in the Sheriff's jurisdiction, they're keeping me posted because of the connection with all the deaths. They're still trying to find out about the tire tracks, too.'

"It seems that so far, they know that the plastic may have come from a theft in Pittsburgh. It's the detonators that have them stumped. If all we had were the bombing of the substation, I'd say it might never be solved. As for the militia angle, that's getting to be kind of a joke with the Feds."

The same shift supervisor spoke again. "What do you think?"

Kelly sat silent for a moment. "It looks like a smokescreen. That's my gut reaction.....this morning."

A rookie detective spoke up. "We're all getting a lot of questions about Brenner. People are asking, is the case closed or not?"

"Far from it. It looks like Brenner may well have been involved. It's not conclusive.'

"March was a soldier. Maybe not real skilled in hand-to-hand, but he did lead an infantry company, so he could take care of himself. Personally, I have a hard time seeing Tommy Brenner overpowering anybody bigger than himself even if it was an ambush from the back seat of a car. I must say, though, Brenner could have been a driver. That's much more likely in my own mind. That brings me to something else on the agenda.'

"There seems to be two sides to this whole mess. The power station was obviously done swiftly and well. Traffic isn't heavy out there but that job had to be razor-sharp. It contrasts to the armory, where old deteriorating dynamite was used. The fragments tell the ATF that it was a leading brand used in the 60's and 70's, made by a firm that went out of business several years ago. Regular fuses were lit, not much more sophisticated that you'd find on a cherry bomb on the Fourth of July.'

"According to reports of the sounds made by the blasts, it seems that at least the fuses were cut with enough knowledge to make a couple of the bundles blow at about the same time. Some of the others were set off by neighboring blasts rather than the fuses.'

"The armory bombing has some similarities to March's murder. There seems to be a lot of recklessness….almost too much self-confidence.'

"When I look at all the incidents collectively, I'd say that this…..group……gang, whatever, almost seems to have a split personality. One possesses stealth and cunning….the other has more balls than brains. There may be a situation in which part of this group is sort of out of control, doing things their own way even if they're working together. It's just the pattern I see."

CHAPTER 4

Kelly stood motionless in the front row of the crowd that surrounded Chester's gravesite and was jarred when the firing squad's volley split the air. A bugler from the American Legion played "Taps", the mournful sounds rolling across the level burial grounds. Mollie felt Kelly tremble and clutched his arm tightly.

Kelly scanned the scene out of habit although the Sheriff's Department secured the area. News vans were present but at a reverent distance. Reporters at the ceremony assumed the stance and solemnity of mourners.

After a ceremony at which Kelly spoke, but could not remember, the throng filed away slowly. Kelly thought it sad that for the widowed childless man there was no home in which family and friends would gather afterward. He stood by Mollie for a moment, his gaze fixed upon the silver coffin suspended over the vault, bathed in the brilliant noon sun.

Once Kelly and Mollie had taken several steps away from the grave, reporters finally approached with questions.

"No. There is no reason to suspect this was anything but a suicide....Yes. We were very close. I'm going to miss him very much....I'm sorry. This happened so soon after the other cities were attacked, I haven't been able to come to any conclusions."

They neared his car and Mollie leaned against the door before opening it. "Do you have to go right back?"

"Not right away. This isn't going to be a very productive afternoon. No rush right now."

"Come home for lunch?"

Once they had settled into the vehicle, Kelly laid his arm on the back of the seat. "I know this sounds kind of funny.....but now that the funeral's over I have an appetite for the first time in days. Let's go to the Haven House."

Mollie stared. "The Haven House? We haven't been there for months. Won't we need reservations?"

Kelly shook his head. "It's been a while now since any restaurant here has needed reservations." He called into the department to tell where he would be and then drove to the south end of Averton to what had been their favorite restaurant while dating.

Once they had been seated and their orders taken, Kelly glanced around at the elegant furnishings. He seemed to be examining his surroundings.

Mollie took his hand. "Why did you want to come here.?"

Kelly shrugged. "I'm hungry. They serve large portions here."

Mollie looked at him with the special scolding frown she had used so often when he would evade a question. She cleared her throat theatrically and Kelly recognized that as her signal that she intended for him to answer her.

He smiled and nodded his head. "I wanted a reminder that some things have stayed the same. This has always been a place we could look forward to coming to. A retreat, I suppose." Kelly gestured to the window, through which they could view the pond. "You know how looking at the water has always put me at ease."

Mollie rubbed her foot against Kelly's leg. "I remember the last time we were here. It was our last anniversary." Kelly noticed that her face was turning red.

Mollie leaned closer. "It was our anniversary. We went home and celebrated on the sofa, then an hour later……".

Kelly laughed. "Yeh. We went to bed and celebrated again."

Mollie grasped his hands tightly. "I'm happy to see you a little more relaxed."

Kelly sighed. "I suppose I was worried I'd break down at the funeral. I was wound as tight as a spring.'

"I hope that over the last day or so, I've got most of it out of my system. I still feel uncomfortable about how everything got to me. But....I remembered what Chester said to me in the hospital. I wish he hadn't decided to deal with it the way he did. But, if he could end it the way he saw fit, who are the rest of us to grieve over his choice?"

Kelly held up his glass of water and gazed into it. "Chester wasn't very religious, you know."

Mollie shook her head. "He never talked about it when I was around him."

Kelly looked back toward the pond. "He only talked to me about it once. Funny....he was talking about death. It was before he even knew Sarah was sick. He told me he didn't know a lot but he believed in an afterlife. He said that if you believed in that you didn't have to fear dying."

"But, isn't that sort of hard to reconcile with suicide?"

"You could say that, I suppose. Any of us free of the physical pain he was feeling....the sadness he felt after Sarah died.....we can say that. I agree it doesn't make sense." Kelly looked up and saw their orders coming. "I just don't think that he was dealing with his normal senses the past few days."

Kelly picked up his fork and speared his salad then sat the utensil back down. "He couldn't have been himself. I remember years ago when a cousin of his put a gun to his own head. Chester ranted about how cowardly that was....leaving himself for a loved one to find. Unless it was the pain....".

~~~

Kelly arrived back in the department in the early afternoon. The office was bustling, but the subdued attitudes of those who worked there were more than obvious.

He went to his office, sat down, reviewed faxed bulletins, and printed e-mails on his desk. There were no solid leads for any of the more recent attacks but vague descriptions of vehicles were being broadcast nationwide. Remnants of the panel truck containing the fertilizer bomb at Cornell indicated that a vehicle had been assembled from untraceable parts.

So far, there were no suspicious purchases of materials that matched the quantities needed for such an act. Kelly read with eagerness a memo from the ATF that residues from plastic explosives were being compared to those from the local power station wreckage.

He strolled to the break room to see the news channels, and view the latest images of the damage from the attacks. He turned to CNN in time to see Averton noted on a national map along with all the other targets.

Back in his office he began sorting through more faxed messages and e-mails from around the country. The more he read of the other attacks, the more attention to Averton was diluted and the more minutes passed since the funeral Kelly found himself unwinding.

It was just after five o'clock when his phone buzzed and he heard the welcome sound of Mollie's voice. "How you doing? Getting past the funeral okay?"

"Better than I thought I would. Yeah."

"Does anyone know yet what's going on? Who's behind all this?"

Kelly laughed quietly. "No. It's still my case because of everything that happened here, but now I'm sharing it with a lot of others. It's hard to imagine Averton being a part of some nationwide plot."

"Think you can stand leaving work at a reasonable time twice in one week? Katie just called. They opened The Bitterroot today. Frank told her something about you picking out a book."

Kelly laughed. "A freebie even."

"Well, Katie said to tell you they're open until six. Frank thinks that if you have a book sitting around to read you'll cut back on your hours and unwind."

Kelly sat silent for a moment and pondered the prospect of walking out of the office. "Okay. I'll get out of here right now. See you in a while."

Kelly leaned back in his chair and stretched, then turned the remaining reports on his desk upside down. The vision of Chester lying in the coffin came to his mind and he felt a cold clammy sensation surge through his veins. He walked to the front desk to tell the dispatcher that he was leaving and then went outside into the very warm late June day.

The Bitterroot was located in what had been a house three blocks from the police department. It was on a section of street full of such former dwellings now serving as barbershops, flower shops and real estate offices. It was the lure of such a setting that had attracted the former owner, Anna Nolan, who had opened the Bitterroot and operated it until her recent retirement.

The lower floor retained its homey characteristics. Each room housed a type of books, including the kitchen full of cookbooks.

The upper floor of the modest home was remodeled into a loft area, divided between a small living space and storage area. Over the years numerous college students had found employment and housing at the site of the Bitterroot. Kelly had been a customer for many years and many of the young assistants had come to know and like the police officer who always browsed the science fiction room.

As Kelly came to the block on which the store was located, he saw two women leaving the store with bags in their hands. Coming to the front of the building, he stopped to look at the display window and the various books placed among small settings of straw flowers.

He opened the door and walked in but saw no one. He took a couple of steps toward the counter but there was only silence. His attention was drawn to what he initially thought was a sale flyer on the counter but he returned it when he saw that it was a page of instructions on how to operate the cash register.

"Katie…..Katie…..it's Kelly."

A voice called out. "Be right there. Go ahead and look around." Kelly smiled to himself as he recognized the voice as belonging to Laura Bond.

Kelly wandered through the room, seeing that Katie had arranged the books in very different manner than the previous owner. Glancing into an adjacent room, he saw the section he was looking for and was soon lost in thoughts of evenings sprawled on the sofa reading himself to sleep.

"Chief Hastings?", the same voice called out from behind him.

"Not Chief….not…..we'll see. I'm still a captain. Hello, Laura. Sorry I had to leave so abruptly when we met."

Laura walked close to Kelly while shaking her head. "I understand, Captain. I know you're never off-duty."

"Call me Kelly."

Laura had just leaned against the shelves a few inches from Kelly when a chime on the door signaled another arrival. She placed her hand on his shoulder as she strolled away.

"Be right back." Her fingertips seemed to linger as she departed and Kelly became aware of the sweet scent of her perfume as he watched her swaying form beneath the silky beige dress and the curling red hair that swept across her back.

His eyes followed until she was gone from view. He was initially amused at himself for his inability to not watch someone he found enticing. At the same time, he felt the need to admonish himself for reacting so to someone who was virtually family to Katherine Norwood.

In a few minutes, she returned to where she had left Kelly. "Aunt Katie and Frank told me that you really like science fiction." She folded her hands in front of her and looked over the same shelves.

"Ever since I was a kid. Can't tell you how many I've read." He laughed and shook his head. "Not as many as I'd like in the last couple of years. But I always found it to be a great escape from stress if even for just an hour or so."

She leaned against the shelves and tilted her head. "They've been telling me what it's been like for you and your police department. This stuff started just after I got here. I thought I'd made the biggest mistake of my life coming to Averton. It's just been the last week that I've stopped trying to talk myself into leaving as much as I'd hate to go back.....I'm sorry, Cap....Kelly.....I'll learn........Kelly. Is there something I can help you find? I've been given strict orders to not accept a penny for any book you want."

Kelly put his hands in his pockets and smiled. "It's hard to choose. I can't believe there are still a couple of Ray Bradbury books I've never read."

Laura reached for one with his name on the cover. "I think I saw a movie by this name once." She took the book from the shelf and stepped nearer to Kelly, the book open in her hands. She swept the hair away from her face and the tresses landed on his shoulder. She turned slightly toward him, looked at what had happened and then pulled the hair back away.

Kelly noticed that she was blushing. "Ex...excuse me", she stammered then continued talking after taking a step back toward the shelves.

Kelly took the book from her and looked at the back cover, attempting to mask his own feeling of uneasiness. He felt an urgency to suppress what he feared was some visible sign that he was aware of her attractiveness and wondered if her obvious embarrassment over the hair was a sign that she had become aware of his observance.

"I've never read this. I remember seeing a book review once saying it was very good. Can't remember what year that was, though." He looked back at her. "I guess that means I'm way overdue in reading it, huh?"

Laura nodded. "It's yours, then."

They began to walk back to the front room and stopped at the counter. "Thank you, Laura. I'm sure you'll end up liking Averton. I know it's a big change from the life in the fast lane back east."

Laura sighed and then pushed herself up to sit on the counter. "I grew up in a quiet part of Pennsylvania until I went off to college at Georgetown. I don't know if I'll ever go back to Boston. I used to eat, sleep and drink stocks and bonds. I could remember earnings and dividend forecasts easier than my family's birthdays. Now I just want to set a canvas on an easel and paint a landscape."

Kelly shrugged. "Couldn't you do both?"

Laura leaned forward and laughed. "I don't want to. I'll turn forty-one soon and I need to try new things. That other life's behind me. The way things turned out….well, it still hurts."

"Being let go?"

Laura shook her head slowly. "It's the way it happened. The business was tightening up….and…well, there were two of us in line for one surviving senior analyst position. My rival for the job…..well, while I thought I was going up the corporate ladder, she was messing around with the CEO." She stopped for a moment, her face flushed red. "This whole thing just has me so….I'm sorry. It's just that things like that should never happen. Not in this day and age."

Kelly noticed that tears had formed in her eyes. He recalled the manner in which he has exhorted himself moments ago but he felt recklessness, a desire to pursue if only for the experience of doing so. He reached into his jacket pocket for a handkerchief and began dabbing gently at her eyes.

As he did so, he saw that Laura had closed her eyes and begun to smile. "Thank you Kelly. I must look a mess now. Good thing I changed the sign to 'Closed'. I'd hate for anyone else to see me like this."

"You...you look fine. I didn't mean to upset you."

Laura smiled. "You didn't. But I shouldn't impose my problems on you. I'm sure you really don't have the time to spare."

"Today of all days, I'm not in any hurry. I'm not going back to the department. We buried my boss and my friend today. I've lived here all my life but things will never be the same again. The bombings, the Chief's suicide...I suppose when all this is over Averton will still be a good place to live."

Laura leaned toward him. "But never the same. I understand. It's like when my father died. For a while at least, we still lived in the same house, my mother still looked the same....I saw the same teenage girl in the mirror. But...it was never the same."

Kelly heard her voice quivering and saw that her eyes were once again filling with tears. He watched as she dabbed at her eyes once again with his handkerchief before she began to laugh.

"I'm really making a great impression on you huh? I'm sure Aunt Katie wouldn't appreciate me depressing the customers."

She took a deep breath and laughed again. "I'm sorry to cry like that." She crossed her legs, took Kelly's hand and pressed the handkerchief into it, then rested their hands upon her knee. "You're just like Katie and Frank described you."

Kelly drew his hand away slowly. "They may overestimate me."

Laura shook her head slowly. "Somehow, I doubt that."

Kelly stepped away reluctantly and then waved the book toward her. "Tell Katie thanks, until I see her myself."

He walked slowly toward the door and Laura slid off the counter and followed him. She flipped the door lock and then placed her hand on Kelly's shoulder.

"Kelly, thanks for listening."

Kelly nodded. "I'm sure I'll see you soon." He walked out the door and as soon as the door closed, he saw the lights dim in the room.

He lingered in front of the store pretending to examine the books on display on the window shelf. Instead, he fixed his gaze upon Laura Bond, now standing in the glow of the light of the display case below the counter.

Her back was to the door and he watched as she straightened up the counter. He saw her reach into her purse and withdraw a compact, then watched as she looked into the tiny mirror and touched her left eye.

Kelly stared as she put the compact away, then picked up a book from the counter and stood back and examined the displays. Finally, the petite woman leaned over the counter on her tiptoes, her feet finally leaving the floor as she stretched across the glass surface and placed a book on a shelf. All the time Kelly gazed as her dress slid up on her thighs, almost to the shapely bottom outlined beneath the sheer, silky dress.

Kelly turned away and began walking rapidly back to the department where his car was still parked. The farther he got from the store, the faster he walked and had nearly broken into a jog by the time he came to the parking lot.

He took off his sport coat and tossed it over the seat of the car, then got in and rubbed his hands over his eyes. The interior of the car had been heated by the warm sun, so he started the engine and air conditioner and leaned back against the headrest. He then became aware that he was still detecting a pleasant fragrance he had noticed in the store. He looked to his side and saw that the right shoulder of his coat was closest, the one from which Laura had swept her perfumed hair.

He drove home slowly, arriving without even remembering the streets and stops along the way. He turned the car off and picked up the book. For a split second, he had an impulse to hide it from Mollie, lest she would detect his brush with flirtation.

He walked into the house and found Mollie mixing some iced tea in the kitchen. "Got anything stronger in here?"

She turned to look at him with an expression of sympathy and pointed toward a cabinet over the counter. "I think there's still some bourbon in there. How was the rest of the day?"

Kelly walked over and kissed her and she felt surprised by how tightly he hugged her.

"Considering everything, once I got past the funeral, not so bad." He found the bourbon and poured some into a small glass. He sat at the table and Mollie watched as he swirled the glass absentmindedly.

Mollie placed the pitcher of tea in the refrigerator and sat down next to him. She picked up the book and scanned the cover. "I see you made it to the store. How did Katie think the first day went?"

Kelly felt his face growing warm. "Oh, Katie wasn't there. Laura was there, though." He took a sip from the glass.

Mollie laughed. "Maybe I should chaperone when you go to the Bitterroot. That Laura's quite a hottie."

Kelly tried to fabricate a laugh. "Well….she may make more men come to the store to browse."

Mollie reached over and playfully twisted his ear. "You can look….that's all. By the way, there's a pizza on the way. I have a meeting, so you just relax tonight."

~~~

Kelly lay on the bed reading, his head propped up with pillows, an empty beer can on the nightstand and an empty pizza box on the floor. He read rapidly at first but within an hour, the tension of the day and those before made him doze.

The book fell slowly to his chest and he slept for nearly three hours, not waking until he was stirred by Mollie opening the closet door. He nodded off again and then opened his eyes to see her standing beside him in her robe, taking the book from where it had fallen on the bed. Thinking he was asleep, Mollie turned off the lamp and walked into the living room.

Kelly drifted off again, only to be roused an hour later when Mollie crawled into bed attempting to get under the covers while he was laying on top of them. He lay still for a while, alternating between levels of consciousness until he found himself suddenly wide awake. He relived the time in the bookstore, the way Laura's fingertips lingered on his shoulder and the scent of the perfumed hair that had crossed his chest.

He wondered at himself, at how he had been so quick to wish to toy with the self-restraint he had practiced since his relationship began with Mollie. Still, he had not actually made an advance.

He had wanted to. That acknowledgement caused him to feel as if the blood in his veins had suddenly turned cool.

Her gestures maddened him as he remembered. He felt an abrupt flash of anger toward her because of them, and then was overwhelmed by the flood of shame that washed over him for having so considered the mannerisms and expressions of a friendly and careworn woman.

Not all of the recriminations could make him relinquish the desire to relive those minutes repeatedly. He loved Mollie deeply and was now transfixed by the momentary touch of a virtual stranger.

His thoughts maddened him as he tried to convince himself that Laura had meant nothing by her actions and that he had seen her through predatory eyes. Concurrently he marveled at the possibility that she had meant it all innocently but had unconsciously betrayed her own initial reaction.

He recalled the vision of her through the window as he was leaving the store, the rounded form of her bottom and the shapely legs. Resigning himself to the fact that he could not help but appreciate such an attractive woman and that his reaction was normal, he began to relax.

Mollie scooted next to him, and noticing his expression she asked, "Is that smile for me?"

~~~

The morning shift at Averton Brass Products reported at seven o'clock, so at 8:30 Kelly walked out to the dispatch desk and looked over the chart to see which officer would be closest to the foundry. He radioed the patrol officer, instructing him to check the fence around the foundry yard to see if the gates were open and to do so several times during the day.

He glanced toward his door in time to see Marcia Young begin to knock. He beckoned for her to enter and she pulled up the chair in front of his desk, immediately opening a file.

"We've already been busy on yesterday's marching orders. A lot of overtime, I know, but we did a lot last evening." She laid a stack of papers in front of the folder. "A lot of this stuff   just amounts to confirming what we already had. Everybody still maintains that March was the genuine thing. The theme is that he never gave up on his brother, but some of the family members go so far as to suspect that he set him up to get busted after he couldn't talk him into going straight.'

"If March and Brenner more than knew each other in passing, we can't see it. We asked everyone a second time. No one in March's family even remembers him mentioning Brenner's name. Wally's brother is the black sheep of the family. These guys didn't travel in the same circles."

Kelly drummed the desk with his fingers. "I saw that list came in on the dynamite handlers."

"As soon as we finish these re-interviews we'll be on that. I already talked to a guy who used to blast for the quarries around here. He told me no one he ever knew would be crazy enough to pull a stunt like that if he lived in the area. Blasters are too rare a breed. He said that either somebody came in from the outside, or if he's local, no one would know that he even knew dynamite. Otherwise, there'd be too much risk."

"That's being logical Marcia."

She leaned forward and rubbed her eyes. "Look, Kelly. It's all we have. We're looking for a van, one that's probably out of state, painted or chopped up by now. We're checking all the body shops around just in case they'd be stupid enough to have it painted around here. But anybody with a garage or barn and an air compressor can do it."

Kelly started toward the wall. "I'm afraid that unless the Feds break something we're stuck in the mud." Kelly watched as Marcia sighed before gathering her documents and walking wearily out the door.

The day had been another full of frustration. Reports had indicated that the gates around the foundry were sporadically open, giving Kelly no conclusive information. He wanted to go home but he knew better than to beg off the meeting with Franklin and his friends.

~~~

It was nearly seven o'clock that evening when Kelly pulled his car into the tree-lined driveway of the lodge. He pulled up next to several other mostly unfamiliar cars and then walked around the side of the structure. He was surprised to see that the outer walls of the new living addition were already completed and could tell from the wooden debris that much work had been done that very day.

He walked back toward the lodge door and saw Franklin standing in the doorway. "What do you think? Living out here on the outskirts will be just fine, won't it?"

Kelly walked up onto the porch and entered while Franklin held the door open wide. Kelly gestured to the outside. "You're not wasting any time on the construction."

The men walked through the corridor toward the lodge's meeting room. "No reason to hesitate. I had this planned out, so I had the crew lined up. Only needed to sign all the papers."

Entering the conference room Kelly saw that there were several men sitting around the room talking. The richly furnished room was dimly lit and the curtains had been drawn.

Scanning the room, Kelly saw that walnut planking covered the walls. The floors were of freshly installed hardwood and the light fixtures appeared to be made from the finest brass.

Franklin began introducing the men to Kelly. Louie Welch's presence made him feel uncomfortable but he quickly saw that the foundry foreman was welcome in Franklin's lodge.

Kelly also remembered having briefly met Don Hart. A retired Air Force colonel, he had returned to Manchester County and started a construction company, the one that was building the addition to the lodge.

He was escorted to a pair of men talking quietly in a corner of the room. Franklin introduced him to Hal Simon, another long-term employee of Franklin's at the foundry who had been the personnel manager for the last ten years. The other was Tommy Rose, a man to whom Kelly had often heard Franklin refer in recounting tales of hunting trips. It had been Kelly's impression that the two had not spent a lot of time together aside from their sporting adventures.

Walking back to the middle of the room, Kelly noticed a man who appeared to be in his early fifties sitting alone in a chair several feet away from the others. He appeared to be lost in his thoughts and just when Kelly was about to ask his identity the host began to speak.

Franklin stood in the middle of the circle of chairs and with a silent gesturing sweep of his hand, everyone grew silent and sat down except for the one who had remained solitary. He was a trim man with jet-black hair, dressed in a white shirt and khaki slacks, but with no tie. He rose and came to stand next to Franklin. After the room had fallen silent Franklin looked around at his gathering with a thin smile on his lips and then placed a hand on the other man's shoulder.

"To recount what's happened to Averton and Manchester County would be quite unnecessary. The outrage we all feel can never go away." He raised his voice. "It never should go away." He stood silent for a moment.

"I want all of you to meet Pat Milland. Pat's name came to me from some friends back east. Now, I've flown him in from New York state because Pat's helped other communities set up citizen groups interested in making life a little more safe and secure." Franklin stepped away and took an empty chair.

Milland placed his fingertips inside his slacks pockets and began to slowly pace the floor. "Thank you, Frank. As Frank told you, I have some experience in setting up groups needed to provide local law enforcement with that little extra assist that can make so much difference." He gestured toward Kelly. "I believe that you now command the Averton police?"

Kelly nodded to him.

"Well, I guess I've never met a chief or sheriff yet who wouldn't welcome some assistance from the populace, right?"

Kelly forced a smile and outstretched his hands as if to receive a gift. Milland returned the smile and continued.

"I must say, though that since 9-11, I've never come to a community that had to face what you good people here have seen. I know that some of the other more recent attacks had more casualties but your town suffered more overall damage and disruption. Averton's only apparent distinction was its small-town innocence and isolation.'

"Frank and I have talked a lot over the phone during the past few days and we concur on something very important – this is likely the work of some far-left.....perhaps some anarchist group. And they picked your community for a reason, a reason still known only to them." Milland resumed his pacing. "I'm not really expecting the federal government to find them out and with all due respect, Chief Hastings, local law enforcement agencies just don't have the manpower, the funds and the intelligence-gathering capacity needed for something like this.'

"All of you have to understand that the seriousness of leftist groups may not seem as real to the government now that the Soviet empire is history. You see, every radical bunch before was looked upon as a potential client of or front for the Communists. Always lurking in the back of everyone's minds was the possibility that every leftist organization would collectively weaken from within our will to preserve our democracy.'

"That particular threat is gone but I've become fearful of something different. I believe that we will now face those who would abandon the need for a cohesive American government, preferring instead just a nation of over three hundred million beings with no loyalty other than to their own individual agendas. They would rather barter than bank, or maybe collectivize and eventually, in their warped vision of the world, undermine our ability to protect ourselves. They may see the globe as a place where we will all meld into one harmonious people while ignoring the evils that still rule many parts of the world.'

"Perhaps even worse, the world…this very nation contains those who would toss away all that our society has ever stood for. They want us to give up our values, to accept a lowering of our dedication to orderly society, the importance of our families and our religious beliefs.'

"Another motive could be to simply take us down a few notches, to make us have to retreat from the world stage, perhaps back off from combating radical Islam."

Milland paused and rubbed his chin, and seemed to be choosing his next words carefully. "Of course, unless America gives up we can't be defeated. If the Soviet Union was never able to topple us these assorted cells of crackpots can't either.'

"The danger lies in the fact that there are those who do not understand this. In the process, they can cost many lives and damage our economy. Using the internet and e-mail an organization can spring up quickly composed of men who have never even met.'

"When the first attack on the World Trade Center took place in 1993 it was just assumed that the perpetrators were foreign. The thought of a domestic movement is even more terrifying because it can be someone who looks just like you, who speaks the same language with the same accent.'

"When something like this happens you have to protect yourselves, especially if you've already been picked as a target.'

"I believe that these mysterious enemies want to make the point that the government is impotent to protect you, and therefore, irrelevant and obsolete.'

"You may wonder why I feel so sure of myself. All I can say is that over the years I have talked people who believed in just the types of things I've told you. It may be true that I've never talked to anyone claiming to have plans to attack American towns and cities, and if I had, I'd already have called the F.B.I.. The problem is, people like this can be transients. They are not likely to own a home and have a mortgage or belong to the Rotary Club. For all I know I may have talked to someone during my college days at Syracuse who went on the form this very terrorist group.'

"The hard reality that you need to face is that unless you can establish confidence in yourselves and your community that such a thing will never be allowed to happen again, the jitters will never go away. Your job base will suffer over a long-term basis and this stigma will remain. You were the first attacked, so the name of this town will be as synonymous with terror as the phrase '9-11'.'

"The underlying danger is that the nation could break apart. The divisive politics we've experienced over the past several elections has served to weaken the bonds of our people. Now, fear is rampant. Hopefully, our nation will remain unified. But if the nation would fragment, people like us…people like you in this room will stand ready to preserve order in what could evolve as a heartland nation.'

"When Frank called me I thought long and hard about your situation. This goes beyond what you need to head off burglaries, more than your normal neighborhood lookout program. I know that Frank has some reservations about this but he agreed to hear me out.'

"I believe that you need to establish an aggressive posture, to the point that the word gets out that if anyone comes into Manchester County or the town of Averton with the intent to disrupt or endanger your lives, that there will be a group of citizens ready to help seal off the roads before they can escape or even try to help apprehend them.'

"Those other communities are facing the prospect of seeing the National Guard units withdraw. They are also being forced to come to terms with deciding how they can best protect themselves. I know they are looking to you as an example."

Franklin stood up, surveying the room. "I know that what Pat's proposing sounds a bit extreme but I feel we need to listen to every possible idea."

He turned to where Kelly sat, the expression on his face one of obvious discomfort. "Kelly we certainly wouldn't want to do anything that would hinder official activities and, most of all, nothing illegal. What do you think?"

Kelly squirmed uncomfortably. "Well…nothing you're talking about is illegal in and of itself. I'm the last person to say that we wouldn't want citizens to help apprehend a lawbreaker but there are a lot of conditions.'

"First of all, and most important, we wouldn't want anyone getting hurt in the process. Naturally, the issue of being armed would default to Ohio law in general. I can't speak for the Sheriff but I see it as unlikely that he would deputize anyone unless they went through training and became regular auxiliary deputies. If that were the case their actions would be under his command and he may not sanction something like this."

Milland put his fingertips to his forehead and took a quick stride toward Kelly. "But…supposing there were no legal problems with weapons possession…if anyone carrying a concealed gun had a permit, and guns being carried in vehicles we done so in accordance with the law, you see nothing that would prevent citizens from voluntarily practicing tactics of roadblocks…manhunts….things like that?"

Kelly found himself nearly stammering. "Well…you…you couldn't actually block roadways to practice."

Milland wheeled around quickly to face Franklin. "Is there a place…somewhere on private property where folks could train, be ready, even store gear?"

Tommy Rose sat forward and stretched his arms out wide. "Hell, Frank. You've got all this land across the road. There's some lanes and driveways. There are acres of hills and woods. Maybe some stuff can be stored in that old barn." Rose turned toward Don Hart. "You've trained military police for the Air Force. What do you think?"

Hart rested his chin on his clasped hands and stared at the floor. "I've trained men under less desirable conditions. I think it all comes down to whether Frank wants his Shangri-La to be used for something like that."

Kelly felt the urge to shout out some type of warning, to say something to deter them. He has been unprepared for the discussion to go so far. All the faces turned toward Franklin who was now pacing the floor while Milland stood motionless waiting for his host to speak.

Franklin leaned on the back of the chair in which he been sitting quietly. "I've known that we'd need to take some kind of action. When anyone else talked about such things, I've talked them out of it because I was afraid of the very potential problems Kelly pointed out here tonight. I wanted to set something up in a safe, sane fashion". He took a couple of steps toward Kelly. "I don't mind letting my land be used in such a manner. But…it has to be understood that I'll feel the need to run a lot of stuff past Kelly here to be sure we're not running afoul of the law or getting in the way of him or the Sheriff. If everyone agrees to that I'll go along".

Immediately, Milland slapped his hands together sharply and nodded vigorously. "Good. I'm flying back tonight but I'll be in contact with Frank and we'll arrange to all get together again. For now, let's discuss some of the more immediate fears being expressed by the community". Milland then spent the next hour soliciting comments from the group.

~~~

Franklin walked over to Kelly, who was rising from his chair for the first time since the meeting began. He coaxed him to a spot near the door, away from the others. "Son, I'm sorry things moved so fast. It kind of took me by surprise".

Kelly shook his head and exhaled an exaggerated, deep breath. "Things can quickly take on a life of their own, can't they? What's this stuff Pat Milland was spouting about the nation breaking up? It reminded me of some comments you made when Mollie and I hosted that cookout right after the attacks."

Franklin stared at the ground for a moment. "He shares one of my greatest fears. The differences among Americans have gone beyond mere disagreement. Too many see their opponents as belonging in another country….literally. What if that other country was carved out of the U.S. as we know it? Can you imagine the sense of loss…the confusion…the pain? That's why we have to do all that we can to keep order."

Franklin nodded toward the center of the room. "Look, I've got to have a few words with Pat before he heads back to the airport but I can promise you I'll keep this thing from getting out of hand. I only get taken by surprise once".

Kelly nodded and walked out into the night air that had become humid after a hot day. He shed his jacket and tossed it onto the back of his car. He sat down behind the wheel but felt suddenly overwhelmed once again by fatigue. He closed his eyes and rested his head against the back of the seat.

He argued with himself as to whether he should go back inside and emphasize to Franklin just how concerned he was about what Milland had proposed. Instead he decided that he may fare better on another day and when he was about to put the key in the ignition he noticed movement outside the lodge. Two figures were standing in what little sunlight came through the trees. He strained to see who stood next to where the addition to the lodge had been built, then realized that he was looking at Franklin and Louie Welch. He lowered his window and although the two now appeared to be having an intense exchange he realized that they were doing so quietly. Although he was only eighty feet away, he could barely make out their voices.

He was startled to see the two men move suddenly closer and it appeared that Welch attempted to grab Franklin's shirt. Kelly instinctively unsnapped his holster but when it appeared that the confrontation would go no further, he did not draw the weapon.

Welch stepped away and threw his arms up as if disgusted with something and turned his back on Franklin before slowly turning to face him once again. Kelly could see that the two men were once again talking, as they did for another minute before both heading to the back door, each shaking his head.

When he felt that no one would see he started the car and, without turning on the headlights, backed slowly out of the parking area. He crept slowly enough that he could avoid touching the brakes and activating the brake lights.

He drove slowly down the dark lane, barely touching the accelerator and straining to take care to stay in the lane. He glanced in the mirror to detect any other unusual activities before the lodge left his view totally. Not until he was out on the road and a hundred yards from the lane did he switch on the headlights and drive slowly toward his home. However, all the while the scene he had just witnessed rattled him.

~~~

Kelly woke from a restless night during which his mind had roused him on several occasions to what had provoked the flash of anger between his friend and Welch. Even though he had felt an immediate dislike for Welch, Franklin's comments about him had sounded almost affectionate in tone.

He felt the need to pursue the matter for his own peace of mind, so immediately upon his arrival at the department he sat down at the dispatch desk and began a computer check against Welch's name. He would try to find out if there was ever any police record on the man and reassure himself that the foundry foreman was not a threat to Franklin. The name entered, he set about reviewing the activities of the force during the night.

It was nearly mid-morning when the dispatcher knocked on his door and dropped off a computer printout. Kelly read it with concern to see that the year before he had joined the force, Welch had been charged with simple assault right there in Averton. He considered that that decades had passed since then but he could not gloss over it if Welch was any danger to his friend.

He called the county courthouse and spoke to Cecil Powers, the most senior of Manchester County's probation officers with whom he had a close and long-term working relationship. "Cecil...I need to have a really old file checked out...".

~~~

Marcia Young had little information to present to Kelly when she met with him late in the morning. There was nothing turning up in the interviews with those who were related to or had known Wally March and Tommy Brenner. Similarly, in the use of dynamite, no one seemed to have any useful insights or hints.

Feeling strained, Kelly thanked her for her efforts and as soon as she left the office, grabbed his sport coat and walked to the front desk to check out for lunch. He looked through the window to the lobby to see Cecil Powers walk in. Kelly went to the door and greeted him.

Kelly looked down and saw that the probation officer was carrying a briefcase. "That for me?"

Powers smiled. "It is if you buy me lunch. I need some fresh air and sunshine".

The two men made small talk as they stopped at a root beer stand and picked up some sandwiches, then drove to a nearby park and found a picnic table. Powers unzipped the briefcase and pulled out a manila file.

"These are all copies of course. Nothing in the records themselves stood out. This Welch guy was arrested for beating on his wife one night, causing enough ruckus that the neighbors called the police. He was arrested and even got rough with the officers in the process. He got a suspended sentence and probation. His wife left town and divorced him right after that.'

"A few months later he was involved in a fender-bender. Some teenage boy backed into him. Welch got into an argument with the kid and slugged him. He got two weeks in the county motel for that."

Powers pulled out another sheet of paper. "Here's mention of something in Pennsylvania."

Kelly stopped him. "You said Pennsylvania?"

"Yeah. He was also charged with a minor assault there too. It was a tavern fight. Nothing remarkable there either."

Powers put that paper away and then took out yet another. "This is a copy of the inside of the file jacket". He pointed to a phone number with a circle around it. "That's the number of the Cincinnati F.B.I. office. Old stuff, but I wanted you to have it. Here's the guy's Social Security number if you want to push it any further."

Kelly thanked his friend and then returned to making small talk as they enjoyed their lunch and drove back to the Department.

All the while, he was wondering what to do with the information he had just received.

As soon as he arrived back in his office he called Calvin Meyers and was relieved that he was at his desk. "I wondered if you could check someone out". Kelly read him Welch's name and Social Security number. "I'd like for this to stay under the radar but it's possible your office may have something on him. Your office number was written in his county probation file."

"Is this very old?"

"Quite so."

"We won't have it here. It could be a few days if you want to keep this discreet."

"Understood. It would be stretching it to say that this is crucial to the big case…thanks, Meyers."

~~~

Kelly spent a slowly passing Saturday morning and early afternoon in his office reviewing cases which still were backlogged because of the bombings. He sorted them by urgency, placing those requiring the most immediate investigations in a tray on Marcia Young's desk.

Once again taking a seat behind his desk, he picked up another file and then let it fall to the desk. He leaned back and began rubbing his eyes when the phone rang.

"Hastings, Acting Chief. Can I help you?"

"When did you start answering the phone like that?" Mollie asked.

"Ugh. Sounds bad, huh?"

"Just a little awkward…like you're having an identity crisis. Say, Katie called. She wants to know if we'd like to have a nice grilled steak. She promises it will be real beef, no surprises. And she says that Frank picked up some of that imported beer you like."

Kelly found himself nodding. "Yes….I can't wait to get out of this place."

"I'll tell her we're coming. She said her niece will be there, too."

Mollie waited for a few seconds. "You still there?"

"Yeah....I'm still here. Sorry, just kind of tired. I'll be home in a little while, then we can walk over."

He stared back down at the files on his desk and then forced himself to examine the papers until he became concerned that his attention was not adequately focused on his work.

He was uneasy at the prospect of seeing Laura Bond again. He could not help but wonder if she had noticed his attraction to her although he had neither said nor done anything improper.

He labored away with paperwork until he could remain at the office no longer. He sighed and put down the paper in his hand and left to go home.

All the while strolling to the Norwoods' house, they made small talk. Mollie dismissed his distracted demeanor to the pressures that she been accustomed to seeing him deal with over the past several weeks.

Upon their arrival, they heard voices coming from behind the house. As they walked to the patio they were greeted by Franklin, so Mollie went on to look for Katie while the two men struck up a conversation at the corner of the dwelling.

While Franklin commented upon the degree to which the weather suited him Kelly glanced toward where three women sat in white metal chairs around an umbrella table. Katherine sat in the middle while Mollie sat facing Laura Bond. Kelly found himself once again captivated by her appearance, his mind racing with recrimination.

He waved to them and took care to stay close to Franklin, helping him with the cooking but unable to totally avert his eyes from the red-haired woman in the short green sundress. As she chatted with the others Kelly cringed to think that Mollie could somehow sense that the young woman with whom she was talking was holding the attention of her husband.

Finally, the steaks were cooked and all were now seated around the table, talking first of the weather, then the plans the Norwoods had for entertaining at the lodge. Afterward the hosts carried the dishes inside, insisting that their guests remain seated.

Mollie reached over and placed her hand on Kelly's wrist. "Laura told me that she's originally from Pennsylvania. I told her how we've always wanted to go camping there."

Laura seemed to stare into space for a moment. "Some days I miss it very much."

Katherine calling from a bedroom window distracted their attention. "Mollie…can you come in for a minute and mark the hem on these new slacks?" Mollie got up from the table and walked into the house.

Laura turned to Kelly. "I'm sorry I got into so much of my unhappy past in the store the other day. I don't know what came over me."

Kelly shook his head, all the while glancing toward the house. "I'm glad you felt that you can talk to me."

Laura folded her hands and leaned toward Kelly. She began nodding her head and launched into a voice that sounded just like Katherine Hepburn: "Well, you're a real nice person just like everyone told me you were."

Her face turned red and she leaned back and laughed. "I wanted to tell you what I found in a box in this big closet in the loft over the store this morning. Did they tell you I'm living there?"

Kelly nodded. "I knew that."

"Well, there was this old musty cardboard box full of paperback books. I don't know how old some of them must be but some of them are science fiction and Aunt Katie said you should have them. The box is pretty heavy so we left it in my room so that you can carry it down. Just stop by some day after work and you can pick them up after I close the store. Just call ahead and make sure I'm there. There's going to be a student from the college working there some days."

His first instinct was to again glance at the window through which he could hear Mollie and Katherine talking. "Sue. I'll be giving you a call in a few days. Someday I'll have to find myself with enough time to do all this reading."

Laura stood up and took a step toward the house. "I'm going to get a drink. Can I get you anything?" Kelly shook his head, and then watched her walk through the back door, entranced by the sway of her hips. No sooner was she gone from his sight than Kelly was once again chastising himself.

A minute later Franklin rejoined his guest and began describing his next hunting trip. Soon after, the three women emerged from the house. Another hour was passed in small talk and cold drinks before the Hastings began walking home.

Mollie walked alongside her husband, all the time shaking her head. "Isn't that Laura a sweet thing? I hope she can use her time here to decompress."

"Yeah. She still seems really stressed out. Working in a book store and moonlighting as an anonymous loft artist….it sounds so Bohemian."

Mollie let out a loud sigh and elbowed Kelly playfully. "May be she'll be as lucky as I was and find a good man here in Averton." She leaned her head against his arm as they walked and Kelly decided to wait several days before arranging to pick up the books from Laura's loft.

CHAPTER 5

Kelly glanced at his Blackberry the following Wednesday afternoon and realized that a full month had now passed since the bombings. Although he was obsessed by the situation, much of the department's time was still devoted to the case, even though with each day the intensity ebbed. Leads went nowhere and it seemed that whoever had terrorized the town had come in a swift, brutal and pointless night of destruction.

He had been asked by Franklin to come to the lodge once again that evening from another meeting to organize the citizens' group. In addition, he was concerned that he would find himself in yet another situation of conflicting sentiments. He could only hope that his friend could help to prevent the community's fears from creating additional dangers.

He did not wish to go home before that meeting so he worked late then drove to the edge of the town to a fast-food stand before going on to the lodge. When he got there, he was surprised to see the gate across the drive closed, behind which stood a man he recognized from the previous meeting as Hal Simon. Simon was holding a walkie-talkie near his face while opening the gate and motioning for Kelly to drive through.

Kelly entered, and then began glancing in the rear-view mirror as he made his way down the gravel lane. He could see Simon closing the gate behind him and once again talking into the headset.

He pulled into a parking space near the sidewalk in front of the lodge and saw Franklin standing in front of the structure. He was talking to men Kelly had never seen before and when Franklin saw him get out of the car he appeared to dismiss the others before walking toward Kelly.

"Thanks for coming out again, son. I know you'd rather be spending your evenings at home."

Kelly pointed in the direction of the lane. "What's with the gate? Problems with trespassers?"

"Nah. Some of the guys thought that we should maintain some security because we don't want a bunch of gawkers who won't understand what we're trying to do out here."

Kelly shook his head, and then spoke in a hushed voice. "Walkie-talkies…security….I'm not sure what's going on either."

Franklin put his arm around Kelly's shoulder and began guiding him toward the open yard in front of the lodge which led him down to a pond. They walked through freshly cut grass clippings, the air still fragrant from the cutting.

Franklin pointed down toward the pond to where two men could be seen examining the ground. He directed his index finger toward the men. "You remember Tommy Rose. He's showing that other fellow, a neighbor of his, how to follow tracks made by a motorcycle."

Kelly turned sharply. "Why a motorcycle?"

Franklin shrugged. "Tommy wanted to give the fellows some realistic training. We read in the newspaper how the Sheriff had asked anyone seeing a motorcycle in the area of the power station to call the office. Tommy thought that it would add some gravity. So the old guy drove his Honda around the grounds last night and we're having the boys take turns following the course he took."

Franklin took another step toward the pond. "I guess we need to make this sort of entertaining. We have to start somewhere. Don Hart has a couple more across the road in the woods waiting for nightfall. They're gonna practice approaching the lodge and see if they can get close before we detect them. Some of the rest of us are gonna have another little meeting in a few minutes. That's why I wanted you back out here tonight. Pat Milland's back."

Kelly stood next to him as a cool breeze broke the irritating monotony of the humid day. "Frank, this isn't easy for me to say….I don't like the looks of this."

Franklin stood with his hands thrust into his pockets, not looking at Kelly. "Then tell me, son. Just what is it that bothers you so much?"

"It looks like some of these guys can't decide if they want to be Boy Scouts or play soldier. It makes me nervous. After all, Frank...this lodge is in my jurisdiction."

Franklin heaved a loud sigh. "That's part of why I want you out here. I want you to know everything that's going on to see there's nothing wrong, that nothing illegal is going on."

Kelly was silent for a moment, the quiet disturbed only by a distant truck engine. "What other reasons do you have for wanting me to be out here?"

"I want you to be part of this. Remember, it's people like you we want to assist. We want to help you make the people feel safe and secure, to feel like someone's always there."

The breeze picked up once again and a light misty rain began to dampen their faces. They walked slowly toward the lodge before Franklin spoke again.

"Please, Kelly. Just help see me through this. I sometimes wish I'd never gotten up in front of that meeting at the hall. Katie's bent out of shape at me. I'd promised to spend a lot of time with her when I retired. Help me convince these folks that they're doing something...anything. They just need something to make them feel okay'

"It will all blow over in time. I just know that if you keep an eye on things with me that we can kill several birds with one stone, so to speak."

Kelly nodded, and then the two men walked back into the lodge. Kelly followed his friend to the same richly furnished conference room in which they had assembled before. As with the previous meeting, Pat Milland stood before the group. Franklin and Kelly sat down in two rocking chairs placed side by side.

As Kelly looked around, he noticed that while two of the men who had attended at the last meeting were absent, there were now two unfamiliar faces. Within a few seconds of their taking their seats Milland began speaking.

"I've been in touch with Frank and I'm glad to hear that there haven't been any more problems in this community in spite of what has happened elsewhere. That could be a good sign. Still, you have to be careful to not allow yourselves to be lulled into complacency."

One of the men Kelly did not know spoke up. "I know that a couple of my neighbors told me that they feel better already just knowing that this group right here's getting something together."

Milland nodded approvingly. "That's the point. Hopefully the training and skills we'll be providing to you will never be needed. But at least Averton and Manchester County will not walk with heads down and feeling helpless. Feeling that you are ready for any contingency provides you with confidence.'

"I'm sure you've all heard the theories about how someone who walks down a dark street at night upright and confident discourages attackers. The same principle applies to a community. You've been victimized once but it's imperative that you never relegate yourselves to the role of victims. Fight back."

Milland began to pace the floor. "And you fight back by being ready to use any means…let me say any legal means to make it known, most of all to yourselves, that your homes and lives will be fought for and protected."

The other unfamiliar man leaned forward in his chair and raised his hand. "You make it sound like you think we'll be attacked again. We don't even know why it happened the first time."

Milland stepped quickly back to the center of the group and turned to look at each of them. "Brad just brought up a good point. Yes, I do believe that you could be a target again. To do so would show boldness on the part of these terrorists. That's a major reason it's so important that you be ready. Secondly, I want you to think of your obligation to the rest of this great nation.'

"The rest of the country, most of all the ones who attacked your community, is watching to see how you'll react. True, we need to exercise discretion in letting many people know the exact details of what we're doing. It's sufficient for now to tell the local public that we're undertaking a substantial community watchdog program. But that's only part of the picture.'

"This may be a nation of more than three hundred million people. But don't underestimate what an impact a handful of people can make. Think back to how narrow some of our elections have been. The same holds true in terms of involvement and commitment as in voting. Most people live their lives sitting back allowing others to make the decisions and take action.'

"For example, a small group of political activists can encourage or discourage a person in terms of running for major office. Only a tiny segment of our population takes an intense interest in foreign affairs and just a few of those people will end up as ambassadors.'

"When you boil it down to the portion of our populace that's willing to become serious activists, you become a force to be considered and respected. All movements of substance begin with an idea and a small core of believers in that cause. On the negative side, what would appear to be a small band of heartless thugs has turned your lives upside down and captured the attention of the world. Now you can provide a counter-balance by demonstrating what's generally referred to as the eternal strength of the human spirit."

Milland halted, and then once again scanned the room, the only sound now the increasingly forceful patter of rain against the windows. "Some of you will find that your talents lie in recruiting others to participate. Some of you or your spouses may want to do the typing and mailing that come along with the operation of any organization.'

"I have been pleased, also, to find out how much enthusiasm there is for learning to handle small arms and to study such procedures as citizen arrest and sealing off escape routes."

Kelly fidgeted uneasily in his chair. "Pat, just a minute." He glanced over to Franklin and then continued. "I need to go on record and say I'm not at all comfortable about some of these things, like I told Frank earlier. Just how far are you from planning to go with this stuff about small arms?"

Milland shrugged. "No actual firing in the city limits, in accordance with city ordinances. I've emphasized all along that we absolutely do not wish to break any laws. If we want to make some noise we can find a farm further from town. But as for terrain and concealment, this camp is excellent."

Kelly stood up. "I'm sorry. I don't think that I can be expected to play a role in all this." He stalked out of the room and toward the door, Franklin following close on his heels. Kelly felt his friend's hand on his shoulder and then stopped at the screen door as rain beat upon the steps outside.

"Kelly, give me some time with all this."

He turned quickly toward Franklin. "You keep talking like you're some reluctant participant in this. I've never known you to be anything other than a rock of resolve. Now you seem to be bullied by these…..these people who seem to have wandered into my world."

"Calm down. You know, I'm just trying to channel all this nervous energy in some controlled manner."

Kelly slammed his hand against the sill of the door surprising both men who had never shared a cross word. "Why did you have to bring this guy in from another state?"

"Son, you've heard him talk. He can keep folks reasonable and make sure these guys don't hurt themselves or anyone else in the process. He's an organizer. They'll all have their fill of this before long and the group will fade away."

Kelly stared out through the rusting screen. "Frank…please be careful…real careful. Don't do anything to bring me out here on business. This talk of arms…I don't know…".

"Kelly, we won't do anything illegal. I promise. I just hoped we could work together on this."

Kelly placed his hands on his waist and glared. "Frank, this has all the potential for one of these guys getting you in trouble. Just what I've already heard is enough to give me cause to keep an eye on this bunch." Kelly tossed the door open, and then walked down the steps, down the sidewalk to his car. In his anger, he ignored the puddles in the driveway that soaked his shoes on the way.

~~~

It was six-thirty the next morning when Kelly sat alone at the dinette table in the kitchen. Sipping on his second cup of coffee, he held out hope that the brew would sooth his sense of distress.

He thought back to the previous evening, still unsettled by the unprecedented harsh words with Franklin. He felt a cold chill at the prospect of his friend having gotten himself involved in a situation spiraling out of control around him, a scenario so out of character.

At the same time, Kelly chastised himself for being naively lured into attending the meetings, especially in light of the fact that his promotion to Chief was still subject to some final bureaucratic steps. He could tolerate no hint of improprieties or let a misstep force him to retire under a cloud after such a stellar career.

A bolt of lightning illuminated the outdoors and the thunder rattled the dwelling. Kelly wondered if the storm would wake Mollie, who he had not even seen the night before. He sipped the coffee and fought to remember details of some of the case files he had read the previous evening after going back to the office after the encounter at the lodge.

He walked to his car and as the wipers kept up their monotone beat, he felt the starkest loneliness he had ever known. He should have gone home the prior evening to talk with Mollie about the clash with Franklin but the pain of that confrontation was compounded by another doubt: he wondered if Mollie would possibly ally herself with

Franklin. He felt oppressed, that in the course of an evening two of his closest confidants may be unknowingly at odds in his own mind while a third had been recently relegated by death to a memory.

~~~

His morning was a series of heights and depths as reports of frustration in the bombings and murder were alternated with an arrest of a suspect wanted in a series of recent burglaries that had made the shaken town feel more on edge. Yet, far into the afternoon, the feeling of being alienated haunted him in spite of being surrounded by other officers who had recently treated him as a peer.

He had decided to take Mollie out to dinner that evening. They would go to a nearby town, any other town, but he was to be preempted when she called him first.

"Hey, Chief. How you doing?"

"Not so wonderful. It's nice to hear your voice."

"Uh-oh. Maybe this isn't such a good idea."

"What's that?"

Mollie hesitated. "Katie called. She wants me to go shopping with her in Columbus. We'd leave soon and we wouldn't be back until late this evening. Kelly…maybe I should tell her I'll go with her another time. I'm concerned by the sound of your voice."

Kelly's head sank to his forearms on the desk. "No, really, that's okay. I'm just tired. Go and get yourself some things."

"Honey, really, I don't have to….".

Kelly interrupted her. "No, I want you to. I'll make the best of things. I'll have a couple of quiet beers and do some reading."

"You sure?"

"I'm sure." Kelly looked out the window and saw that the rain was once again heavy. "Katie's driving?"

"Yes. She's even treating me to lunch and dinner."

Kelly peered out at the rain once more. "You two be careful."

~~~

Kelly's vision began to blur from reading files and reports so he wandered through the Department speaking to officers and making small talk. It was near the end of the day shift, the point at which under normal circumstances he would begin to think of going home.

He had not been away from his desk for five minutes when he was paged to take a phone call.

"Chief Hastings."

"Chief....Kelly? This is Laura Bond. How are you?"

"Just fine. What can I do for you?"

"Remember those books I told you we found?"

"Sure. I've been looking forward to seeing them."

"Are you free to come to the store when you're done at the office?"

Kelly looked at the clock and felt queasiness in his stomach. "Say when. Mollie and your aunt took off, so I can be there in a little while."

"Tell you what. This is my afternoon off at the store so I'm going to my water aerobics class now. I'll be back at 7:00. The place will already be closed so just ring the doorbell at the back door."

"Thanks, Laura. I'll see you then."

~~~

Kelly glanced at his watch as he walked out of the Department. He had remained there to review personnel files, as he felt uncomfortable with going home before leaving for the bookstore.

He felt like walking and there was a fortunate break in the rain but as he began the short walk to the Bitterroot, he took an umbrella. As he walked beneath the rain dripping from the trees that lined the sidewalks he felt a sense of unease in reliving what he hoped was merely a momentary fixation with the woman he was about to visit. He took pains to recall similar passing reactions he had experienced with other women to convince himself that this was really nothing unusual.

He came to the store, the back of the building darkened as the sun was setting. He pressed the button next to the door but found himself looking around nervously. A moment later he was taken aback to see Laura descending the ladder to the loft dressed in a thigh-length beach robe over a sparse two-piece swimsuit. She opened the door and began shaking her head as if to apologize.

"I'm sorry, Kelly. I got back a little later than I expected. It started raining at the pool so we got under a shelter. Time was passing by so I just picked up my stuff and drove home. I thought I would be dressed before you got here."

Kelly shook his head and laughed. "I'm certainly not offended." He immediately winced at his own words but Laura only smiled.

She tilted her head toward the overhead loft. "The box of books is still up in the apartment. It's too heavy for me. Let's go on up." Laura stopped, took on a perfect Mae West pose and voice, purring, "In other words, why don't you come up and see me some time?"

Both laughed as she took a step toward the ladder and then glanced down at her garb. She gestured for Kelly to mount the ladder. "Maybe you should go first."

Kelly nodded and then went up the ladder into the loft, Laura behind him. He looked around at the sparse furnishings and then saw a box of books next to the single bed, the only place to sit.

The only light that was on was a table lamp on the other side of the bed.

Along the far wall rested an artist's easel with a small table holding paints and brushes. In a corner was a narrow two-burner stovetop over a dormitory-style refrigerator next to a single-basin sink.

Laura motioned toward the bed. "I'm sorry for the lack of furniture. This bed also serves as my reading chair and sofa. It's a far cry from my condo on Boston Harbor.'

"I'll be getting some furniture next week....stuff that can come up the ladder." Laura gave a theatrical turn with her arms outward. "But I must say I love it the way it is. I love it because it's so different from where I moved from. I always wanted to live in a place like this."

She pointed to a door next to her bed and laughed. "The bathroom is smaller than the shower in my condo. But....who wouldn't want to spend some time in a loft apartment over a bookstore with all the time in the world to paint? It feels so....right."

Laura sat down on the bed and gestured for Kelly to also be seated. He looked at her and laughed as he sat down a couple of feet away. "How many investment analysts would find happiness in a loft?"

Laura leaned back against the wall and smiled. "Only those who pretended to be someone they're not and then finally find their true selves."

"You were a beatnik trapped inside the body of a broker?"

"Something like that. I mean, I was good at my job. Dealing in junk bonds can be quite a rush."

"Not to pry.....I mean, this is really none of my business, but I'm sure you were making some great money. Now....".

Laura laughed. "I don't want to phrase this in any boasting way. But, yes, I was doing quite well. I put a lot away. And I got one fine severance package when they let me go. Between the fact that I made them a lot of money and I knew where the bodies were buried, well…. you know."

Laura stopped and giggled. "I suppose that's not a good choice of words when talking to a police chief."

Kelly laughed. "Maybe you should show me that box of books now."

Laura pointed to a wooden crate in the corner. Kelly went over to retrieve it and set it in front of the bed. He sat once again and Laura scooted closer.

He immediately began looking at the musty books, commenting on them as he explored and telling Laura about the authors with whom he was familiar. As they chatted, Kelly was distracted by the glimpses of her through openings in the robe. When he was talking but not looking at her the fragrance of chlorine reminded him of her state of dress.

After he had browsed through all the books Kelly glanced at his watch. "I wonder how the girls are doing with their shopping."

Laura leaned forward and smiled. "I'm sure they're having a good time. I know why Mollie likes to spend time with Aunt Katie. Even though I didn't see her very often I always looked forward to spending time with her."

Kelly looked back down at the books. "Why didn't you see more of her? I don't think I was aware she had much family back east."

Laura nodded. "Katie's first husband borrowed some money from my parents. Then he avoided our family….sort of kept us separated from Aunt Katie while they were married. He didn't tell Katie why. She was hurt. She never could talk about it."

"But she ended up with Frank. At least that turned out well."

Laura placed her hands on her knees then rose and began pacing the floor. "He's wonderful. He's become family to me. But I'm worried about him. So is Katie."

Kelly stared at her. "Why is Katie worried about him? Is he ill?"

Laura shook her head. "It's probably nothing. I shouldn't even mention it."

"No. Please....tell me. Mollie and I care a lot about him, you know. Is there something to be concerned about?"

Laura walked slowly back to the bed and sat down close to Kelly. "It's this stuff going on at the lodge. Katie's afraid that Frank's being taken advantage of. He has a lot of money and he's always been generous. But she said he's been buying airline tickets to fly in some speaker or something and she's really worried about one fellow who used to work for Frank at the foundry."

"What did she say about him?"

She shook her head. "It was something about this guy being kind of a bully. She's mentioned him being hot-tempered and she's afraid he'll get Frank in trouble."

"What else did she say?"

Laura hesitated. "She says....she would be more worried except that she knows you're looking over Frank's shoulder. She told me it was her suggestion to Frank that he invite you to those meetings, but she didn't tell him the real reason she hoped you would be there."

Kelly stared at the floor until Laura placed her hand on his knee. "Did I say something wrong?"

"No. I'm just glad you told me that. Sometimes things aren't what they appear to be. I'll try to keep up with things. I owe it to them."

"I feel better hearing that. They're wonderful people. I can't thank them enough for helping to make this sabbatical of mine possible."

Kelly looked over at her. "Sabbatical.....does that mean you may go back?"

Laura sighed. "Maybe back to Boston. Not to the same business. The day before I was told they were going to let me go, that night I had gone home and typed my letter of resignation. How ironic was that?'

"I was working seventy-hour weeks, constantly. Just a couple of days before I left the firm I was dumped by the guy I thought was finally the one. I was in the pits. Then my biggest client called and reamed me out because I hadn't correctly predicted the size of an interest rate hike.'

"I hung up the phone and put my head down on my desk and started sobbing. I went home and poured myself a glass of bourbon and wrote my resignation letter.'

"The next morning I walked into my boss' office to quit and before I could hand him the letter he broke the news that I was getting the axe." Laura laughed. "I made out much better that way. The bastard had a well-earned guilty conscience."

Laura looked around at her surroundings and smiled widely. "Now I earn minimum wage, I've got a place to live with more atmosphere than anywhere I've lived before and I've never felt more content."

"But after living in Boston aren't you going to feel like you've moved to the end of the Earth?"

"That's why I came here. 'The end of the Earth'….that sounds so inviting." Laura laughed. "It's not like Averton is the Yukon."

"No, I mean….compared to Boston….".

Laura stood and walked toward the window. "Believe me….even with what has happened recently, Averton compares well to Boston….to anywhere else."

Laura reached toward the window and drew the curtain closed, then undid the robe and let it fall to the floor. Without saying a word, she walked back to the bed and sat beside the stunned man.

She traced a finger down the side of Kelly's ashen face. "I told you a lie. I wasn't delayed getting home from the pool. I wanted to still be in this bikini when you got here."

She placed her nose directly against Kelly's. "The question....", she whispered, "is 'How soon will I be out of it'?"

Kelly quickly stood upright and stepped away shaking his head. "Uh-oh. I don't think so....".

Laura rose and stood next to him grasping his arms. "Kelly, I'm sorry if I...I'm not a loose woman, Kelly. I've never been like this before. I never even slept with the guy I was dating for nearly a year. There's just something about you, Kelly.'

"I've argued with myself all day. I kept thinking I might chicken out, just behave myself when you came over. But I don't want to behave."

Kelly stepped back. "Laura.....".

Laura reached for Kelly's tie and began to slowly undo the knot. Pulling it out from under his collar, she reached both hands to his neck and began unbuttoning his shirt. "You can leave if you want. After all, you're armed."

Kelly gently took the tie from Laura and tucked it into the pocket of his sport coat. "Laura....I don't handle regret well."

She reached to her nightstand and opened the top drawer. She took Kelly's hand and placed a key in his palm. "The invitation is always there."

Kelly felt as if an unseen force was pressing his hand toward his pocket as he dropped the key into it. He turned reluctantly and in silence began his way slowly down the ladder out of the loft.

He stepped outside into a light rain, checking the door behind him to be sure it had locked. He walked around the side of the building to the street, nervously glancing around. He finally came to the corner around the street from the department, behind which his car was still parked.

He stood in the drizzle for a moment and then looked down at his watch. He got in the car and sat for a few minutes. Finally, he started the engine, then at the last second turned toward the street running behind the Bitterroot and parked a half block from the store.

At first walking slowly and deliberately, his pace and heartbeat quickened as he neared the shop and walked around to the back. He reached into his pocket for the key, and then took a step away to leave.

However, he continued to turn, back toward the door. He carefully unlocked it and stepped in as though he had never been there before. He stood at the foot of the ladder and took a deep breath.

"Laura?", he called out. He waited for a few seconds then called out to her again before she appeared at the top of the ladder still in the bikini. Kelly bounded up the ladder, and then placed his arm around her waist before carrying her toward the bed, all the while Laura squealing with laughter.

~~~

It was 1:30 in the morning when Kelly sat alone in his kitchen. He was sipping on a can of beer, unaware of the time, aware only of a mosaic of emotions. The deepest remorse he had ever known alternated with a sense of euphoria. He was in his own home, yet felt as if he did not belong, that he had relinquished his right to walk further into the dwelling.

Those feelings exhausted him as much as the manic romp with Laura Bond and he wondered if he should simply fall asleep in the living room. He was so absorbed in his thoughts he did not hear the slippered footsteps behind him. When Mollie placed her hands on his shoulders, he nearly leaped from the chair, spilling beer onto the floor.

"I....I'm sorry. I didn't mean to startle you."

Kelly sank back into the chair and rested his face in his hands. "It's okay....just didn't hear you. Have fun shopping?"

Mollie pulled out another chair and sat down beside him. "We had a great time. I expected to find you at home reading. Something go wrong?"

Kelly shrugged, then shook his head. "You know how it goes. I just had some things to take care of. It'll all settle down some day. I'll have my evenings off."

Mollie pulled her chair around in front of him. "I'm worried about you Kelly." She pressed her hand to his cheek. "How are you ever going to know when you can't handle any more?"

He placed his hand on hers. "I'll be okay. I promise."

Mollie stood up and placed her arms around his shoulders. "You feel all tensed up. I know it's really late but maybe I can give you a good workout."

Kelly stood up suddenly. "No." The word came out of him so quickly that Mollie was left to stand staring at him in confusion. He walked over and hugged her, then faked a quiet laugh. "I'm sorry. I'm wound as tight as a spring tonight. Some things just do that to me. I don't think anything would work.'

"I'm so tired I'm getting flakey. I just need rest. That's all I need."

~~~

Operating on a minimum of sleep, his mid full of guilt and excitement, Kelly drove to the department to find the town quiet on a Saturday morning. Five minutes late for the eight o'clock meeting he himself had called, he was nonetheless too worn to rush into the office. Already waiting in his office were the equally unenthusiastic Marcia Young along with Neal Penn, the officer with the most years in the detective division.

He had never been fond of Penn, three years his junior. Penn had been outwardly disappointed at being passed over when Kelly was named Chief Detective and even more antagonized by Marcia Young's recent designation. But he was a dedicated cop and always put the needs of the department first. Because of that, Kelly knew that Penn could be counted on to track down the whereabouts of Tommy Brenner on the evening of Wally March's death.

Kelly was beyond trying to pretend to be in an energetic state so he simply sat down and began talking. "Thanks for giving up yet another Saturday morning. What do you have so far?"

Penn opened a file folder and began reading from a sheet of notes. "Marilyn Brenner claims that she hadn't even seen Tommy for two weeks. That was when she saw him walking on a sidewalk, and she claims she turned around and went the other way.'

"Cynthia Hammonds' kids were at their paternal grandparents' house that night. Everyone tells me that happens a lot. She'd go on binges, get into some beer, do some drugs or some guy....it'd go on for three or four days, then she'd pick up the kids like she'd just gone to the beauty parlor. She got welfare but the grandparents helped out a lot so the kids wouldn't go without in spite of her.'

"Those folks couldn't help any. They never went in her house more than a few times a year and they have no idea whether Brenner would have been there that night."

Kelly's expression grew dark. "Neighbors?"

"She rented that little green cottage down by the old train depot, that junky looking place. The neighbors can't see her place from their own windows or yards. I know, because when I was interviewing them we walked all around their properties. They're not afraid of talking. They really are blocked from the view."

Penn pulled out another sheet of notes. "All I have is that an uncle of Brenner's said that he sometimes took off camping with some guys from Cincinnati. Supposedly, they'd taken off for the eastern side of the state, camping in the back of this guy's pickup truck. At least he swears that Brenner claimed they were camping. He suspects they were doing a little drug dealing, 'cause whenever he'd come back from one of those little trips, he'd be flashing some money around. Then he'd get lean and put in more hours laying carpet to tide him over until another trip with this guy. And this other guy has a history of minor dealing.'

"Ken Morrison says that he thinks Tommy was in his apartment a couple of days before the murder because he hadn't worked enough to pay his rent and he collected a few bucks from him one morning that week. But he also said the guy was so transitory he didn't pay much attention.'

"We're still trying to find his camping buddy so that we can have some lead as to when he saw Brenner or if anyone else can place them in Cincinnati on that day. Brenner's buddy doesn't seem to have a real good address. Just a flea-ridden truck from what we hear."

Kelly sat in silence so long that his two subordinates began glancing at each other and each wishing the other to break the silence. Finally Kelly looked up, the frustration apparent. "Before you go, anything else?"

Marcia shrugged. "We have inquiries out all around the state on both of these guys, seeing if they did anything to get themselves noticed. No, nothing else."

Kelly nodded, once again staring down at his desk before forcing a barely audible "Thanks". He once again fell silent, prompting the two officers to slowly get up and walk out. Kelly leaned back in his chair, resting his now pounding head back against the leather. He closed his eyes and did not notice the door open once again a minute later.

He became aware of a frowning Marcia Young staring at him and then once again closed his eyes. "What? I have a killer headache."

Marcia shook her head and spoke through clenched teeth. "Penn's busted his ass on this. I know you don't like him….".

He waved her suggestion away. "I'll apologize to him Monday. It has nothing to do with Penn….or you. I'm sorry. Nothing's coming together. This whole nightmare's totally illogical. No one knows where anyone was….it's too much."

"Sounds like you don't want to be chief."

"I didn't say that." Kelly slammed his hand on the desk.

Marcia got up and opened the door again. "You might as well say it. After all your time here, you're still expecting the low-life to live neatly packaged lives? Check in with us before they go out and do their nasty deeds?"

The door slammed behind her and seconds later, it was assaulted by an empty coffee cup that shattered and fell to the carpet in small pieces. Kelly walked around the desk, sat down on the floor, then pulled a waste can next to him and began the tedious task of picking up the pieces.

Sitting there, he cringed to think of the following day, a Sunday afternoon gathering of Mollie's family surrounded by her siblings, aunts, uncles, nieces and nephews. He recalled how she would always cling to him at such times, showing off her detective husband, and could only imagine what that day in the park would be like now that his face had been seen on news footage across the nation and world.

Every eye would contain a knowing glance, a sharp point lodged in his heart as he pretended fidelity and mocked Mollie's trust.

CHAPTER 6

Kelly had no more than arrived at the department at seven-thirty on Monday morning when he was paged to a telephone call. Shaking his head, wondering if a call that early was an omen pointing to another stressful week, he reluctantly answered.

"Calvin Meyers here. I have a little surprise on that inquiry on that Welch fellow. Can I drive up this morning and see you? I've got a file to show you."

"Of course. I thought it was going to take some time."

"Same here. See you soon."

Kelly hung up and immediately recalled the exchange between Franklin and Welch and how concerned he had been. He thought of the comment Laura had made as to how Katherine was worried over her husband's involvement with him.

The next thirty minutes passed quickly as Kelly met with Marcia Young and the shift supervisor so that they could update him on some of the more routine business taking place over the weekend. Although the usual break-ins and assaults continued as normal, nothing else regarding the bombings and killings had surfaced and Kelly began hoping for some stunning unsolicited confession to occur.

Just when the meeting was ending, he was notified on the intercom that the F.B.I. agent had arrived to see him. Eagerly he fetched Calvin Meyers from the lobby and took him to his office.

Meyers sat down and immediately opened his briefcase and pulled out a manila folder. He shook his head as he shuffled through the papers. "I don't know the meaning of all this." He peered over his glasses toward Kelly and grinned. "Of course, you never told me why you wanted this stuff on Welch. This is not the complete file. They just sent me the high points. This stuff is so old it was never scanned and put on the database."

"When my buddy in the records archives saw what was in the file he decided to expedite it to me. Tell me, Hastings, how much do you know about the Minutemen? Not the guys watching the border with Mexico. I mean the super-patriot extremists from the sixties and seventies."

Kelly felt a chill. "I remember a seminar on domestic terrorism at the Academy that included some information on them."

Meyers grunted. "I suppose you and I were just learning to kiss girls when these guys were all over the news."

Kelly nodded. "They kicked up a lot of dust."

Meyers shook his head. "I suppose, depending on your point of view, they were either misguided patriots or dangerous out of control paramilitary nut-jobs. Their theory was that the U.S. government was sure to surrender to the Communists. They were going to be the last line of defense."

Kelly sighed. "I read how they held training exercises, stored arms, then started robbing banks to keep themselves afloat. Didn't they come to an end with a shoot-out with some state police?"

Meyers pulled a yellowing sheet of paper from the folder. "That's correct. They scattered, but not all went away. And it seems that this Louie Welch was right in the middle. He was young, just twenty or so, but he was right in the mix."

Kelly's back stiffened. "Welch was a Minuteman?"

"Welch was never charged with anything but it seems that he was around when a number of things happened. Most of his activity was in Pennsylvania."

Kelly's eyebrows shot up at the mention of the state. "I think that may be where he met Frank Norwood. And Frank's wife has a niece that grew up there who just came to town." At just the mention of her, Kelly felt himself wanting to walk away from the conversation.

Meyers continued. "Welch may have been used as a scout, watching law enforcement activities, picking out banks and so on. But, he was a suspect in several cases of serious assault. The Bureau thinks he may have been an enforcer for various Minutemen cells. In nearly every case he was investigated for, it involved someone who was starting to talk, or maybe dropped out of the movement."

Kelly's mind began to race. "What else?"

Meyers stabbed his finger at another sheet of paper. "Welch was also suspected of helping procure a shipment of restricted weapons for a guy named Marvin Symington. But as always, Welch covered his tracks….never charged."

Kelly let out a loud sigh. "I never met Welch until recently even though he and I have lived within a few miles of each other for years. I looked up his address and he lives a mile outside of town, down by the river. I must say…..I sensed that this guy was bad news right away."

Meyers shrugged. "Remember, most of these guys were simply convinced they were going to save the country. Some went way too far. As far as Welch goes, the Bureau just plain never knew where he was coming from. But….it gets better."

Kelly leaned toward Meyers as he went on. "This report says that in the early seventies there was a splinter group that went off on their own. They thought the Minutemen were too moderate. They wanted more action, less political chatter."

Kelly whistled. "And Welch?"

"Welch was one of them. They called themselves the Continental Army. According to our notes, they were more personality-driven around this Symington. They didn't last long. When Symington got sent to the federal pen the group fell apart.'

"Some went back to the Minutemen, a few later got involved in militias and a couple even got into the racist white-power groups.'

"Symington had copped a plea on a lower-level weapons-possession charge so he was paroled after three years. Then he disappeared. That's where the file on Welch ends. He seemed to be clean after Symington took off."

Meyers tossed the entire folder across the desk to Kelly. "How well do you know Welch?"

Kelly laughed. "I really just came to know of him since the bombings. He worked for my friend. It doesn't fit that Frank knows about all this. Welch has had a couple of incidents here over the years. And he is hot-tempered."

"Well, Hastings. We are talking about a lot of years ago. He's sixty-two now."

Kelly seemed to be gazing somewhere else. "I suppose you're right."

Meyers began to chuckle. "But you'd like to see if there's anything else, so you can stop worrying about your friend?"

The agent shook his head. "Without any formal investigation…I'll see what I can do."

Kelly nodded. "I can't thank you enough. And if this is all the Bureau has I'll understand."

~~~

It was lunchtime when Kelly began thinking of her again, constantly and wantonly. He sat at a stool in a nearby restaurant exchanging greetings with those who walked by, yet consumed by memories of an evening he should have not known.

He felt a wave of shame as he recalled leaving the note to Mollie on the kitchen table: "Be home late this evening, Love you."

He had no plans to work late but rationalized that he really did not know from day to day now. He knew in his heart that he was giving himself an opportunity. It would simply discourage Mollie to become inquisitive if he should not be home at a reasonable hour.

Throughout the afternoon, he fought to concentrate on his work but found that the combination of yearning and guilt was disorienting. He was in a loving marriage and he considered any problems to be more or less imagined by Mollie, although he found the repeated references to them trying as time went on. Still, a few weeks ago he would have considered himself settled in for life, his sometimes ravenous libido in the care of a meticulous custodian in Mollie.

Nothing he could say to himself would justify what he had done. Still, knowing that he could not impregnate a woman and having found Laura Bond so alluring, he was even more enthralled by the recent athletic and adventurous coupling in the loft.

He left the restaurant and almost passed one of his officers on the sidewalk without seeing him. Each storefront, each corner on his way back to the department reminded him of Mollie, of some conversation, something for their home purchased there or a mutual friend working there.

The ability of others to deceive and carry on falsehoods was something which he could never before relate to. Now he was himself rehearsing answers to questions that may never be asked, concocting false scenarios of cases needing evening time. All the while, he marveled at himself at how his desire to be with that other woman was again beginning to overshadow his formerly unyielding ethics.

~~~

Louie Welch sat in his back yard as the sun sat along the banks of the Manchester River. The water flowed along the back of his cottage-like home a mile outside of Averton. There he sat in a metal lawn chair on many a warm day, often fishing for catfish and carp. On this evening, he was in a more pensive mood. All that sat on the cedar table beside him were a small glass and half-empty bottle of sipping whiskey.

There was a transistor radio there as well but Louie Welch cared little for much of what he heard whenever the news was broadcast or he scoured the internet. For his own tastes, he heard too many reports of what to him was the disintegration of the orderliness he sought in society and the world. His America had become too soft, too lethargic in its efforts to rein in those who violated its customs and laws. Too much latitude was granted to those who threatened men who grew older as they sat along the side of a river and fished.

He reached down instinctively to the grass beside his chair and felt for the pistol then glanced back toward the cottage. He looked at the back door, the one that had been broken open three times in the past two years. Enraged at the arrogance of the thieves and the lack of fear they had shown, he recalled how they had even once broken down the door with the house illuminated by lights and the television.

Welch was awestruck to come out of the bathroom and find that his television had been taken while he was home, dusk having barely fallen. Before he could retrieve his gun from beneath the pillow on his bed, the robbers had also taken the power tools from the small attached garage.

This was about as bad as random crime got in Averton and Manchester County, where time between murders was typically measured in years. However, the attitude of the anonymous thieves grated on Welch. He also chafed at the notion that they did not know who they were taunting, a man who did not feel free to show his true mettle.

He looked at the whiskey bottle and remembered the first time he had sampled that brand. It was on the front porch of a cousin's home in Baltimore and he had gone there to avoid going directly to his home in Pennsylvania after he had been sent on a courier mission for the Minutemen in 1968.

He had caught a flight to Omaha, and then taken a cab straight to a grimy motel where he checked in and waited for a phone call. The call came within an hour of his arrival and he waited patiently and watched for a black Chevy Bel-Air station wagon to rattle into the parking lot. His left hand was in a death-grip around the handles of a green gym bag and his right hand reassuringly patted the .45 caliber pistol tucked into his waistband.

Once the car had stopped, Welch stepped from the room and locked the door behind him. Although his most trusted fellow Minuteman had vouched for the stranger he was meeting, Welch truly trusted only himself.

As Welch entered the car, the two men traded passwords. Then the driver half-turned in the seat, raised his shirt and revealed a Nazi SS "Death's Head" tattoo on the small of his back, yet another pre-arranged verification. In return, Welch pulled up the left sleeve on his t-shirt to display the inked image of a coiled snake and the legend "Don't tread on me". The gym bag was then tossed onto the back seat.

Mutually satisfied, the driver opened the glove box and retrieved a pair of sunglasses that he gave to Welch, who put them on to find that the insides of the lenses had been coated with black paint. Without speaking, the men drove for nearly twenty minutes before pulling up in front of a garage in a part of town consisting mainly of warehouses and closed factories.

The driver retrieved a remote control door opener from his shirt pocket and raised the garage door while Welch sat quietly, unsure of what was going on around him. Next, the station wagon drove in and after the driver got out and closed the door Welch could see that a light had been flipped on in the small building. Finally Welch heard the driver's voice when he opened the passenger door and said abruptly, "Take 'em off and get out."

Looking around at the dingy garage full of metal barrels and crates, Welch watched casually as his companion pulled a tarpaulin from over two five-foot crates and a battered footlocker. The driver walked to the back of the station wagon and opened the rear door. Each man grabbed an end of each crate and scooted them into the cargo area. Then each struggled with a handle on the locker and lifted it into the vehicle also, straining and grunting at the weight. As a final touch the driver reached into a corner of the garage and retrieved an old quilt littered with bits of straw and spots of pigeon droppings, and covered the cargo.

Still silent, the driver pointed to his eyes. Welch angrily donned the darkened glasses and both men got into the car. Retrieving the remote once again, the driver opened the door, backed the car out and lowered the door again.

They drove for what Welch estimated to be a half hour before stopping in the parking lot of a shopping center. In an instant, the driver got out with the station wagon still running, opened the back door to retrieve the gym bag and then walked nonchalantly to a rusty green pickup truck. Seconds after he got in, the truck pulled away.

Welch was frozen in place for a minute, holding his breath at the prospect that at any moment police would surround him. He felt certain that his temporary partner had not been wired for sound but he had made it a point to avoid conversation. Still, Welch knew that the entire swap could have been a set-up.

Welch slid slowly across the seat, his right hand now holding the gun he had pulled out. He reached over, opened the glove box, and pulled out an envelope. Inside he found the fictitious title to the station wagon in the name of a man who never existed, and a fake registration to match both the name on the title and the stolen license plates. There was also a map of Omaha with a red "X" marking the location of where he now sat. Without further incident, he drove out of the parking lot, hit the state highway and began the long drive to Albany, New York.

For Welch the mission was a fair and just trade. Money from two bank robberies in the Dallas area has purchased some "redirected" U.S. Army M-16's and the needed ammunition for use by the Minutemen. Now he would deliver them to a cell in Albany and make his way to Baltimore to stay low for a while.

He was not at all pleased that the transaction was with a group of would-be Nazis who kept a nice piece of the action to finance what Welch considered nonsense. One of Welch's favorite memories was sitting on the lap of his Jewish grandfather in Philadelphia and listening to stories. In addition, when his family moved to Allentown some of his neighborhood playmates were black children he missed to this day. However, more than anything else, Welch was a pragmatist, so if there were neo-Nazi fingerprints on his tools of combat, so be it.

~~~

Night had fallen by the time Kelly told his wife that he felt like taking a long walk. In truth, he needed to talk to Franklin but did not wish to alarm Mollie. She may inquire about the reason for the need to see Franklin or wish to go along for the visit.

Katherine met him at the door and guided him through the living room. It was now filling with boxed belongings in preparation for the upcoming move to the lodge. Kelly made his way to the den where he found Franklin dozing with a book on his lap. Kelly leaned down and gently shook the older man until he finally stirred.

Franklin rubbed his eyes and leaned forward to his desk. "I hope you kids haven't been here long."

Kelly pulled a chair near the desk and say down. "I'm alone. I'm out on a walk. I'd rather neither of you told Mollie I came here."

"What's wrong?"

"First thing, I'm sorry I stormed out of the lodge."

"No need to apologize. You care. It never happened....over with. Now, what else is on your mind?"

"It's about Louie Welch. I heard some stuff about him that I suppose you may know about his past....about a group called the Continental Army?"

Franklin leaned back with a slight grin. "Continental Army! My, I haven't heard of those fellows in a long time. How did you ever come to know of them?"

"Just in relation to Welch. Did you know about his involvement with them?"

Franklin nodded. "Look son, I can tell from the few moments I've seen the two of you together, let alone your comments about him, that you don't like him. But I can tell you this. Welch is a flawed man, like all of us. One thing he is not is a liar.'

"Back when I hired him he told me all about his past, including the Continental Army. But he had foundry experience back east and a friend of mine called me about him. Welch needed a job really bad and he came clean about everything. I got a good foreman and made sure he got set up with a fine pension to look forward to."

Kelly felt himself becoming agitated. "If you knew about the kind of group he was involved in why would you want him out at that lodge surrounding himself with a bunch of guys who think they're….".

Kelly sank back into the chair and began shaking his head. "I'm sorry, Frank. I guess I can't stop worrying about that group you're forming and what some of these guys may try to make of it. Throw in some guy who was in some para-military extremist group….".

Franklin leaned toward Kelly and smiled. "It's good to have a friend who cares so much. Trust me, Kelly. Louie's changed a lot since those days. He's just a frightened man like so many others here now. He sees retirement coming and he's afraid everything he's worked for will go down the drain.'

"Look, I didn't mean to recruit him to the group, but he heard about it through the grapevine and he called me. He may seem tough as nails and when he was younger he did some things, I'm sure. Now he's just scared to death and he sees some manifestation of the "Reds" he always ranted about. If you could have seen how upset he was, well, you wouldn't have expected me to turn him away."

Kelly got up slowly, and then shook his head. "I just don't want to see someone take advantage of your charitable nature."

The older man placed his arm on Kelly's shoulder as they walked toward the hallway. "I know you're a cop but I'm a good judge of character. Welch worked for me for a lot of years and even though he got into a couple of scrapes, he's just fine."

Kelly nodded, and then went out the door, all the while Franklin watching while he strolled slowly down the sidewalk and around the corner. Once Kelly was gone from sight, Franklin walked into the bedroom where Katherine sat in front of a footlocker sorting old blankets. He sat down on the bed and Katherine turned to see the look of concern on his face. "Frank....?"

He shook his head and looked at the floor. "Kelly just left. Somehow he found out that Louie was involved with the Continental Army."

Katherine looked toward him with a puzzled look. "It's not surprising that he could find that out. But after all these years, why now?"

"I didn't want to make a big deal of it. But Louie's spooked him enough to make him check him out."

Katherine got up and sat next to him on the bed. "This means that Kelly's gone beyond any local records. Louie hasn't been in any trouble around here."

"Nothing major. I just thought after all this time the coast was clear with Louie. It's always been so important to me that those things were never known."

~~~

It was nearly five in the morning when the phone next to Kelly's side of the bed rang. He instinctively grabbed for it quickly so that Mollie would not be disturbed. He half-spoke, half-mumbled into the set.

"Chief, Lawton here."

Kelly went silent.

"Lawton, sir. Night dispatcher?.....I'm new."

Kelly cleared his throat. "I'm sorry, Lawton. What is it?"

"Something came in a little while ago about that Brenner guy."

Kelly forced himself to put on a suit, and then rushed to the department. He went down the hallway shouting out the name of the shift supervisor, almost knocking over Tom Meadows from the detective unit, who went chasing after his boss.

"Chief, Chief. I'm acting tonight. I have the file."

Kelly spun around, nearly stammering in embarrassment for his lack of calm. He motioned for the detective to follow him to his office.

Meadows opened the file containing just one typed note. "I followed up on this phone call before I called you. This came from a small-town cop near Wheeling, West Virginia. He's a retired guy who was filling in the night of the bombings and March's murder. He's been fishing in Ontario for a while. He left the morning after and last night he heard about Brenner and saw his picture for the first time.'

"Brenner was there that evening. He pulled him over and just gave him a warning for speeding. But he did see his license. He also remembers that Brenner was driving an older dark blue Dodge panel van. He didn't like the looks of the guy so he followed Brenner around for a while and watched him go into a house they've been watching for drug activity. He left a report for his chief and then forgot about it."

Kelly slammed his fist to the desk. "There's way too much distance for Brenner to have been behind anything here that night."

Meadows sighed. "I know. Anything else I can do?"

"No. But thanks. Good job."

Meadows stared down at his dejected boss then quietly left the room as Kelly began reading reports of the scant activity that had taken place overnight. He glanced at his watch and saw that it would be a couple of hours before his main assistants would arrive.

He got up from the desk and walked out into the still-dark morning and the cool night air. He walked quickly along the sidewalks of the neighborhoods near the department, losing track of his location until he came to sit on a low stone wall around a once-elegant home. There was the sudden sensation of being out of his element, incapable of living the life in which he had found himself.

Kelly wanted to strike out, to seek some sort of refuge from the frustration he felt. He thought of Mollie and her lingering insecurities, then of Laura, as if she were a right to which he was entitled. Finally, the fresh pain of losing his boss and friend overwhelmed him. He stood to walk again and as he walked, the frustration turned to rationalization.

Kelly spent the morning briefing Marcia Young and the other supervisory staff on the development of Brenner's alibi. They discussed what options to explore next and whether to inform the public that Brenner could not have killed March.

The confusion of the morning caused time to pass mercifully fast until just before noon when Kelly was paged to the phone. Collapsing into the chair, he answered the phone impatiently.

"Hastings here."

"Hi. Sounds like you've already had it. I just wanted to know if everything's alright. I always worry when you get called out of bed."

He sank back in his chair and tried to soften his demeanor. "I lost my suspect."

"What? Who?"

"Tommy Brenner. He's been cleared of being anywhere close to Averton. It wasn't his van near the armory. He didn't kill anyone or blow anything up. Now we don't have a clue."

"I'm so sorry. You sound so down."

"That doesn't quite describe it."

"You'll be home late tonight?"

"If at all. I don't know how this can get mangled up any more. I just want to control the release of this to the public. This is pretty crazy, running the department and still being short-handed. I still have a lot of my old job to do."

"Well, I won't tell anyone who would cause the news to get out. You take care of yourself."

"I'll keep hanging on. I just feel so discouraged….like nothing's going right. Bye."

Mollie placed the phone back on the receiver, then turned glumly to where Franklin and Katherine sat. They both placed their coffee on the table in front of them and prepared to listen to what had so distressed their younger friend.

Kelly had just returned from eating a carried-in lunch at his desk when his phone buzzed.

"Hastings here."

"Can you talk? Should I call back?"

Kelly sat silent for a moment.

"It's me, Laura. Should I call back?"

"Uh, no. I'm sorry. I'm….uh….just not very used to your voice on the phone. How are you?"

"Missing you, that's how. Look, Kelly, I don't want to seem presumptuous or brash or anything like that but….oh gosh. I want to know if you can get away with me for a little time together. I'm sorry, I know it's not reasonable for me to ask but….I want you to lie, do anything just to be with me again."

Kelly found himself nodding his head, as a rush of exhilaration, a giddiness overwhelmed him. He spoke immediately.

"Okay, I'll do it. I want to….". He took a deep breath and lowered his voice. "I can't wait to. Just say when."

"Well….since I'm pushing my luck….is this too crazy? How about this afternoon? Can you find a way to get away, for a few hours even?"

"Let's see. I'm embroiled in a terrorism case with the world watching….of course. I take it you have some ideas?"

Her voice grew softer. "Yeh, I have some ideas alright. We can go out of town to be safer. Meet me at the Holiday Inn at the south end of Dayton. We can get a room with a whirlpool tub. I'll meet up with you in the lobby."

Out of habit, Kelly jotted down the meeting place then whispered good-bye. As soon as he hung up the phone, he sent the note through his shredder then tore off the sheet below it and destroyed it too, lest it have an impression of his note. He placed his face in his hands and began shaking, trembling like a schoolboy invited into the lair of some adolescent fantasy.

Regaining his concentration, he picked up the phone and began making arrangements to meet with Marcia Young and the city manager the next morning to discuss the manner in which the public would be informed that Tommy Brenner was no longer suspected of killing Wally March. He also called the F.B.I. office in Cincinnati and left a voicemail for Calvin Meyers and asked that he call him in the morning.

Kelly thought of his liaison with Laura only days before and the fevered pitch with which they savored each other. His stomach fluttered, he felt his heart palpitate and he wondered if it all was from excitement or guilt.

~~~

Late in the morning, Kelly called Marcia Young into his office and asked her to keep something confidential. He was experiencing great bouts of anxiety and he was going to be gone for some hours. He was going to go to a park and take a stroll around a lake or just sit for some time in the shade of a tree.

He knew that if Mollie had to contact him she would ask for Marcia. She was to tell Mollie that he would be tied up conducting interviews regarding the bombings. It was imperative that Marcia not tell Mollie how stressed he was.

~~~

Though it took less than an hour, the drive to the south Dayton suburbs seemed like an eternity. He finally pulled into the parking lot and spotted the black BMW he had seen at the Norwood house.

Sitting in the car, he felt the contrast of the impulse to drive away and the one to go into the hotel. As he thought of Mollie, a wave of guilt rolled over him but he also thought back to the fevered previous encounter with Laura. His shaking hand finally grabbed the door lever and he stepped out into the warm sun.

In spite of the warm temperature, as he approached the door of the lobby he experienced a chill and he suddenly turned to scan the scene to see if anyone was watching him. Stepping quickly into the more subdued light of the lobby he glanced toward the door to the restaurant.

Standing in the doorway he spotted Laura seated in a booth along the side dressed in jeans and a t-shirt. As she saw him, she lifted a wine glass with one hand and with the other motioned for him to join her. Again looking around, Kelly strode quickly to the booth and sat down. He scooted toward the wall, knowing that he had been on national television and had even been interviewed by three Dayton stations.

As soon as he had sat down, he felt a weight leave his shoulders. Rather than discuss their last time together they instead launched into a rapid conversation of the events of the most recent days. Kelly surprised himself with his willingness to tell Laura of the developments surrounding Tommy Brenner and was equally amazed at how little he cared at that particular moment in time.

Even after the meal was served they talked while dining. It was a great relief to him that he had made up the story to Marcia and felt no need to rush through the day. He was laughing, feeling a lightheartedness that he had forgotten

The meal finished, the check and tip on the table, they sipped at their coffee until the talk finally gave way to silence.

They found themselves simply glancing at each other until he felt Laura's foot rubbing against his ankle.

Kelly noticed her expression change and her face look down toward the table. He reached across, placed his hand under her chin, and turned her head upward. "What's wrong all of a sudden?"

She tilted her head. "Nothing's wrong except that I call you to do this when you're the one who has everything at stake. It's selfish of me. I've been feeling that way ever since I got here and signed for the room."

Kelly placed his hand on her forearm and began caressing it. "Did you think that I was reluctant to come here?"

She shook her head slowly. "No. That's just it. Coming here seems to make this all the more serious….a higher level of indiscretion. Kind of like, it heightens the sensation of doing wrong."

Kelly patted her arm. "Let's be frank. It is wrong. But it's more wrong for me that it is for you." He smiled. "I'm cheating on my wife. You're just being a bad girl."

Laura laughed. "Yeh, And in a little while we can go up to the room and I'll show you all over again just how bad I can be."

Kelly woke in the dimly lit hotel room to the sound of a car horn blaring in the parking lot. He glanced at his watch on the nightstand and saw that it was nearly seven o'clock, then reached beneath the sheet and patted Laura on the backside to wake her. She turned over, nuzzled against his neck and yawned. "You're a cop. Tell me. Why does this make you sleepy?"

"I think it has something to do with oxygen."

Laura crawled over on top of him and he began stroking her back. He moved his hand lower and began circling an area at the top of her right leg where it rose to form the buttock. "I felt that rough patch the last time. You get burned sometime?"

"No. The day before I moved to Averton I decided to take a final dip in the pool at my condo complex. I was talking to a neighbor, not watching where I was going and slipped in a puddle of water. I fell in and scraped myself on the concrete edge on the way down."

"That must have smarted."

"It hurt my pride more than my flesh. Plus, I ruined a perfectly good swimsuit." She rested her face on his chest. "This has been one incredible day."

Kelly kissed her on the forehead. "It's evening now. I think I'd better get going. It's seven. If I take a quick shower and leave right away I'll get back to Averton by eight."

"It won't take long to add some hot water to that bubbling tub over there. How about getting back to Averton by nine?"

It was ten-thirty that evening before Kelly would allow himself to stop pacing the perimeter of the bombed-out power station. He began to obsess with wondering who had visited it with explosives, watching with little interest the deputies who still guarded the mobile power trucks next to the newly rigged transmission wires. He wondered what the scene must have looked like and who had turned his life upside down and ended several others.

He finally walked to his car and sank into the seat. He was exhausted and yearned to tell someone of the level of fatigue he felt after experiencing several hours in a hotel room with a woman named Laura Bond.

At nine-thirty the next morning Kelly and Marcia Young waited until Carol Moon, the city manager, and the mayor Samuel Wyatt arrived in his office. As they exchanged pleasantries, Kelly was still grasping for the right words but simply blurted them out as soon as everyone had settled into their chairs.

"Tommy Brenner didn't kill Wally March or take part in the bombings. He was several hours away in West Virginia at the time." He paused and watched their expressions darken. "We'll keep working with the feds on the bombings, but as for the murder….it's back to square one."

Carol drummed her fingers on the table. "Kelly, he was our only hope for a resolution. It's like everyone just disappeared or vanished into thin air."

Kelly stood up and began to pace. "I think I should just call the local paper and radio station, tell them what came up."

The city manager leaned toward him. "I keep seeing all those talking heads on TV saying how there is no Fourth World…. Kelly, we need to keep folks calm. Give it a couple more days. Right now, it could make a difference with the population. Every uneventful day is precious….and healing. We can share the heat if anyone barks at you. Right Mayor?"

Wyatt nodded.

Kelly leaned back and sighed. "If you wish. But a couple more days won't make this town go back to normal."

The manager smiled. "I know. But the weather's been nice. More and more people are getting out. The pool's been busier and some of the youth baseball teams are starting a short season to take the kids' minds off things. And it won't be long before the county fair comes around. After that, we need to get past what I guess will be a rough first week of school. We're already talking about how to plan some special holiday events for December, hoping to not seem insensitive. There aren't any definite answers. But please, wait a couple of days."

Kelly nodded, then Carol Moon patted him on the shoulder and left the room. He turned and looked at Marcia. "You know, and I know, that we're done with the murder for all practical purposes."

Marcia began to nervously click her ballpoint pen. "And the feds are stumped on the rest."

Marcia tilted her head back at Kelly until he finally stared back with a look of annoyance. "Okay. What are you looking at?"

She shook her head. "You need to take some more time off. You look like hell."

Kelly shrugged. "I took that time off yesterday. But I ended up going to the power station last night."

Marcia again shook her head. "You and Miss Mollie are gonna forget what the other looks like if you keep this up."

Kelly glanced at the clock on the office wall. Seeing that it was nearly six he pushed away the stack of papers that would await his arrival the next morning. He rose wearily from his chair and reached to take his coat from a hook on the door when an officer opened the door while still knocking.

"Chief, a driver lost control of his car and knocked down a power pole. A couple of blocks lost power and some people are freaking out. We're getting calls about another attack. Worst of all, the National Bank's doors won't open. They're programmed to lock if the bank losses power but they malfunctioned and no one can get out. Some people were still working there and we're getting panic calls.'

"It's like they don't believe us. They think the bank may be a target. People are hiding under desks and trying to break windows to get out. Should we use loudspeakers?"

"Yeah. And call the radio station and tell them it's an auto accident. Tell the reporters in the lobby so the networks will have it right away."

The area affected was only a block from the department and Kelly ran there to find reporters and citizens milling around outside darkened stores. He darted past people shoving microphones toward him and spoke instead to clusters of residents. Within a minute, a cruiser came by with a loudspeaker broadcasting the message that all was well.

An hour of chaos and hurried conversation passed before the power was restored and Kelly was stunned at how much fear was triggered by a mere confined blackout. It took another hour and a half before he had given attention to all of those who seemed intent on speaking with him.

Initial comments were about the power outage, but would usually drift over into discussions of the unsolved crimes. Those in the downtown area who still did not know him by sight quickly found others pointing him out to them.

Unable to politely pull away from a group of business owners who had gathered around him, Kelly decided to join them for lunch at a café that had been blacked out and tried to act nonchalant about the afternoon's events. He strained to be attentive but wanted only to go home and put the day behind him.

All the while, he also dreaded being in Mollie's presence for fear that she would somehow sense his infidelity. As he drove home, he realized that his foot was shaking on the accelerator and his hands were unsteady on the steering wheel.

He pulled into the driveway to see Mollie standing on the front steps taking the mail from their box. Upon seeing him, she began shaking her head sympathetically and walked over to meet him as he got out of the car.

"You poor guy. What else can go wrong in this town? I've been watching the TV and people have called to ask if I'd heard….".

Kelly placed his arm around her as they walked into the house. "Under any other circumstances, except for the folks trapped in the bank it would have been a mere inconvenience."

They walked into the living room and Kelly dropped into the reclining chair. Mollie sat down on the arm. "So, what's been going on with you for the last couple of days?"

Kelly avoided looking up at her. "Dead ends. I don't know if the public is gonna accept that but it's the way it is. We don't know who killed March, we don't know if the Fourth World even exists. After five weeks nothing is going anywhere.'

"We don't know if we'll ever be struck again or if something in town is gonna be blown to bits tonight. And I'm so tired I can't think straight."

Mollie began rubbing his shoulder. "It's only eight, I know, but why don't you go to bed. Turn off your cell and I'll unplug the house phone. I won't let anyone disturb you unless it's a major disaster, okay?"

He stood up and placed his hands on her waist. "That sounds great. Thanks."

She put her arms around him and held him tightly. "Oh, I can't tell you how much I love you. I can't wait until all these troubles are over."

She kissed him then let go of her embrace. He forced a smile in spite of the chagrin he was feeling. He walked into the bedroom, turned off his phone and got undressed as weariness overtook his recrimination.

He fell asleep immediately but experienced vivid dreams of his time in the hotel room with Laura. He was once again stepping into the room with her, watching in anticipation as she draped her clothing over a chair. He saw her joining him in the swirling water in the oversized tub and relived their laughter and teasing as they dried each other off and hurried to the bed.

He drifted in and out of slumber, so disoriented by his exhaustion that he was unsure of his actual whereabouts and as to where dream and reality ended and began. His subconscious struggled to settle into one state or the other. When Mollie entered the room later that night dressed in her robe after a shower, Kelly's restlessness was so obvious that she tried to avoid any noise of opening drawers or the noisy closet doors. She simply pulled back the covers and lay down on the bed to wait until he settled down.

He turned over with his eyes still closed. His hand touched her bare stomach where the robe had fallen open and Mollie found herself being pulled to him. She began to laugh at his sleepy antics, wondering whether he would suddenly fall into a deeper sleep and stop or continue on and give her a story to tease him with the rest of their lives.

When his lips found their way to her throat and began to inch down her neck, she opened her robe to ease his descent to her breast. When he did so, she reveled in the humor of the scenario as well as the pleasant sensations. However, as he continued downward to her lower abdomen, Mollie began to squirm and try pushing him away. She finally began to shake him and call out his name. "Kelly....KELLY! Stop that. I don't like that."

When he was finally awake, he found Mollie standing next to the bed, tying her robe's cord closed around her waist. He shook his head and sat upright. "What's wrong?"

Mollie sat down next to him. "Don't you remember? It was nice for a while...".

He rubbed his face, and then began to tremble when his confused mind finally provided him with a realization of what had taken place. He put his hand on her leg. "Sorry. I didn't know what I was doing."

She began running her hand over his arm. "It's okay, Honey. Just try to go back to sleep. You really need rest."

He stood and ran his hand over her shoulder. "I'll be right back. Go ahead and turn off the light."

Kelly walked to the bathroom and found a bottle of antacid tablets, for he felt that he could become sick to his stomach. As he strolled back to the bedroom, he wondered if he had called Laura's name, and felt afraid to go back to sleep for fear that he would do so.

Sarah Talbert had worked for the Averton Call since she graduated from college with a degree in journalism three years before. Now only twenty-five she was the paper's most versatile general assignment. She also ventured into what little investigative reporting the small publication would attempt.

The inquisitive young woman looked up at the brilliant July morning sky and climbed into the cockpit of a small Cessna. She strapped herself into the seat next to her uncle, a pilot for thirty years. She watched with intrigue as he tinkered with controls and examined gauges, the numbers on which meant nothing to her. A minute later, she felt her stomach drop as the plane lifted off and they began a leisurely ascent.

The silver-haired man leaned over to speak above the noise of the engine. "How did you hear about the stuff that's supposed to be going on out there?"

"Why Mack, I'm surprised you haven't heard the rumors yet yourself."

"Ehhh....I stay to myself too much I suppose."

Sarah gazed out at the scenery. "The girl in the apartment next to me said that her best friend's uncle had a little too much scotch one night last week and started telling that he's part of the group that's going to 'kick ass' if anyone messed with the town again. And he went on about how they were training and going to get guns, the whole works."

"So, what are you expecting to see from the air?"

"I want to see if there really are men in camouflage running around the woods playing with guns. Uncle Mack, do you know Franklin Norwood? I've only met him briefly myself."

Mack shook his head. "It's not that I know him so much as I know of him. From what I gather it would be unlikely that he'd let anything out of bounds go on out there."

Sarah leaned toward the window. "We'll soon know. How low can you get?"

The uncle laughed. "Low enough that you can see what they're doing but if you want to keep it a secret as to who's watching...".

"And of course, I do."

The plane banked as soon as the Norwood properties came into sight and they had no sooner passed over the edge of the wooded area than Sarah nearly strangled herself with the camera strap in her haste to focus. "I can't believe this luck", she nearly screamed. "There's two guys with rifles that just hopped over that fence and I got it. I just hope my settings were right."

She continued to scan the scene as the plane turned toward the interior of the property while Mack began to tense up on the controls. "Now Sarah, we're not going to get shot at are we?"

She craned her neck at the window. "That would make some great material wouldn't it? Imagine a photo of a rifle pointed up at us."

Suddenly Mack began pointing frantically to the window next to him, turned, and banked the plane sharply. "Look. Right there. Look."

Sarah peered down to see three men, one of whom was pointing up at them. The other two were rushing toward some apparatus that they proceeded to cover with a tarpaulin. She tugged at his sleeve. "Uncle Mack, what is that?"

He picked up speed and headed away from the woods. He shook his head, and then laughed. "I can't believe it. I was in Vietnam for two years. That my dear, was a .50 caliber. You get the picture?"

The young woman slapped the knee of her jeans in disgust as she hurriedly looked over the digital image. "A tree had it partially blocked. But we saw it, we both saw it. Mack, can you go over the pond?"

He turned the plane back and heaved a sigh. "I'm too old for this. I don't have the reflexes anymore."

Sarah readied the camera once again. "You're doing fine. Can you slow it at all?"

"What do you see now?"

She began taking pictures rapidly. "Rubber rafts right along the edge of the pond where the bulldozers have been making it bigger." Mack held his breath as he listened to the clicking of the camera.

Sarah pointed again. "Can you make a pass over those pickup trucks?" She fumbled as she retrieved a longer-range lens from her bag. "I want to get those license numbers."

Mack went into a steep climb, shaking his head as he flew. "Good heavens, girl. You know, they may get the markings off this plane. Then what do you do?"

Sarah laughed. "I suppose I'll just stay away from you for a while."

~~~

Kelly rose slowly the next morning and while standing in the shower attempting to wake up, realized that it was now Friday. In two hours, he would be standing in front of the police department for the press conference he had called the previous afternoon. In telling the public that Tommy Brenner had been cleared of the murder of Wally March and any involvement in the bombings, it would be a fitting end to a week of occupational frustration and personal turmoil and confusion.

For both a change of pace and dramatic effect he put on the dress uniform that had been out of the closet only once in the past year, the day of Chester Todd's funeral. He cared little for formality but conceded that he felt more like a cop in the uniform.

Driving to the department, he anticipated his early morning meeting with Calvin Meyers, who would also be present for the press conference. He felt embarrassed when he reached the parking lot and saw that the F.B.I. agent was already there.

He warmly greeted Meyers in the lobby and invited his into his office. The federal agent had no more than sat down when he began shaking his head. "I don't mean this in any critical way, I want you to understand. But, I've been thinking about something since the last time we met.'

"You asked me to check out Louie Welch, and you never really told me why. You didn't seem that concerned about him at the time. I wonder, are you now?"

Kelly shrugged. "Not really. Why?"

Meyers leaned forward and clasped his hands on the desk. "I started thinking more about the days when the Minutemen were in their heyday and how the off-shoot Continental Army went over the edge. Have you considered that Welch may have had a role in the recent goings-on here?"

Kelly shook his head. "Not at all. I must say, I have concerns about what he may do in the future as part of my friend's watchdog group.'

"I don't like the guy at all. But Frank Norwood vouches for him. He assures me that he knew about Welch's past when he hired him. Being an asshole doesn't make him a murderer or worse."

Meyers sighed. "Look, Chief. I had some files on the Continental Army e-mailed to me. What action they did get in on was pretty dramatic. One of their tactics was to create a diversionary event to distract everyone's attention. I guess it just looked similar and considering a former member of the Continental Army lived here....".

Kelly got up and gazed out the window. "I've done some reading about such groups....a puzzling bunch. On one hand, they see themselves as super-patriots. On the other hand, they feel justified in violence because they think that they can make the country better in the end. I just have a hard time seeing a motive in what happened here. But then, I can't wrap my brain around that kind of thinking. But....I have a hard time seeing anyone I've met being of that stripe."

"I understand, Hastings. But while the Continental Army had their anti-communist agenda, they were quite personality-driven. They centered around this Symington guy I mentioned. It wasn't exactly a cult. But, I understand that once he was compromised, little more happened. But Welch was there. Never charged with anything, but I would suggest you keep an eye on him."

Kelly resumed his place in his chair. "This friend of mine, Frank Norwood...I was told that his wife has some concerns about Welch hanging around him." Kelly began tapping his pen on the desk. "Maybe I will pursue that. Maybe my dislike for Welch is for good reason. At least, because of our mutual friend I will have the opportunity to be around him from time to time without arousing his suspicion."

They were interrupted by a buzzing sound and Meyers reached into his coat pocket and retrieved his cell phone. He listened intently for a minute, then said, "Okay. Have a couple copies made for me to give to the police and sheriff here."

Meyers snapped the cell closed with a flourish. "We have an e-mail coming for you. It's a message from the Fourth World sent to Homeland Security. And, it's to your attention. That's all I know."

"And it's addressed to me?"

"I guess they see you as the man in the forefront. It looks like they're going to start taunting you. That is, if they're even for real."

Kelly slapped his hand on the desk. "How are we going to know?"

Meyers shook his head. "Well, every communication opens an opportunity for us to track something down. You know, we could issue a statement that we doubt their existence. Then one of three things would happen. Either they'd come out in the open enough to convince us or it would die out. The third possibility is that they are for real and do something really nasty to prove it."

Kelly again got out of his chair and began pacing the floor. "I can't take that chance. I'd be inviting them to strike again, but they get to pick the target. It's too risky."

Meyers nodded. "That says to me you think they could be for real."

"Somebody came in and blew the hell out of this town."

"Your choice of words tells me that you still don't give much consideration to it being somebody local."

Kelly allowed a smile. "Hey, look. I went the full route trying to tie Brenner to this. Besides, you keep telling me that the feds can't verify the existence of the "Fourth World".

Meyers laughed. "I'm sixty miles away. I'm some guy from Cincinnati nobody knows. I'd love to see you break this case wide open."

Kelly sat down and began rubbing his forehead. "I think the locals must believe that the bigger the crime the more leads we must have. They are a lot more patient when we're trying to solve some routine rash of burglaries." He glanced at his watch. "Time to meet the press."

They stood and headed toward the lobby and could see that outside the department, a crowd of reporters ringed the steps and a line of vans with broadcast satellites lined the street. A cluster of microphones was placed several feet from the door of the department.

Glancing again at his watch, Kelly walked to the microphones. "We have substantial evidence that Thomas Brenner was out of state at the time that National Guard Captain Walter March was murdered and the explosions took place in and around Averton." He paused as a murmur went through the group that included townspeople listening in and a staccato of camera clicks ensued. "I cannot reveal the source of this information because it would jeopardize a criminal investigation in another jurisdiction. I need to add that I'm not implying that Mr. Brenner was conducting any criminal activity there." Kelly took a deep breath. "As we stand right now the murder remains unsolved."

Several reporters began to speak at once but Kelly simply put up his hands. "I'm sorry, but I really can't tell you anymore. We're just going to press ahead. I can't answer any questions." He turned quickly and reentered the department. He did not notice the young blonde woman in the short denim skirt stand aside to let the network correspondents recap what had taken place.

Sarah Talbert strolled down the block as equipment and media left little by little. Lingering a few more minutes, she finally walked into the lobby to the front desk and smiled at the dispatcher as she handed him her card. "Think I can speak to the Chief if I promise to not ask about Tommy Brenner?"

She waited anxiously as the dispatcher picked up the phone and relayed her request. She could not help but relive the hours she had spent the previous evening printing out photos and comparing them to images she and her gun-collecting uncle found on internet sites.

Finally, the dispatcher let her in and pointed to the chief's office where Kelly was waiting for her with the door open. He gestured to the guest chair and they both sat down.

"So, you have a non-Brenner question?"

Sarah opened a steno pad and posed a pen at the ready. "There are rumors going around about things happening at the old church lodge, the one that Mr. Norwood bought. Is your department conducting any investigations regarding any illegal activities there?"

Kelly felt his veins go cold and then began shaking his head slowly back and forth. "To my knowledge there's nothing illegal going on there. And no, we're not conducting any type of investigation."

She leaned close to the desk. "I understand that you and Mr. Norwood are close friends."

Kelly nodded. "Yes. Yes we are."

"If there were a reason to conduct an investigation would you call in another law enforcement agency….say for the sake of avoiding any personal conflicts of interest?"

Kelly leaned back in his chair and opened his arms in an expression of exasperation. "Sarah, you're asking what-if questions. First of all, there's no investigation. Secondly, if the situation were to come up I'd have to step aside if an actual conflict arose.'

"Last of all Sarah, remember that this is a small town. It's hard to avoid relationships. That helps us more than it gets in our way."

The reporter pretended to ignore the comment. "I've also heard a rumor about people seeing weapons one evening recently. Rifles, things like that. Any comment?"

Kelly found he was fighting the urge to abruptly halt the interview. "Sarah, people may be out target shooting. That's fine as long as they're not within the city limits. Unless there is some reason to believe that the weapons are illegal there would be no reason to investigate."

"Does it concern you that some military-style weapons are out there?"

Kelly shrugged his shoulders and folded his hands on his stomach. "Like what?"

Sarah wanted to scream out that she had seen a .50 caliber. "For instance, supposedly a man was seen carrying a Barrett .416 caliber sniper rifle."

Kelly shook his head. "Some guys like to use those in long-range shooting contests."

The reporter looked back down at her notepad. "I understand that another was seen with a Heckler and Kock MP5. A gun like that goes for over $10,000. And it's not for squirrel hunting."

"Again, Sarah.....nothing illegal there. Personally, I would rather buy a nice boat with that kind of money."

Sarah began to ask another question, then shook her head and smiled to Kelly before closing her pad and standing. "Thanks, Chief. I'll be talking to you again." She waved at him with the pen and disappeared through the door.

Kelly quickly got up and closed the door. He found himself breathing rapidly, fearing that his greatest concerns for Franklin Norwood were coming to pass.

Sitting once again, he tried to recall each word, trying to determine if he had lied. That was something he had always pledged to himself he would not do. Then he thought of Mollie and

Laura and recognized that he was indeed quite capable of deception after all.

~~~

It was early afternoon when Kelly drove the curving road that lead to the Norwood's lodge home. The sky had clouded over quickly and what had begun as a brilliantly sunny morning had given way to and overcast drizzly mid-day.

As he watched the windshield wipers wave back and forth he recalled the telephone call he had received from Mollie and hour earlier. Franklin and Katherine were spending the day at the lodge moving in their final belongings and Mollie was sad that her friend and confidant would be a little less handy.

Upon his arrival, there was no guard at the gate, and he was able to drive in without the slightest impediment. Pulling up to the lodge he could see that the only vehicles present were a truck belonging to the contractor, Don Hart, and the Norwood's' own car.

He was surprised at the progress made on the attached garage being added. He walked to the front door and knocked, then heard Franklin calling for him to come in.

He found the older couple sitting on the couch in the meeting room unwrapping a box of plates and saucers. The sound of a hammer came from the basement and other unopened boxes filled the room. Franklin stood up, gestured to the boxes and shook his head.

"This is the last time I do this."

Katherine nodded in agreement but was smiling. "I think I'll take a break and do some unpacking in the bedroom while you boys chat."

The two men watched in silence as the graceful gray-haired woman departed. As soon as she was outside, Kelly's expression grew grim and he turned to face Franklin.

"I've had some questions, Frank. Questions about guns....are you still able to assure me that everything's okay out here?"

Franklin's demeanor changed and he leaned toward his friend. "As far as I know, of course." He leaned back and sighed. "I must say, though, there have been some days when I haven't been around here and some of the boys did come out and....I don't know. I can't think any of them would do anything wrong."

Kelly shook his head. "It's not been suggested to me that anything illegal had gone on. But even legal arms can make it look like hell's going to break loose."

"I understand. I can assure you I'll stop anything that can even give the wrong appearance."

"Frank, was Louie Welch out here?"

Franklin shrugged. "Could be. He might have been out here that evening."

Kelly tensed as he pondered the next comment. "Frank, I never mentioned anything about an evening."

The older man's eyebrows arched and he momentarily appeared to be angered, but only shook his head. "I can ask some questions. Now as far as guns, sure, some of the boys had their rifles out here, that is, in the woods, out of the city limits. Some of them like to target shoot. I even had some of them out for a paintball gun war game. It was fun. I should have invited you."

Kelly sighed as he looked down at the floor. "This type of thing....it's just what I told you I was afraid might happen." He looked up at Franklin. "Some of these guys are going to get you in trouble. What if somebody comes to me with some evidence of something you don't even know that's going on out here? How can I ignore that? Frank....the feds are still involved in this town. This could turn into some nightmare, me having to send officers out here with a search warrant or some guys with U.S. Marshal badges waltzing into here. Call these guys off. Tell them to go home and play cards."

Franklin reached over and placed his hand on Kelly's shoulder. "I promise I'll take this real serious. If I find out anything isn't the way they promised me I'll toss them out on their butts. I'd never put you in a position like that."

Kelly nodded, then got up and began to walk slowly toward the door. "Looks like everything's coming along quickly."

Franklin smiled as he gestured toward the maze of stacked boxes. "This will be our first night here. I'm not even sure where the pillows are, but we're here."

Kelly fumbled with the door latch. "Mollie's going to miss having Katie within walking distance."

"Oh, once she comes out here a few times she'll realize just how close we still are. Speaking of beautiful girls, have you been back to the store and talked to Laura lately?"

Kelly felt his face flush. "The last time I was there was to pick up some old books."

The two men walked outside together. "Well, I know that she was used to the fast lane in Boston. But I hope that she may find some nice down-to-earth fellow here in Averton. She's certainly been unlucky in that respect. For all the power and money she's seen she's still kind of the shy and vulnerable type. I think she needs someone to keep an eye on her besides a couple of oldsters like Katie and I."

Kelly nodded, and then waved as he hurried to his car. Once inside he picked up a clipboard on the seat and pretended to examine it until he saw Franklin walk back into the lodge.

CHAPTER 7

Kelly arrived home at 9:00 that evening, his eyes burning from reading forms and reports throughout the afternoon and early evening. His temples throbbed in pain from the strain of the tedium coupled with interspersed reminders of yet another uncomfortable talk with Franklin.

He walked in to find Mollie once again dozing on the couch, having fallen asleep reading, her curriculum planning being her primary source of company and refuge. He leaned down and kissed her on the cheek, waking her, and she reached to squeeze his hand.

He stroked her head, and then walked into the bedroom. She remained alone on the couch, where she buried her face in a pillow and sighed.

~~~

Two miles away the meeting room in the lodge was brilliantly lit, though the curtains were drawn. Franklin paced furiously next to a coffee table in the middle of the room ringed by the seated figures of Louie Welch, Pat Milland, Tommy Rose, and Don Hart. In the background, Katherine watched from a doorway with her arms folded and a look of concern on her face.

Franklin stepped toward Welch, vigorously shaking a fist in the man's face and shouting. "A .50 caliber. You brought that .50 caliber here. You dumb ass."

Welch got up slowly but unafraid and shook his own finger toward the much taller man. "Don't lose your head, Frank. No one has anything to go on."

Don Hart spoke when the others fell silent. "What about the plane?"

Franklin turned toward him sharply. "Plane? What's this about a plane?" he yelled.

Welch sat down and waved his hand to trivialize the issue. "It's nothing. The other evening there was some little plane buzzing around out here."

Franklin scanned the room to see Pat Milland sitting with a shocked incredulous look on his face. Welch remained nonchalant but Rose and Hart looked down to avoid eye contact.

Franklin shouted. "Who was in the plane?" He again stepped toward Welch. "What could they have seen?"

Rose shuffled his feet, and then began to speak with a trembling voice. "We don't know who was in the plane. But....the .50 caliber was exposed when they flew over. I don't think we covered it in time."

"Damn you Welch", Franklin thundered, kicking over the coffee table, sending coffee and beer over the plank flooring. "There was no good reason for you to be playing around with that .50 caliber in broad daylight. What will the public think if they hear about this? It's my reputation, my image, that's going to make this thing work."

Hart shook his head. "Look, Frank. The day's going to come soon when the public is going to find out we're more than they think right now."

Milland stood up, arms crossed and one index finger on his chin. "The point you have to understand, Colonel Hart, is that in the proper time and place the mention of us having a .50 caliber would be no big news at all. What Frank's trying to get you to understand is that until the populace is so frightened that they become ready to accept us as their ongoing protectors with no questions asked and no reservations we have to take a very moderate approach."

He stood for a moment in silence, pondering a thought. "In reality the chances are negligible that from overhead anyone would have been able to identify a .50 caliber, especially when flying so low and needing to concentrate on keeping the plane under control. Did anyone specifically see a passenger?"

All sat in silence, either shaking their heads or shrugging. Milland clasped his hands together. "Good. I feel very certain that you can write this incident off to a close call and a lesson well-learned. This is to be the beginning of a national movement, one that will restore the society handed us by our fathers. Right here in Averton and Manchester County is the origin of the move to reclaim a nation.'

"The heartland states will take it upon themselves to take care of business. The Continental Army and the Minutemen before them were formed to preserve the union as the republic that was formed in the 1770's. But we have to accept reality…portions of this nation are lost. Let them do without the Americans who still revere the Founders. Let them get by without those who see the sweat of the brow as the precious nectar that nourishes America."

He looked down at his watch. "I have to catch a flight back east." He scanned the room. "I suggest that each of you listen very closely to Frank. He is going to brief you now on how we continue our national movement. And remember, this is his property and he's taken responsibility for what each of you does in this organization."

It was not often of late that Kelly would wake in a room lit by daylight. He glanced over at the clock to see that it was ten o'clock, twelve hours since he had fallen into a deep sleep. Sitting up slowly on the side of the bed, he stood stiffly and opened a drawer containing his favorite well-worn jeans and Cleveland Browns tee shirt, long neglected since the bombing.

He looked once again at the time and decided that he would go to the office for a while, but only after eating a leisurely breakfast. Walking out of the bedroom and nearing the kitchen, he saw a note on the dinette table. "Went to get some groceries. Might buy some new clothes. Be back before lunch."

He put on some coffee, then went back to the living room and reached for the remote control to turn on the television. However, just then, his cell phone rang and upon answering, he was greeted by the rapid voice of Marcia Young telling him to check his e-mail for the message she had forwarded to him.

Sorting through an accumulation of spam, he finally found the forwarded message and opened it.

"Chief Hastings:

It is apparent that those of us in the Fourth World know much more about you, than you of us. This is because police officers are so identifiable, while one or more of us can (and do) come and go as we please into and out of Averton, watching, observing, and learning. For instance, we know that Mollie frequents the Value-Right food market on the north end of the town, and that she frequently visits the home of the Norwoods, the man of the house who fancies himself to be some sort of civic leader, not seeing the truth, that his only true agenda is to preserve the status quo of Averton – Averton, which looks so much like the U.S., a microcosm of life in America, regulated, measured, divided and unyielding.

Averton is symbolic to us, chosen by a pair of darts, the first tossed toward a map of the U.S., and striking Ohio, and the second dart thrown at a map of Ohio. It was your fate that the dart simply landed nearest to Averton.

That it was Averton has no meaning to us, however, it would make no difference. No matter which state or town it would have been, there would have been the same plainness, the same stifling rules and traditions, and robotic obedience.

The fame of Averton has begun to fade, now. That will not be the case for long, however.

Farewell, Chief. Hail to the chief. You will hear from us again within days as we once again demonstrate the impotence of the state to protect its dependent wards. Wave to every unfamiliar face you see, for it will be us."

Kelly read the message repeatedly in stunned disbelief, reeling from the blatancy of the threats. He called Marcia back and ordered her to activate their recently developed system of summoning all command-level staff to meet at the department at noon. Kelly arrived at the office precisely at noon himself after spending the intervening time making notes to himself and pondering the possible new targets of any new attacks on the town. Most of all he struggled to maintain his temper at the length of time it took for the federal authorities to make the e-mail available to him, especially considering the reference to and implied threat against Mollie.

Even as Kelly entered the conference room, he was uncertain as to what he would say. Therefore, he began the meeting by simply reading the message and when he had concluded simply sat down on the edge of a table. "Since I've been on the force we've never had to go on a precautionary special alert. I wish I knew just what we need to be looking out for. Whatever we do it must be done without drawing a lot of attention."

Kelly stood up and gripped the back of a chair tightly. "We can't panic the town. Right now, we have no way of knowing if this message is a hoax. If it isn't, we run the risk of having someone hurt. If we make an announcement the whole town is going to evacuate itself, for all practical purposes. Then if nothing happens, we'll be even more at the mercy of whoever sent this e-mail, whether it really was the Fourth World, whether they exist or not. Any suggestions?"

Marcia Young spoke up. "Kelly, wouldn't it be best to err on the side of safety and notify the public that we have received a threat? Each and every person could decide for themselves or their family what to do."

Tom Mott, who served as one of the shift supervisors, shook his head. "I think we could have this junk pulled on us every week. The town could eventually die off from something like this."

Kelly stood silent for a moment looking down at the conference table. "I'm worried about the reference to something being imminent. I want the shifts full. No days off for anyone until further notice. Each shift supervisor, you pick one or two officers at random to drive their own cars out of uniform. We don't have enough squad cars anyway but that'll keep us more inconspicuous. Tell all the force to keep their mouths shut about this as much as possible. I have to let just a handful of city officials in on this, but let's control this as much as we can. Watch the night."

Kelly soon wearied of making calls and relaying the news of the e-mail. He put the receiver down after leaving a message for Calvin Meyers then walked to the dispatch desk, marked himself out for an hour and went outside to his car.

In less than fifteen minutes, he was entering the unguarded lane that led to the Norwoods' new home and as he approached, he could see that the only car present was their own. Pulling up in front, he found the older couple sitting at a picnic table to the side of the building playing cards.

Kelly walked toward them, gesturing to the parking area. "I haven't seen the two of you alone out here before."

Franklin patted the bench next to him, where Kelly took a seat. "The remodeling's done, and….I've thought a lot about what you've said to me over the last couple of weeks. I'm sorry, son. I've always had a stubborn streak when it comes to listening to someone younger. I told the boys to cool it for a while with the training. You were right. Some of them just wouldn't listen to me. They were having some fun but there was some lack of judgment. If I let them come back it's going to be with some real clear understandings."

Kelly cleared his throat. "There's something you need to know. This could be a hoax. But, I got an e-mail, allegedly from that Fourth World group. Frank, they mentioned you, sort of in a mocking way. Here's a copy. See what you think."

Katherine came around the table and audibly gasped as she read the references to her husband and to Mollie. Kelly took the copy back and placed it in his sport coat pocket. "You want police protection? Maybe the two of you shouldn't stay here alone."

Franklin sighed and placed his hand on his wife's arm. "I never thought I'd bring about a reaction like this. But....I think we'll be okay out here. It's not like they threatened us. It's the reference to Mollie that scares me."

Kelly nodded in agreement. "I know I'll never talk her into taking a leave of absence from her job. I can't let anything happen to her. That's the husband in me talking. As for the cop in me I couldn't think straight if I thought she was really in danger."

The afternoon had become warm and close and Mollie sighed as she closed her suitcase. Kelly sat on the bedside finding words difficult. "I would have retired months ago if I had ever thought you'd be threatened."

Mollie looked at him and smiled, then knelt on the bed and leaned over and kissed him. "At least I get to spend a few days with my sister. Then I come home and finish planning the new school year." She ran her hand over his cheek. "I knew you were a cop when I married you. I knew some unpredictability came along with that."

Kelly shrugged. "I felt too uneasy about you leaving alone in the evening."

Mollie patted his shoulder. "Don't worry. Beside, with an unmarked car following me, I'll be safe."

Kelly stood, holding on to her hand. "I have to go back to the office. Best not to call me for a couple of days. If this bunch really exists....well, we don't know their capabilities."

Kelly kissed her again. He took a few steps toward the bedroom door, and then turned. "So much has changed, hasn't it?"

Kelly arrived home at nine o'clock that evening but was so restless and concerned about Mollie that he decided to simply go back to his car and join the expanded patrol of the town. All the while, he tried to calculate how far Mollie had driven so far and assumed she was by then nearing Indianapolis.

He cruised for hours scanning vulnerable targets in the darkness imaging how they could be attacked. Next, he began calculating the days since the bombings and murder of Wally March, forty-two days that mocked him and his career, rendering his talents and training impotent. Those days had also seen him succumb to betrayal of the woman who had been gone for mere hours but he missed dearly.

He arrived back home at two A.M., took one of his Xanax and attempted to sleep. However, he only tossed and turned fitfully until seven, then rose and began dressing quickly. He felt nearly manic when he recalled the wording of the e-mail, wondering whether he would receive another communication or face something more drastic.

Driving to the department he passed through a town only beginning to stir, past homes in which the still sleepy inhabitants were dressing and eating breakfast before departing for one of the twenty churches in Averton or spending the morning perusing thick Sunday newspapers. At intersections, he waved to some acquaintances who might have wondered if he knew things they did not.

He arrived at the department that was already more full of activity than typical for a Sunday morning, even since the attacks. The evening shift supervisors were still tracking locations of officers on patrol, much the same activity that was being repeated a mile away at the offices of the Manchester County Sheriff's office. Rural roads leading to the town were also being subjected to increased surveillance. As soon as Kelly walked into his office, he received a phone call from the Adjutant General of the Ohio National Guard advising him of which units were subject to activation if needed.

The morning proceeded at a frenzied pace, giving way quickly to a humid afternoon. Officers called in to report locations, many doing so on personal cell phones to avoid heavy air traffic that could be picked up on personal police scanners, sales of which had multiplied in the community over the previous weeks. Patrols became more concentrated around the most vital buildings as the evening drew near and church activities ended, with few situations in the town involving clusters of citizens.

Most of all Kelly was relieved that the media had not received any leaked information regarding the e-mail. Even though there were more officers than normal on duty, the scene was not so out of the ordinary as to stir the imagination of the few disgruntled correspondents and video technicians on duty around the department.

As the evening wore on, the churches empty, the parks deserted, and the last movie over at the theater, the atmosphere in the department began to lighten up. Still, Kelly kept reminding everyone that the message had implied an imminent threat. However, as the evening shift gave way to the expanded night shift Kelly felt enough at ease to go to his office and doze in his high-backed chair.

In the rear of the building housing the Averton Police Department along with one of the city's two fire stations was an air intake vent eight feet above the pavement. On this warm humid Sunday night, it was the source of the air being chilled by the cooling system for the entire building.

A plain white van pulled up below the intake and a disinterested-looking man in tan shirt and slacks casually got out. He strolled to the sliding side door, retrieved a step stool from inside, and placed it next to the van. Then he took out a satellite dish and carried it to the top of the vehicle. His actions did not draw any attention from his apparent broadcast rivals within sixty feet in another white van and they would not notice his plastic gloves.

But instead of activating the dish, he pulled a canister from a tool pouch and quickly unscrewed the lid. Once the lid was removed and the canister was placed directly below the air intake, a small lever was depressed and the worker scurried quickly down to the street. The driver then walked quickly away in the sparse light, taking off and discarding the tan clothing and assuming the persona of a jogger.

Inside the building, police officers, firefighters and paramedics began to feel their throats burn and their eyes water. Within a minute, they were fleeing the building, the tear gas causing them to seek fresh air and ease the irritated tear ducts. The nausea caused many to kneel in front of the curb in front of the building.

All the while, network cameras captured the humiliating sight of the police department being forced to flee their own building. Within minutes, the news networks were broadcasting the chaotic scene live across the nation.

No sooner than most had assembled outside the sound of explosions once again rocked the town, though not nearly as strong as those that had leveled the armory and power station. In spite of the illumination of the street lights, they could see sparks, flames, and plumes of smoke on the far side of the city.

The scene was one of chaos in the darkness of the Manchester County Sheriff's office, as confused and injured deputies made their way through the building, shouting to each other, their voices confused with those of frightened prisoners contained in the attached jail. Unknown to them another small explosion had taken place a mile away at their radio tower. Throughout the town and county officers and deputies attempted in vain to communicate with their command officers who were either overcome with smoke or plunged into darkness.

Roger Steadman, Chief Deputy and officer in charge, found a flashlight in his desk drawer. He made his way to the outside to join the deputies already at work in assisting the firefighters who arrived from the nearby fire station unaffected by the night's incidents. He was greeted by a scene of electrical wires lying across the ground from power poles sheared at their bases by the explosions. He ran to the back of the building where two deputies were already inspecting the smoldering remains of the emergency power generator.

Throughout the area, the police scanners aired the confused and urgent attempts at communication while citizen band and ham radio operators frantically exchanged information and rumors. Once again the night in and around Averton was bathed in throbbing red and blue lights.

~~~

At all the intersections of roads and highways providing access to Averton, vehicles were assembling from which men emerged carrying spotlights. They positioned their cars and trucks so as to impede traffic, turning on their emergency flashers to draw the attention of drivers and using their beams of the spotlights to motion traffic to stop. The men at the crossroads would step back passively when emergency vehicles would pass through but stop all private ones and speak to the drivers and take note of unfamiliar license plates.

In the town itself, a group of three men took positions around the building that housed the telephone company. A similar deployment took place at the water plant.

Throughout the entire town men carrying hand-held radios and flashlights walked the streets talking to those frightened residents who had not huddled in fear within their houses and apartments. In addition, when dawn arrived, as National Guard troops once again entered the town, the band of men organized by Franklin Norwood was relieved by the company of troops, but not before hearing many expressions of gratitude from police officers, deputies and countless citizens.

By early morning the daylight had brought the restoration of power to the section of town around the sheriff's office as linemen rigged temporary connections. Even the office itself was once again functional within three hours of the blasts, courtesy of a generator brought to the scene by the National Guard. This time there were no deaths, just a few needing attention after being exposed to tear gas. The main lingering problem was the loss of the communications tower and with it the ability to dispatch cruisers and receive information in return. The blasts had been surgical this time, powerful enough to render the police agencies useless for several hours but limited to property damage. Before lunch, new power poles had been hoisted and the old splintered ones were being hauled away. ATF agents were analyzing the plastic explosive charges used to take down the poles and remote tower and destroy the generator.

Helicopters from the National Guard, ATF, and Ohio State Highway Patrol weaved through the skies over Averton and Manchester County looking for unusual activities. In addition, the volunteers scrambled by Franklin Norwood patrolled the roads with their radios, relaying messages to officers.

At the police department the F.B.I. agents called in were examining the canister that had contained the tear gas, looking over the aerosol-type trigger that had been pressed down to allow the pressurized gas to escape. Kelly was huddled in the conference room with the supervisory staff, straining to contain his fury and embarrassment. It was a taunting beyond anything he had ever known, the sight of state and federal forces once again brought in to protect his town, the very protectors themselves driven from their fortress while Franklin's group of largely untrained citizens provided the only continuity of vigilance through the night.

In the background, a television with the sound turned off displayed images of the other previously attacked cities' reactions to the new Averton incidents and clips from a press conference by the Director of Homeland Security. Once again, Averton was the focus of the nation.

That meeting over, Kelly contacted the Sheriff and arranged for an impromptu joint press conference in the city council chambers. To a room full of media they announced a curfew and requested that traffic and phone calls be held to a minimum. They brushed aside questions regarding the group of private citizens who had come to the aid of the town and then the two lawmen went back to their departments to understand what had happened.

Upon his arrival at his office Marcia Young, who held a dispatch sheet, greeted Kelly and he found himself following her to his office. Once inside she handed him the sheet. "We got a call from your friend, Mr. Norwood. He didn't want to bother anyone with this until now but his house was riddled with gunfire last night. He said he heard it at the same time the explosions took place. He could hear them at his place.'

Marcia continued. "We did get a couple of calls around that time about hearing rapid shots but the officers on patrol didn't see anything and that lodge is pretty-well hidden. Of course, everyone responded to the explosions."

Kelly looked up at her with a look of frantic concern. "No one was hit?"

Marcia shook her head. "The windows to their bedroom were shot out but they were already in bed and the bullets either passed over them or lodged in the walls on the outside. One of the feds is already out there with Mott retrieving slugs. They called in and told me that at first glance it looks like it was an automatic weapon."

Kelly stared down at his desk, and then slammed his fist. "I feel partly responsible for this. He tries to help and then someone tries to kill him."

Marcia shook her head. "At least it got him some more notoriety. The story got around and one of the networks arranged to interview him. Look for him on a screen near you any time now."

Kelly sat down and leaned back in his chair. "I haven't heard from Mollie. I'd love to see the look on her face when she sees this."

There was a knock on the door just as Marcia was walking out. Calvin Meyers stepped in waving a sheath of papers. "Just got this from ATF. The power poles, the generator and radio tower....they were all blown with the same variety of plastic used at the power station."

"The detonators?"

"The same as before. It's unbelievable, Hastings. We're dealing with some ballsy folks here. The color of the plastic does sort of blend in with the poles but someone had to manage to press these into place without being noticed."

Kelly rubbed his forehead. "Those are busy streets. People are on those sidewalks all the time. Someone could stop there and pretend to tie a shoelace and not draw notice. Now, with all the media and gawkers around all the time someone could actually benefit from the presence of so many people. It's ironic, Meyers....in a small town like this we don't concentrate much on protecting the cops."

Meyers seemed to stare at Kelly. "I know that you didn't have any serious casualties this time but you seem so much calmer this time."

Kelly laughed. "Getting hyper didn't help me the first time around, did it? I'm just more angry this time. Someone's really yanking my chain. The e-mail, following Mollie, that attack on Frank's home....it's gotten real personal."

Meyers sat down and leaned across the desk. "That shooting out there...there's never been any shooting before. Why wouldn't they try to blow up his house? They blow up everything else."

Kelly threw up his hands. "I wish I knew. I'm just glad they weren't hurt."

"What about this Welch? You picked up anything new about him lately?"

Kelly shook his head. "Not a thing. I have to admit I've let that slide for now. You seem to think he's suspicious, don't you?"

Meyers began to speak slowly. "I'll do anything I can to help you figure all this out. One thing I can do is bring a detached outsider's point of view."

Kelly nodded. "I don't like this Welch, but I see nothing to link him to anything."

Meyers stood. "I hope you don't feel like I'm encroaching."

Kelly shook his head slowly and wearily. "Any help, any type."

Meyers slapped Kelly reassuringly on the shoulder then walked out the door. Driving back to Cincinnati he fought the urge to drive much too fast and it seemed like an eternity before he arrived back in his office. Before he had even settled into his chair he had his phone off the receiver and was pushing buttons as he sat down.

As Kelly woke on a cot in the locker room the next morning, after having three hours of sleep in the last two nights, he found that it took a mighty effort to push himself onto the side of the narrow bed. The hours before he had taken refuge there were a blur of interviews, phone calls, and meetings. He went into the restroom and splashed some cold water on his face, too tired to take a shower.

He trudged to the conference room to see what was on the television and was once again greeted by the image of a network correspondent speaking from his town.

"This is Cynthia Yardley reporting live from Averton, Ohio, a town still settling its nerves after the second wave of terror bombings in seven weeks. Fortunately there were no fatal injuries this time in contrast to the many deaths and scores of wounds suffered in the previous attacks.'

"To update the situation, the law enforcement officials report that all communications have been fully restored".

Kelly watched another replay of the interview he had given shortly after midnight.

"A corps of National Guard engineers has hastily rigged a temporary radio dispatching tower to be used for local emergency and police communications and all residents of Averton and Manchester County now have electricity. In spite of the damage caused at the back of the office when a generator was blown up the Sheriff reports that the office is now fully operational, as is the Averton Police Department. That agency was rendered helpless for an hour after tear gas was released into the ventilation system.'

"A story we are following with much interest is a group of citizens who
        had formed a community watch organization then found themselves pressed into action much more quickly than expected. We have with us this morning the local resident who formed the group, Mr. Frank Norwood."

The scene immediately included Franklin standing next to the reporter. "Mr. Norwood, thank you for speaking with us this morning. I must say you have quickly become somewhat of a local hero here as there have been countless comments regarding how you and your group helped to secure the area while the law enforcement agencies were temporarily disabled." Kelly winced at the comment. "Mr. Norwood, could you tell us a little bit about how the group formed?"

Franklin gave a meek smile, and then began to glance confidently back and forth between the reporter and the camera. "After the initial bombings, as well as the senseless death of Captain March, it became evident that the citizens felt a need to do a little something more to protect themselves and to assist the local law enforcement. Some of us got together and started talking about what we could do. It was unfortunate that we were attacked again but I'm glad we were able to help out."

"Mr. Norwood, is this an organization with a name or formal leadership?"

"We are the Manchester County Citizen Defense Organization." Kelly set down the cup of coffee he had just poured, stunned to hear that the group had a name. "We have roughly seventy members, nearly sixty of whom were activated early Monday morning when the Fourth World launched its attack." Kelly remained motionless, listening to Franklin's words in disbelief.

"You sound convinced that there really is a group called the Fourth World behind these incidents."

Franklin nodded without hesitation. "I've told everyone I've spoken to that I believe that group to be authentic. We should all have seen this coming for years. None of this happened without warning. We've allowed our nation to slip into complacency in terms of individual responsibility and the need to set a clear sense of purpose as a people. We shouldn't be surprised when we now see radicals taking the right of freedom of expression to this extreme, to believe that they can do anything, hurt anyone, to force the whole country to abandon its soul and self out of fear and lack of resolve. That won't happen here. We'll defend ourselves and every other community had better be ready to do the same."

"On that point, Mr. Norwood, have you been contacted by other communities for advice?"

Franklin smiled meekly. "Well, for what any advice from me could be worth, yes, we have been contacted by citizens in all the other communities that were attacked as well as others not. Some people who have worked with us have already traveled to some of those communities and we can expect to see similar organizations being formed around the country."

"And last of all, Mr. Norwood, I understand that your own home was attacked by gunfire during the night. Do you believe there is a connection?"

"I've lived here for many years with no incidents. I can't draw any other conclusion."

The young woman turned back toward the camera. "I'm certain that we will be hearing more from Mr. Norwood and his organization as the situation here unfolds. We also have word that the local police chief received a message two days ago from someone alleging to represent the Fourth World stating that three would be further activities by the terrorist group. I must add that I have not yet verified the existence of that message, nor the means by which it was transmitted. It is not known if the message was even legitimate or merely an eerie coincidence. This is Cynthia Yardley reporting live from Averton, Ohio."

Kelly muted the sound on the television, then sat back and sighed. For all that he had been through over the past few weeks he had never felt so weary and disheartened, and so willing to walk away from the job.

Back in his office, he played mental games, wondering who may have leaked the existence of the message. He knew that he had been forced to disclose it to more people than he would have cared to. He knew that Calvin Meyers would be incapable of such a slip and he reminded himself that the Fourth World itself could have done so to taunt him further.

His thoughts were interrupted when he heard a knock on the door and Marcia Young peered in. "Kelly, we have a live one out here. You need to hear this."

Kelly nodded and a few seconds later Marcia ushered in a pale nervous young man dressed in faded jeans and a blue work shirt. Kelly motioned for him to sit down.

"What's your name?"

"Bobby....Robert Aiken. I live out by the old church lodge, about a half-mile down the road."

Kelly leaned forward in his chair. "What did you come to tell us?"

"I....I was out during the night when Mr. Norwood's house was shot up. I'm sorry I didn't come in sooner....I wasn't supposed to be out in the middle of the night."

"How old are you?"

"Seventeen. My folks were in bed but I went to set some traps along Edgar Creek." The boy grew more nervous. "I didn't come in because I was afraid to turn myself in for trapping out of season….and trespassing." He hesitated, waiting for Kelly to say something.

Kelly shook his head. "Let's don't worry about that. You just tell us what you saw."

The young man breathed a sigh of relief. "I was trying to set some traps on the section of the creek that flows near the lodge. I was gonna' just walk in if I could instead of climbing the fence. I got there and their gate had a lock on it but I just climbed over the gate."

"What time was this?"

"I think it would have been about one, because I saw the clock in the kitchen when I went out the door of the house and that was a little after twelve-thirty."

"What happened next?"

"I went over the gate and walked across the creek. That took me another five minutes to get to the good section. It took me a while to set the traps and I was about done when I heard what sounded like a car nearby. I got down on the ground but I never saw any headlights so I finished up and got ready to head back."

The boy's face turned even more pale and just as he was about to resume Kelly's phone range. "Meyers here. I'm in your conference room. Sorry to interrupt, but Murphy from ATF got back with me. Those rounds that hit Norwood's place were fired from an UZI. That was indeed automatic fire. But the shots were fired up high. Maybe somebody just wanted to send a message."

Kelly hesitated for a moment. "Come in here and join us."

Within seconds, the door opened and Calvin Meyers joined Kelly, Marcia, and the nervous boy.

"Bobby, this is agent Meyers from the F.B.I..."

The boy's face drained once again. "We want him to listen in to what you're telling us."

The teenager took a deep breath. "I picked up my flashlight and the burlap bag I carry my traps in and all of a sudden I hear these explosions. At the same time I hear this gunfire."

Meyers broke in. "How did it sound?"

"It was real fast, like a machine-gun….like you see in those commando movies. I just stayed down until it stopped. As a matter of fact it only lasted for a few seconds. Then it was silent except I heard a couple more explosions. That was when I heard what sounded like a couple of men…laughing. It was real weird.'

"I started to panic and I took off for the road. I don't know how long it took me to get there because I was trying to hurry but stay low and quiet at the same time.'

"I got to the fence and went over and got down in the ditch. I looked at the road and didn't see any cars so I went across, then got down in the ditch on that side. I was still scared and kind of out of breath. I just laid down to get myself back together before going home.'

"Finally I started to get up, and then I got kind of startled when I saw this truck coming down the road, like out of nowhere."

Kelly put up his hand to stop him. "How far were you from the camp gate?"

"Maybe….maybe a hundred yards by that time. I ducked down again and the truck was driving my way, real slow, without any headlights on." The boy reached into his pocket and pulled out a slip of paper. "He was moving so slow and there was enough moonlight that I got most of the license number, except for the last two digits. Here's what I was able to remember of it."

Kelly turned to Marcia, who nodded. "I already gave it to the dispatcher. They're running it down now."

Kelly looked at the boy once again. "What kind of truck was it?"

"A blue Ford truck, I'd guess late 80's. My uncle had one like it."

Kelly wanted to break into a grin. "Anything else you can tell us?"

The boy shook his head. "Uh-uh. But will I get into any trouble for what I was doing?"

Kelly began to laugh. "I have more gratitude than that. You need to tell your parents about this but tell them I said to keep this quiet. We may need some more help from you."

As the rattled young fellow left, the office Meyers gave him an F.B.I. business card. A moment later, the dispatcher walked in and handed Kelly a sheet of paper. Within a few seconds, his face grew dark while Marcia and Meyers sat watching. Finally, Kelly looked up.

"The truck. It's registered to Louie Welch."

Meyers sat upright. "How about we get a warrant and go in first thing in the morning? He may still have the gun at his house."

Kelly nodded. "That surly bustard…..".

Meyers stood up. "You understand, Hastings, possession of one of those things makes this a federal case. I have to notify ATF about this."

"As long as we get him. That son-of-a-bitch tried to kill some people who are like family to me and Mollie."

Meyers rubbed his forehead. "The kid heard men laughing?"

Kelly nodded. "Must have been two shooters."

Meyers leaned toward Kelly and Marcia. "This is a small town. We have to keep an absolute lid on this. No one else in the department, no spouses, no one until we have him in custody. Agreed?"

Both shook their heads, Kelly somewhat stung by Meyers's tone. Meyers then pulled out his cell phone and left for his office to set the process in motion.

~~~

Two hours later a small, older sedan cruised lazily down Watterman Road, approaching the entrance gate to the lodge. A

Lincoln Continental emerged from the lane going in the same direction and the sedan picked up speed to follow. The driver of the sedan picked up a microphone from a radio mounted under the dash and talked with the pilot of a helicopter overhead while attempting to maintain sight of the Lincoln, yet not be obvious in its pursuit. He followed until the vehicles approached the business district of the town, then circled a block and returned, parking the truck across the street from the eatery.

Inside the restaurant, with no one within several feet, Kelly leaned toward Franklin with a distressed look on his face. "I'm crossing over the line right now Frank, but maybe now you'll listen. Louie Welch riddled your house the other night."

Franklin leaned back and began to scoff at the suggestion. "I can't believe any such thing", he whispered. "After everything I've done for him, why would he try to hurt me and Katie?"

"Look, Frank. I can't answer that. I'm just telling you I don't want to see anything happen to you before we can take care of this. Go away somewhere until tomorrow night. Just get away where he can't hurt you."

Franklin leaned back and shook his head. "I've never been so shocked in my life."

Kelly reached over and placed his hand on Franklin's shoulder, then pulled him nearer. "Take this seriously. I really should not be telling you this. I'm trusting you with some very privileged information."

Franklin sighed. "I don't know for sure what I'll do next. I will promise, though, I'll be careful. If I hear anything out of Welch, I'll call you right away. It would look funny if I suddenly disappeared. He's supposed to come out to the lodge tomorrow night. He called me yesterday and said he wanted to talk to me but didn't want to say anything over the phone."

Kelly looked around nervously. "I hope to be able to give you the all-clear by lunch time tomorrow."

"What do you mean? Is he going to be arrested?"

Kelly looked around. "Things will happen in the morning."

Franklin leaned back, appearing relieved. "I guess I can keep my wits about me until then. I've known him for so long it just seems beyond comprehension."

Across the street in the sedan, Calvin Meyers pushed the bill up on his ball cap and quickly raised his binoculars to his eyes once again for just a second. He put them into the glove box and slammed the lid closed, understanding and sympathetic to what he had seen but fearing that his job could be made more difficult.

~~~

Kelly worked through what would have been his normal lunchtime, spending much of the afternoon on the phone and submitting to yet another on-camera interview with a network news correspondent. All the while, he was secretly cringing that he would once again face a round of ribbing from his staff.

Late in the afternoon, he finally had a lull in the action and had the opportunity to lean his head back against his chair. However, the quiet moment was shattered by another phone call and he answered the call abruptly, assuming it would be another reporter.

"My. It sounds like you're having a rough day."

He sat silent for a second, needing to collect his thoughts. "Laura….how are you? I'm sorry I haven't called."

"Uh-uh. With what you're going through, there's no need to apologize. I understand."

"It has been pretty bad."

"I feel so sorry for you. I thought that maybe….oh, I don't know….maybe I could help you work out some of that tension you're feeling. That sounds good?"

"Yes….it sounds really good."

"And you know what? Today's my birthday. We can celebrate. And there'll be something better than ice cream and cake waiting for you. Come here around ten when it's dark out."

"I appreciate how you're always aware of my need for discretion."

Laura giggled. "It's not like we need light anyway. See you tonight."

Kelly heaved a sigh of relief as he set the phone down. He knew that he would have an eventful day ahead, and with Mollie still away, he would have freedom to give in to his greatest weakness. He rationalized that he needed the evening ahead more than he needed rest.

Working on through the early evening, partaking of a vending machine sandwich for dinner, he went on to agonize through a call to Mollie, expressing words of love for her while glancing at his watch to see how much time remained before he was expected at Laura's apartment.

He rushed home to shower and change into old clothes that would make him much less recognizable. In addition, he decided to drive the extra car usually parked around the side of their garage, one that he rarely used.

Nearing the book store, he once again parked around the corner and walked briskly toward the back of the store to the apartment door, sporting sunglasses in spite of the onset of darkness and a ball cap lowered across his brow. Although the neighboring buildings were dark and safely out of hearing range from the Bitterroot, he turned the key slowly to avoid drawing attention.

Closing the door behind him equally carefully, he did not relax until it was secured behind him. Looking upward to the ladder leading to Laura's loft he could see only minimal light, a glow that flickered and danced as it beckoned him.

Taking each dimly lit step cautiously, Kelly took four steps until he could see the candle burning on a stand several feet from the bed. And, on the bed was Laura, stretched out on her stomach in the nude, glancing toward her visitor with a mischievous smile to greet him.

Kelly laughed and shook his head, then tossed his cap into the lone chair in the room before sitting down on the bed next to the petite redhead. Kelly ran his fingers through the cascading hair that reached to the middle of her back, and then continued his fingertips down the small of her back and over and around her buttocks.

Hearing her purring in response, Kelly reclined next to her and resumed his petting. Rubbing his fingers firmly around the nape of Laura's neck, he was again greeted by a warm smile and moans of contentment.

Kelly kissed her on the shoulder and shook his head. "I can't understand how you can just look so much more.....naked, than any woman I've ever seen."

Laura laughed and raised her head to encourage the neck massage to continue. "Do I want to hear how many women you've seen without any clothes on?"

Kelly continued the caressing. "Actually, I could count them on one hand."

Laura gave a heavy sigh. "Speaking of hands, you have the best. This is a treat."

Kelly shrugged. "It's the least I can do for your birthday. I feel like a piker....not bringing you a nice gift....taking you somewhere nice....".

Laura shook her head, causing the locks to cascade over Kelly's arm. "None of that would be safe." Laura raised herself up on her elbows and then turned to view the modest room. "I'm happy to have you here this evening. We're safe here. This is our refuge....a birthday party for two."

Laura lowered her head and once again rested her head on her forearms. Kelly once again began rubbing his hand across the small of her back, then lower to her upper thighs and buttocks. Laura giggled, then began singing slowly, "Happy.... Birth....day.... to... me....".

Kelly began caressing in smaller circles. "Does all this feel good?"

Laura nuzzled her face against his. "Uh-hmm. What a birthday this is turning out to be."

Kelly pulled her onto her side and embraced her before once again commencing to stroke her lower back. "This is your evening…..whatever the birthday girl wants to do."

Laura grew quiet for a moment, then tilted her head and looked at Kelly with a quizzical look and smile. "You mean my sexual wish is your command?"

Kelly nodded. "Of course. Now you have me intrigued."

Laura crawled over on top of Kelly and gazed down at him. She reached to his belt, and began jingling his handcuffs. "I know what I've always wanted to try."

Even in the dim light, Laura could see Kelly's eyes wide open in surprise. "Uhh…well….I've never…. Handcuffed a woman….I mean for fun."

Laura laughed. "Try it. Because then….I'll show you a real good time."

Kelly let out a deep breath and grinned. "It is quite tempting."

"I remember you telling me I was a bad girl. Arrest me."

At midnight, Kelly finished dressing, and then sat down on the bed next to Laura. "Too bad I have to worry about where I'm seen leaving in the morning."

Laura reached up and kissed him. "I understand. I'll always understand. We'll do this again, real soon. I'll see to it."

Kelly stood and began to step away but hear Laura call to him. "Kelly, please, come back here for a minute." He could hear an uncertainty in her voice replacing the unique combination of sweetness and boldness that typified her demeanor. Feeling rattled by her words he sat down next to her. "What's wrong?"

Laura feathered her fingertips across his arm. "We both know things like this don't last."

Kelly simply nodded silently.

"Kelly, whatever happens from this hour on....I want you to know this was never meaningless for me....never just....".

"I don't think I understand what you're trying to say."

"And I don't know how to say it. Just this, Kelly. This was always more than just a physical act for me. You're a great guy."

Kelly stared down at her. "If I were a great guy we never would have done this."

Laura leaned her head against his side. "This won't go on much longer. And it would be better if neither of us felt anything." She pulled away. "You better go now."

Kelly walked slowly away, haunted by the trembling in her voice. When he reached the ladder, he almost walked back to the bed but in the dim light he could see that she had turned away on her side.

As he went down the ladder, he looked toward the tiny figure beneath the sheet with longing, but proceeded on, leaving the store and locking the door behind. He went out into the fresh night air and was back in the car in two minutes.

In spite of the hour, upon arriving home he took a leisurely shower, and then fell into bed experiencing a combination of exhilaration, remorse, and confusion. As he drifted off in exhaustion, his last thought was that it would be a relief if the affair ended so that he could try to reorient himself to the way life was supposed to be.

Kelly had been asleep for just three hours when he was roused by a tapping on the bedroom window. In one motion, he glanced at the clock and retrieved his pistol from the nightstand.

The tapping resumed and he peered around the edge of the curtain to see Laura glancing in. She had a mischievous look on the face pressed up against the window. Astounded, he motioned to her right and walked through the kitchen and out into the garage where he met her at the back door.

As soon as she had stepped inside, she placed her hands on his shoulders. "I didn't know what kind of reception I'd get doing this. I was real careful not to be seen. I won't stay long, either, so no one will see me leave."

They stepped inside the kitchen, now able to see each other in the glow from the street light in front of the house. Laura reached around him and clasped her hands behind him. "When you left, I told you we'd be doing this again soon. Show me to the bedroom."

Kelly ran his hand over her face and felt her back. "You're soaked in sweat."

Laura placed her face against his chest. "Certain things just bring that out in me. I've just paid a visit to one of Uncle Frank's friends. I can fill you in later. But for now…".

It was an hour later when it was her turn to get dressed and leave. Kelly got up and stood beside her. "I guess I just didn't press all the right buttons this time. Sorry about that."

Laura laughed. "That's okay. I recall my toes doing a lot of curling earlier in the evening. I never had to fake it with you. I wasn't going to do that now."

Laura took a step away. "I should have been more relaxed this time. It's the first time we haven't been on camera."

Kelly stood silently stunned by the words. He hoped that he had misunderstood what she was saying. However, she spoke again, this time her voice quivering and breaking.

"Oh, Kelly….you come to my place…. Fool around with me in a motel room I arrange….You're a dear man, but are you sure you're a cop?"

Kelly grabbed the crying woman by the shoulders and swung her around in front of him but she quickly and painfully knocked his arms down.

"Listen to me, Kelly. Listen closely. You'll do anything I tell you from now on. Anything Frank needs, he gets from you."

She stepped away again. "Anything you have, your job, your marriage, it's all in his basket now."

Seeing his astonishment, she stepped closer again. "It was easy to put the blinders on you, Kelly. Now you call your F.B.I. buddy right now. Tell him you got a phone call from the Fourth World telling you that one of the right-wing extremists in Frank's Civilian Defense Organization is going to die. You start telling everyone you know that you're convinced they exist, that they're behind everything. I'll be in touch. Your phone will ring in a few minutes. Answer it."

She reached into a small leather purse, retrieved a package, and handed it to him. "I have things I have to accomplish out of loyalty. Things I believe in. But in another place and time….". She touched Kelly on the cheek, and then sprinted out of the house.

Kelly opened the package and found two video tapes and a small manila envelope. With trembling fingers, he opened the envelope to find a copy of a faded color photograph. It showed a tall muscular man and two children standing at the rim of the Grand Canyon. Now he knew what Franklin looked like in his younger days. There was no doubt that the little girl with flowing red hair next to him was the woman he now knew as Laura Bond. And the boy in his late teens on the other side of Franklin definitely resembled Pat Milland.

He ran upstairs to his office where he had the only VCR in the house. He frantically closed the blinds, then turned on the set and loaded a tape.

Before he could begin watching the phone rang and when he answered, no one replied. He knew the purpose of the call was to cover the story in case the F.B.I. would later run a records check on his line. He tossed the phone to the floor and began watching the first tape.

His gaze was met by the scene from the motel room near Dayton as he and Laura stepped from the whirlpool tub and made their way to the bed. He stopped the tape and ejected it, his hand shaking. He inserted the other video and watched Laura squealing with laughter as he handcuffed her to the bedposts.

Turning the set off and retrieving the second tape, he took them both to the garage and crushed them in a vise. But he knew that there were other copies so he went back into the bedroom, found his phone, and set about to interrupt Calvin Meyers's slumber.

At 5:00 A.M., the agents of the Federal Bureau of Alcohol, Tobacco, Firearms and Explosives took up positions near the riverside cottage of Louie Welch. During the night, the road had been barricaded and manned by the Sheriff's Department and the occasional motorists coming upon the intersections were told to find an alternate route.

Agents waited in tall grass in the ditches along the road, and after being in position for two hours they finally glimpsed a light come on in the cottage. Their plan was to wait for him to begin backing his truck out of the garage, then bring in a car to block him and surround him in the open rather than giving him the chance to barricade himself in the house and make a stand. A hundred yards down the road a suited agent waited with a federal search warrant in his coat pocket.

The agents waited tensely while Welch ate a quick breakfast and when he raised the garage door and got into the truck, whispered information was passed by hand-held radios.

The truck door closed and the nearest agents expected to hear the truck start. Then they would call for the blocking vehicle to come in. Instead, the truck, garage, and Louie Welch exploded into a ball of flames that immediately consumed the house also. There remained not a shred of unburned paper, nor trace of the overnight intruder who had removed the UZI from the house.

~~~

At seven A.M., the Sheriff barked radio orders to his deputies to control the countryside around the area of the river where curiosity-seekers were walking past the roadblocks to get a view of the smoldering ruins. However, of special interest to the police on hand was the scorched and mangled black 1975 Dodge cargo van found in the garage.

Several feet away, Kelly conversed with Calvin Meyers, who pointed to media helicopters circling overhead. "Most famous small town in America, Hastings."

Meyers looked at Kelly with piercing eyes. "Now, let's go over this again. The phone call, you still don't remember anything hinting that Welch was targeted to die?"

Kelly shook his head. "No, there was nothing that would have singled him out. Have you been able to trace it?"

Meyers swore quietly. "It came from one of those disposable cell phones. Now, did you tell anyone what that kid told us?"

Kelly turned to the agent and snapped at him. "Of course not." He felt himself begin to shake. "I guess the Fourth World had him pegged as being in their way."

"Why? Just because he was a member of Norwood's group?"

"It's quite possible", Kelly stated emphatically.

Meyers took a step away. "Tell me, Hastings. Do you think there's any chance of us finding that UZI out at Norwood's place, or anything else illegal for that matter?"

Kelly shook his head with emphasis. "No way. I know Frank too well."

"But Welch was a friend of Norwood's."

"Yes. He was Welch's boss, remember?"

Meyers stared at the scene in front of them. "I wonder how your friend's taking this. Personally, I mean."

Kelly shrugged. "Not well, I would assume."

Meyers appeared to gaze absentmindedly. "Having his house shot up surely must have rattled him. Have you talked to him the past couple of days?"

Kelly felt his face turn cold. "I talked to him on the phone the day after that happened. And I met him for a cup of coffee yesterday. I just wanted to reassure myself that he was okay."

Meyers gestured toward the smoking remnants of the home. "Norwood's been lucky."

Kelly could not bring himself to look at the agent. "How's that?"

"Well, somebody sure did take out old Welch, here. That National Guard captain got nailed in no uncertain terms. A bunch of civilians get blown away. Tommy Brenner and his sister-in-law weren't even part of this, but we thought they were. Now they're six feet under. But Norwood....Welch shoots up his house, and he doesn't get a scratch. Wild, isn't it?"

Kelly shrugged. "Not all of those things are related."

"No, but just the circumstances....". Meyers walked away toward his car without saying another word. Kelly remained standing in the yard watching with rubbery legs as the body bag emerged from the scene and was loaded into an ambulance.

He told the sheriff that he was leaving the scene, then drove slowly back to the department. However, upon his arrival an agitated Marcia Young immediately greeted him. "Kelly. Come to the conference room. We just taped something you need to see."

"What's going on?"

Marcia sat down at the table in front of a television and video tape player, and then pressed a button. The picture cleared, and then Marcia forwarded the tape. Once again, the screen was full of Franklin Norwood, with a sound receiver in his ear, standing in front of his bullet-riddled lodge and addressing an unseen interviewer.

"Mr. Norwood, please tell us again your reaction to the death of Louis Welch, a member of your Civilian Defense Organization."

Franklin started gravely into the screen. "This is a morning of great personal sadness for me, of course. Mr. Welch was an employee of mine for many years until I retired. That's how I came to know him. He joined my organization more or less as a favor and act of friendship to me. I feel very badly."

The male reporter continued. "Mr. Norwood, are you absolutely convinced that this death was a direct result of his involvement with your organization?"

"Anyone who knew Louie Welch knew that he was a man of great strength and determination. Louie died because the Fourth World viewed him as an impediment to their efforts to bring Averton and Manchester County to its knees so that every community in this country will feel afraid to resist when their turn comes. We're dealing with radical extremists who can never achieve their objectives but will hurt as many people as they feel necessary in the process of trying to prove otherwise.'

"These anarchists don't believe in nationhood. Their philosophy, co-mingled with the rampant decay or morality and order in our society can cause chaos. They may try to frighten people like me but they will only validate the need for citizens to take a much greater role in protecting and preserving our society. Just because Communism is on the decline does not mean that there are no longer forces wishing to bring down our orderly and precious way of life, aside from the radical Islamists."

"Mr. Norwood, as you certainly know, we have heard some rumblings from the residents here that they feel a sense of disappointment in their local law enforcement agencies due to the fact that the first bombings and the murder of the National Guard commander were never solved, and now there have been more bombings, including the one this morning that killed your friend. What's your assessment of the law enforcement efforts here?"

"Brad, that's a good question. I know many of the law enforcement officials here, and they're absolutely top-notch. We have to remember that the federal agencies have also been as frustrated by these events. It's not a problem with the quality of law-enforcement, it's a problem with the fact that law enforcement must usually react after-the-fact. They are called in after a crime has been committed. What our organization is about is prevention through vigilance and strength. There is no competition or tension between our organization and law enforcement. We play different roles and hopefully we can complement each other."

Marcia turned off the tape. "How's that?"

Kelly stared at the frozen image on the screen. "He certainly is a confident man."

Marcia sat down again. "Who's going to keep vigilance over the vigilantes?"

"They're not vigilantes. They've done nothing wrong."

"Sarah Talbert called this morning. She asked to talk to me when she was told you weren't here. She asked if we'd heard any rumors about crates of weapons being delivered to the lodge."

"They're not vigilantes."

CHAPTER 8

Calvin Meyers sat in his Cincinnati office tapping a pencil on the desk until his junior partner, Myron Mead, asked what was bothering him. "You may as well ask me now because I know you're gonna ask me to help."

"Yes. I need for you to begin working on another thing. I want you to start checking some more stuff on Franklin Norwood. Go ahead and get started on some more background information while I'm out this afternoon." He handed Mead a slip of paper. "The only real starting point I have is this company he used to own. Start there and work backwards. Check for military service and employment history through Social Security. I don't want to do much checking around Averton. He's becoming too much of a hero."

"I'll start checking it out right away Cal."

Kelly sat alone in the kitchen in the early evening, an uneaten sandwich sitting before him. His stomach was roiling, unable to accept food. The telephone rang and the caller I.D. screen showed that it was Mollie calling on her cell phone. He allowed it to keep ringing and saw that she left a message.

His mind was a void and he could not comprehend how he had come to this point. Within a few weeks, he was the heir apparent to a job he was uncertain he wanted and was now being blackmailed to remain in it.

He thought of the images on the tapes and envisioned Franklin sitting watching them. He imagined the look on Mollie's face should she see them and resigned himself to the fact that his entire life was now guided by the whims of a man who had pretended to be a friend.

The most agonizing question for him was whether Mollie was in danger. He now knew it was the Norwoods from whom she needed protection.

Calvin Meyers arrived at his office the next morning to see Myron Mead on the phone writing furiously on a legal pad. With the other hand, he pointed to a stack of papers on the corner of Meyers's desk.

The senior agent read the first of the faxed document. It was a Department of Defense form indication that there was no computer match found for military service by Franklin Norwood.

The second was from Social Security indicating that the employment records for Franklin began in 1985 in a Pennsylvania foundry. While Mead continued on the phone, Meyers pondered how a man of Norwood's age could have no recorded work prior to that time.

Mead hung up the phone and peered at Meyers. "Yesterday afternoon I called the Ohio Secretary of State's office to ask when Norwood was issued his incorporation papers. Well, he never filed. His foundry in Averton was in his wife's name. She incorporated it and gave a Pittsburg, Pennsylvania address. She owned it. He was listed as the CEO, not the owner."

~~~

The Averton City Council meeting that evening was held in front of a large but rather silent audience, as had been the case over the past several weeks. The citizens sat in tension, fearful of the assembly yet hopeful of hearing some positive news leading to a return to normal in a town under an indefinite curfew.

After hearing a forced, nearly robotic, and partially fabricated report from the Chief of Police, the council strained to conduct more minor but mandatory pieces of business. When it was time to open the meeting to public comment Franklin rose and walked to the microphone.

The man who had been seen several times on national television recited his name and address, an act of protocol that brought chuckles from some of his admirers in the audience.

"I was so sorry to read in the newspaper yesterday that the county fair is being cancelled. I can't blame the fair board for their concern over possible incidents and the point that they made about their legal liability is hard to argue with. But as a private citizen, I'm willing to take some chances. This community needs a little pick-me-up. So, a week from this Saturday I want to invite anyone in Manchester County to come to my place for a community picnic. I've talked to the owners of the field next to me that will someday be the new industrial park. As long as it doesn't rain too much, we'll have plenty of parking. And we're going to mow the woodlands across the road from the lodge. There should be plenty of room.'

"Anyone who wants to run game booths for the kids or turn burgers on a grill is welcome to call my wife and sign up. It's only a few days away but if we use our imaginations we can have a good time."

Carol Moon the city manager attempted to speak above the sound of applause from the audience. "Mr. Norwood....Mr. Norwood, this is very generous of you, especially in light of the loss of your friend this week, but since the fair was canceled due to security questions, well, don't you have the same concerns?"

Once again, there was laughter from the audience, and Kelly winced at the implications of that reaction.

Franklin stood silently, shaking his head. "No, not at all. The Citizen Defense Organization will provide security." Applause once again filed the chamber as Kelly bowed his head and turned away from the direction of the tall graying man at the microphone.

Marie Mentano waited for the room to grow quieter. "Mr. Norwood, are you proposing armed security by private citizens?"

Franklin held up a hand for emphasis. "I'm talking about a process whereby those entering the grounds would be asked to show a driver's license or some other form of identification to prove that they are local residents. As for your question about arms, only those with previous military or law enforcement experience will carry weapons, and those will be out in the open.

No laws will be violated and there will be no concealed weapons, even if the guard has a permit to carry one."

The councilwoman glanced toward the city attorney, who shrugged, then spoke. "We're not talking about anything in violation of law. I'd like to know what the Chief says."

Before Kelly could begin a response, Franklin spoke up again. "I already asked Kelly earlier today. He said there would be no problem from his standpoint."

Kelly felt himself begin to shake. His future was being mapped before his eyes.

The attorney leaned back in his chair. "Then I have to say, I can't endorse this, but there seems to be no legal impediment."

"Then it's on.", Franklin exclaimed.

~~~

Calvin Meyers and Myron Mead got up from their desks, both feeling the need to stretch. Meyers held up a sheet of paper and waved it in front of his partner. "Every time I get involved with something like this I get afraid of some 'courthouse fire'." He glanced at his watch, not really caring about another late evening at work. Once again, he stared at the faxed copy of the birth certificate and read from it: "Born in Allentown, June 4, 1940. Born Katherine Ann Norwood".

"Now tell me, Myron. Wouldn't that be quite a coincidence, two people named Norwood getting married?"

The junior agent murmured. "I'm trying to get a copy of the marriage license."

Meyers paced the floor. "Needle in a haystack. I wish we knew where he was born."

Mead shrugged. "I know. The regional guys are making some contacts in Allentown and Pittsburgh for us. They're checking with the locals for old Chamber of Commerce records, newspaper clippings, the works."

"How about anything on Welch?"

Mead shook his head. "I talked to ATF today. We figure somebody could come out of the woodwork to claim the remains. Somehow, he's gonna get buried. We're in constant touch with the coroner. Unless you're willing to go to the foundry to see his records, we'll have to take the slow road."

Kelly reached his home at dusk, a solitary dwelling on a Friday evening that only weeks before would have held the promise of sometime in the pool with Mollie or a drive down a tree-lined country road. Instead, he sat alone again in the living room, turning on no lights and sipping beer into an empty churning stomach.

The doorbell rang and he rose reluctantly and wearily. He had feared a visit from Franklin for the purpose of issuing more marching orders. But instead of his former friend Sarah Talbert, her steno pad in her hand, met him at the door. "Sorry to bother you at home. But I really need to ask you something."

Kelly opened the door and gestured for her to come in. He turned on the lights then motioned to the sofa, where they both sat down. The reporter flipped open the pad and gazed at Kelly with a determined look.

"I got a call, an anonymous call, saying that you received a warning call that the Fourth World was going to kill one of the CDO members, Can you confirm this?"

Kelly knew that his directions would call for him to promote the story. "Sarah, I'm going to help you scoop the big guys. Yes. That is true."

The young reporter could hardly contain her enthusiasm. "My anonymous caller also told me that you're convinced that the Fourth World is for real."

Kelly cleared his throat and strained to keep his hands from visibly shaking. "I can't imagine how anyone could claim to know what I believe, but it does happen that I do indeed now believe that the group is real. I see no other explanation for all of this. The power station, the armory, Wally March, the attacks on the other towns, then we have this new wave of explosions. Finally, the murder of Mr. Welch. Yes, I'm convinced."

Sarah found herself breathing rapidly. "I want to go back to something I asked you about once before. I heard from another source that wooden crates, the size that could ship weapons, were being unloaded at Mt. Norwood's property. Are you certain that there's no problem with illegal arms there?"

Kelly shook his head forcefully. "No problems. I'm ready to personally vouch for Mr. Norwood. Everything there is on the up-and-up."

~~~

Calvin Meyers had just sat down at his desk on Monday morning when his phone rang. A secretary from the New York office of the F.B.I. asked him to hold for the field supervisor. "Cal, this is Jim Holbrook."

"Jimmy….I thought you'd retired."

"Next month. We almost missed something, it seems. Close call."

"I don't know what you're talking about."

"A couple of our records guys came to me late Friday afternoon wanting to pick my brain. Something piqued my curiosity. They told me how you were asking about a woman named Norwood. Then one of them mentioned that a while back you inquired about some Welch character.'

"I couldn't sleep that night because something kept ringing a bell. I hadn't made the connection when I hear about that car-bombing. It all linked up yesterday morning when I was leaving for church.'

"We didn't have a file on anyone named Norwood. But I remembered a connection with another case I worked on a long time ago. I was investigating a fellow named Marcus Stanton. He was one of the Minutemen who broke off into a bunch called The Continental Army."

Meyers interrupted. "Welch was a member of The Continental Army."

"Yes, he was. His name came up when I was following Stanton around. We busted Stanton in '67. He went to Leavenworth but he died there a couple of years later from a heart attack.'

"It seems The Continental Army had some rather well-heeled friends to keep them in cash. That's where Katherine Norwood comes in. She was a socialite from a wealthy family that was sympathetic to the Minutemen, then The Continental Army when they broke away. Her sister was married to Marcus Stanton."

Meyers hesitated for a moment. "Did you ever know of Katherine Norwood marrying?"

"No, but remember, after Stanton went to prison and we could never pin anything directly on Welch, any investigations on them were closed."

Holbrook continued. "I'm going to fax you copies of what we have on Katherine Norwood and her family. There's background information and some newspaper clippings.'

"We considered The Continental Army to be pretty much out of commission. The leader, that Marvin Symington, went to prison on the same charges that sent Stanton away. Matter of fact, Symington is the only unfinished business in that whole deal. He was the heart of the group, their guru."

Meyers raised an eyebrow. "You have anything on him you can send me?"

"I will. I didn't know that he was of interest to you. But now I can remember records saying that Symington had strange political ambitions. He's run for office on the banner of some fringe party. He even got involved in some tax-revolt populist movement on the national level once. He was sent to the pen and was released on parole in '82. I say he's unfinished business only because after he was paroled he seemed to disappear. He had a son and a younger daughter, and he took them with him. The Bureau looked for him for a while but the Minutemen and The Continental Army withered away."

Meyers thought for a moment. "Can you get me some physical description of Symington? If you can find a photo, see if you could have one of those age-progression drawings done."

Holbrook sighed. "If I were a few years younger, I'd ask why you want that, but if I ask, it may make me delay my retirement. I'll try to get your enhancement. Have fun."

"Thanks Jimmy. And I'll tell you, we don't believe there's a Fourth World."

Kelly sat alone with a fast-food lunch at a park bench on the warm and breezy Friday afternoon, welcoming the quiet in the shade of a maple tree. He had found respite from the reporters and the microphone-wielding interviewers. He had increased his intake of the Xanax, even exceeding the prescribed dosage.

He had also just that morning stared at the bottle of capsules as an escape from the abyss in which he found himself. He fantasized of calling Mollie and asking her to meet him in secret so that he could say goodbye. At other moments, he considered confessing all to the federal agents and asking for reduced charges in exchange.

He recalled the interview with Sarah Talbert and knew that it only deepened the deceptions. It would be multiplied when the major media picked up the story.

Most of all he relived his brief phone conversation with Mollie, pretending that he could only talk for a few seconds, but telling her how much he loved her.

He did love her. He simply could not understand what he had done. And he seriously wondered if he would ever see Mollie again.

The next morning Calvin Meyers and Myron Mead examined the e-mailed photo sent from Jim Holbrook. It showed Marvin Symington as he was photographed upon imprisonment. Meyers nodded furiously as he opened the second attachment and looked at the age-progression image. "No question. It's Norwood. Norwood is Symington."

Meyers taped his finger on another stack of faxed documents. "Here are the papers filed to obtain a Social Security number under the name of Howard Thomas. Fake birth certificate, the whole works. Now here is the stuff he had an attorney use to have his name changed to Franklin Norwood. He and this Katherine did get married, but the name change took place a month later.'

"Katherine Norwood had inherited a fortune from her grandmother five months before they got married. They must have used that money to buy the foundry in Averton. Looks like her father owned a foundry in Pittsburgh, and Symington....Norwood worked there under the name of Howard Thomas. That's how he learned the business. It also gave him a way to hide out. They killed a lot of birds with one stone when they moved to Averton."

For a Saturday morning, there were an unusual number of people in the Cincinnati office of the F.B.I... Meyers watched in amusement as the thirty year-old Mead, dressed in cut-off jeans and a Rolling Stones tour tee shirt handed out fake drivers' licenses to his "wife" for the day, as well as to another "couple". They were extra agents brought in from Cleveland for the day to attend the community picnic at the Norwood property.

The licenses listed apartment addresses in Manchester County and they hoped that no one would pay much attention. The cars they would be in had Manchester County adhesive stickers placed over those reading "Hamilton".

The woman posing as Mead's wife was Carla Moore, particularly noted within the bureau for her ability to memorize a scene and the distance between buildings. She would carry a purse, and then pay a visit to one of the portable restrooms. From her bra, she would remove a tiny camera that would be attached inside the purse at one end. A button would be attached to the strap, allowing her to take pictures inconspicuously. All the others were to make general observations regarding the number of Defense Organization members on patrol, their attitudes, and the number who appeared to outwardly carry weapons. They would stay together, to not stand out as strangers.

Reaching the parking field at eleven, they were directed by men wearing green military-style clothing. Upon approaching a gate that appeared to have been newly installed for the occasion they saw men holding hunting rifles spaced approximately one-hundred yards along the length of the property on both sides of the road. Two were at the gate itself while two unarmed men checked identification.

Mead noticed that the men were only going through the motions of checking identification. The agents believed that they knew why: there were no terrorists to try to enter the gathering. They passed through with little delay and Mead wondered if the locals even realized that the guards were not even bothering to inspect picnic baskets, purses and bags.

After wandering the grounds for a few minutes, Carla headed for one of the blue portable restrooms to rig her camera. The others waited and watched what appeared to be a giant family reunion taking place around them.

The group strolled near the lodge and Mead saw that the Norwoods were sitting in their yard surrounded by reporters and cameras.

The grounds were alive with laughter and the squeals of children winning small plastic prizes at game booths. The fragrance of grilling hamburgers filed the air and there was the frequent "whishhh" of soft drink cans being opened. Several unarmed men in the green clothing wandered through the crowd with hand-held radios but they seemed to have no compelling reasons to use them.

The agents walked to a corner of the grounds and spread out a plastic ground cloth on which they placed their packed food. Carla would turn her purse, and then press the camera button.

These photos would complement those taken by an ATF helicopter that had been posing as a news chopper.

Having eaten a brief meal they returned to wandering through the crowd while photos were taken of the men in green. The security was so lax that they did not even bother to take the camera out of the purse before they left to muttered good-byes from the guards.

On Monday morning, Meyers, Mead, the Cincinnati agents, and several ATF officers sat around a large table in the Dayton Federal Building. They were reviewing a map of the Norwood property with Tom Ebert, the U.S. Marshall for the area.

Ebert shook his head and laughed. "This is one of the most unusual parole violation raids I've ever been involved with."

Meyers drummed his fingers on the table. "I hope we can hold him long enough to rattle his cage and get him talking."

Ebert continued looking over the map. "I haven't heard you mention the Averton police. This arrest is in their borders."

Meyers let out a deep breath. "There will be some limited involvement. But, small town….you know."

Around seven that evening Meyers sped to Averton and walked briskly into the police department and asked if Kelly was there. Upon being led to his office, he closed the door and walked to where Kelly was standing beside his desk.

Meyers reached out to shake hands and when Kelly's own was in his grasp, he tightened the grip and pulled the shorter man closer. "I don't know what in the hell is going on with you."

Kelly broke the grip and stepped away. "What?"

Meyers sat down and waited for Kelly to do the same. "One time, when I was a detective in Detroit, a partner of mine was accused of being on the take. We all believed it. I did for sure.'

"He left the force and went bankrupt. Two years later proof came out that he was innocent. But by that time, he was a drunken bum. His family broke up and he never held a steady job until he died a few years later."

Kelly found himself beginning to hyperventilate. "Why are you telling me this?"

Meyers looked up at the ceiling and laughed. "After that I always told myself I would always give another cop the benefit of the doubt. But I just know you're in something up to your ass with Norwood and his band."

His accusation did not draw a response. He leaned forward and shook his finger at Kelly. "I have no way of knowing right now what you know or don't know. But your friend Norwood's real name is Marvin Symington. He has a real bad history. He skipped parole, and tonight you're going to help arrest him for that." Meyers watched Kelly's face turn ashen. "I will pick you up here at 8:30. You have one last chance."

~~~

On Watterman Road, two hundred yards from the driveway that led to the lodge, a battered, rusty van was pulled to the side of the road with its hood raised. A man in old clothing was tinkering with things under the hood while the cargo area was a technological warehouse where tow of the Cincinnati agents waited.

Inside the lodge were assembled six people in the conference room. Pat Milland was the only one who stood, except for Katherine, who hovered in the background nervously listening.

"I have to say, I've been wholly impressed by the way you've brought all this together. The people in the other towns you've referred to me have been very enthusiastic, and as a matter of fact, I've been contacted by citizens in forty-seven states. One hundred-twenty other communities have already organized their own defense groups. We've had three positive comments made about us on the Senate floor, and even the Attorney General has been complimentary, but reserved, as we would expect."

Milland scanned the room. "When my grandfather helped found the Minutemen, he had no idea that he had cancer. But he would be proud to see his work improved upon with The Continental Army and now this organization.'

"I suggest that the next step be to take advantage of the pledges of support that have come to Frank. Begin running the newspaper and television ads. As you know, I recommend that Frank be the national CDO Coordinator. He brought about this revival and we could have no better spokesperson and leader. I believe that we can now force the government to either clean up what's ailing this country or face having groups like ours take the initiative."

Milland turned to Franklin. "I understand that as far as the local police department, we have free reign on this property?"

Franklin nodded. "I'm confident. I also believe we would have forewarning of any federal moves as well."

Milland clasped his hands together sharply. "I know that some things have happened here that we all feel badly about. There were some deaths that were never planned. Most of all I feel sorry that Captain March stumbled upon Welch prowling around the armory that morning. Welch tried to do his job but his bumbling did him in….his attitude brought unnecessary attention to him. In case any of you were wondering, no deaths in Averton were actually intended. But you can be in your car on the way to do a good deed and cause an accident that takes lives.'

"What happened here only gives us more reason to press ahead and make sure that good things come of our efforts, to see to it that the whole country benefits from our endeavors. Averton will be known before long as the birthplace of a national resurgence of law and order, a new but smaller nation in which communities will have more local control over their own destinies. We want to be less dependent upon the national and state governments to protect us from the terrorists, the criminals, the drug dealers, and the scum of society.'

"The next steps will also be painful. As our members exert pressure, successfully at some point, to cause states to begin unraveling the ties to the federal government, certain things will sort themselves out. There will be some significant migration as folks decide where they want to settle. Texas will be problematic in regard to the cities. But the treaty that brought Texas into the union calls for breaking it up into four or five states.'

"There will be islands within the states. But technology will eventually iron out the logistics. The Northern Peninsula of Michigan will likely break away, and northern Ohio will likely meld with Pennsylvania, southern Michigan or the Chicago region..'

"It is time now to be more cautious with e-mail. Use texting and Twitter, and keep on top of short-wave broadcasts."

Kelly knew that he may be followed, but left the office just minutes after Meyers left and drove to the Bitterroot. He went to the back door, hesitated, then inserted the key and went inside. As soon as the door closed, he heard a voice. "Come on up."

With a mixture of fear and anger, he slowly climbed the ladder to the loft. There he saw Laura in a tee shirt and shorts reclining on the bed with a magazine.

He walked slowly and stood as she sat up and patted the bed next to her. He sat down slowly. "I really don't think I want to know all that you've done. I'm not sure why I came here."

"You want me to tell you that your conclusions are wrong."

"Are they?"

"Sorry."

"I still can't believe I let this happen."

"You had help. I was good. You know, Katie told me that when a man runs into a lay that's too good to be true, he'll still believe it's true. But I meant what I said about how I felt....feel about you."

Kelly laughed. "I know....another place and time."

He took a deep breath. "And you did this because of what you believe in."

"I was raised to believe in certain things. Dad hit some rough times, but my brother and I helped him carry on."

Kelly shook his head. "What would you have done if it hadn't worked out so smoothly? What if I hadn't become Chief? What if Chester hadn't killed himself?"

Laura remained silent and Kelly slowly turned to face her. He saw a look of sincere pity on her face. Fear welled up inside him and he sprung from the bed.

He found himself nearly unable to breath. "Chester.....Chester committed suicide."

Laura stood and slowly approached him. "He hanged himself, that's correct. He just wasn't alone at the time. No one touched him. He was just given directions. But he needed to be convinced by a phone call."

Kelly forced out the words. "What.....what did he hear on the phone?"

Laura strolled back to sit on the bed. "Let's see, it was something like, 'Chester....it's me....Mollie. They'll kill me if you don't do what they want'."

Kelly began to feel as if the floor were swaying beneath him. He backed toward the ladder and took hold of the top rung, but as he tried to descend, he lost his grip and fell several feet to the floor, twisting his ankle and cutting his forehead on the edge of a table.

He scrambled to get outside, then collapsed on the grass and began vomiting. Laura followed him outside, but simply locked the door and walked away. Kelly remained on the ground, wiping his mouth with a handkerchief and hearing Laura drive away.

His ankle throbbing in pain, and his heart broken by hearing of how his mentor had met death, Kelly tried to appear nonchalant as he walked into the department and into his office. He had been able to stop the bleeding from his forehead, but a red mark was prominent.

He sat down at his desk and opened up his word processing program. With trembling fingers, he typed a four-paragraph narrative and signed it, then composed a one-sentence letter and signed that as well. As soon as he had done so, the desk clerk called to tell him that Calvin Meyers was there to see him.

Kelly placed both letters in the pocket of his blazer, then stood and walked slowly to the lobby. Without saying a word to the agent, Kelly followed him to his car.

Near the lodge, the agents in the van had yet to intercept any phone calls, so they were confident that the raid might indeed have remained a surprise. Myron Mead and Carla Moore were getting restless in the confined space.

A sports car slowed down and turned into the driveway. Mead watched through a periscope as it pulled up near the lodge.

Carla watched as he smiled. "What do you see?"

Mead cleared his throat. "One hot redhead."

Carla gave him an elbow in the ribs. "Down, boy."

Mead's cell phone chimed. He listened for a few seconds, and then took a deep breath. "It's time."

Inside the lodge, Laura stood next to Katherine, listening as Pat Milland continued to speak.

"We're starting to see the cracks in the foundation. Our contacts in the other towns are reporting the same type of reactions we got from the community here. The news coverage reinforces that.'

"The right questions are being asked and the right people are arming themselves. I project that within a few months we will start to be taken seriously in our calls for a new constitutional convention and geographical realignments, the first steps in returning to the orderly society our founders intended."

Officers from two federal agencies were now in Kevlar jackets and helmets, inching nearer the lodge. Fifty feet behind them, Meyers and Kelly stood with the U.S. Marshall Tom Ebert, who held the arrest warrant in his hand.

Meyers took Kelly by the arm and pulled him aside. "I want you to stay out here. This is a federal arrest, so I can say that."

Kelly strained to speak. "Meyers....when this is over, there's something I have to talk to you about."

The F.B.I. man did not look at him, but patted him on the back. "I'm glad to hear you say that."

The agents moved closer and took positions behind the many pine trees surrounding the lodge, totally encircling the building. Tom Ebert, along with Kelly and Meyers, walked cautiously behind. They hoped to move quickly so that any news helicopters would not spoil their surprise.

When he was fifty feet from the lodge an F.B.I. agent handed Ebert a loudspeaker. He took a deep breath and began. "Marvin Symington....we have a federal warrant for your arrest. Come out now and surrender".

In the lodge conference room, confusion broke out. Most in the room did not know who Marvin Symington was. Everyone inside froze while Ebert repeated the command.

Those inside crouched below window level and several drew handguns. Katherine bolted for the living room and the agents spotted her movements.

The ATF agent in charge signaled to one of his officers, who readied a stun grenade. With the next signal, Ebert strode quickly up the two steps to the front door, and the agent ran up to the house, broke a window with a hammer and tossed the grenade into the lodge.

As soon as the stun device was thrown, five more agents rushed to the side of the house. When it went off, two more agents carrying a fence-post driver broke down the door.

However, the grenade's flash and concussion had not sufficiently disabled everyone in the large home, but merely disoriented them. And once the agents were inside, Tommy Rose fired wildly with his revolver. There was pandemonium in the house as those inhabitants who could move did so, in all directions. But Rose lay dead in a pool of blood.

Suddenly there was gunfire in several directions and Franklin found his wife, took her by the sleeve, and dragged her to the door leading to the cellar. Calvin Meyers saw them descend as he entered the lodge and handcuffed a wounded Pat Milland. Kelly stood in the side yard with his gun drawn.

To the sound of sporadic gunfire, Meyers shouted to an ATF agent that the Norwoods had fled to the cellar. The heavily armored agent waited to be joined by another, then threw open the cellar door and tossed another stun grenade after them, one that landed next to a case of C-4 explosive.

The Norwoods met their demise quickly as the resulting blast and flash fire filled the confined space. And Calvin Meyers was knocked to the floor, semi-conscious by the following explosion. The entire house filled quickly with flames, and the old, dry wood floors were engulfed.

As the house burned, stashes of ammunition exploded and shot into the air, and once it was decided that any possible survivors were out of the building all others backed away to avoid the random bullets.

The three survivors from inside the conflagration, all ATF agents, gathered on the roadway with Kelly and the shaken and grieving Myron Mead. Fire trucks and Sheriff cruisers were soon on the scene and numerous helicopters filled the sky.

Once the danger had subsided, Kelly and the federal agents joined the firefighters in attempting to locate bodies. However, as he reached a pile of flaming splintered wood, Kelly reached inside his coat pocket. He placed the typed confession to obstruction of justice into the flames, followed by the letter of resignation addressed to the city manager.

Watterman Road was closed to any non-emergency traffic, but just next to the barricades news crews were setting up equipment in the night lit primarily by red and blue flashing lights several hundred yards away. A reporter watched as her camera operator signaled silently as seconds counted down for her to go on live national television.

"This is Cynthia Yardley reporting live from Averton, Ohio, outside the compound of Civilian Defense Organization leader Franklin Norwood. Reports are sketchy, but we have heard that federal agents were attempting to arrest Mr. Norwood for some outstanding warrant. Obviously, things went terribly wrong, and the lodge that was serving as the Norwoods' house has been destroyed by fire. There are also reports of explosions and bursts of gunfire. We are hoping to get a comment from the Averton Police Chief Kelly Hastings just as soon as possible."

~~~

Two hundred yards from the barricades, Kelly stood in his ash-streaked clothing. Once again, the odor of charred wood and burned human flesh made him want to retch. He closed his cell phone, having finished the painful task of telling a sobbing Mollie that her closest friends were dead and that some even more unbearable news about them was to follow. He walked down the road toward the assembly of media and set about to report on casualties and conspiracies.

~~~

Kelly and Mollie sat on their porch swing, neither speaking much but each considering the last few days. Mollie's eyes were ringed in red and Kelly knew that would be the case for some time.

Kelly placed his hand on her shoulder. "Do you think it would help for you to go see somebody....a counselor?"

"Where would I begin? My best friends used us for their bizarre....what?"

Kelly sighed. "I don't know what to call it either."

Mollie began to cry softly. "They used us....and you could have been killed. That poor Laura died because her family got her wrapped up in all that madness....".

Kelly again felt the sensation of having a hard time breathing.

Mollie leaned her head against Kelly's shoulder. "If Chester hadn't killed himself, he would have been so shocked by all this. What family he had...everybody who knew him....they have to live with that awful memory."

Kelly felt his legs turn to rubber.

Mollie sat up and ran her hand across Kelly's cheek. "I hope you don't regret having to retire so abruptly."

Kelly pulled her close. "There was no choice. I blew my credibility with those comments I made about Frank."

"But he fooled us all."

"But I'm....I was a cop."

Mollie took his hand and kissed it. "Anyway, when I think of what could have happened at that lodge....oh, Kelly, you were so lucky."

Kelly stood up and looked at the ground. "Yeah. I was lucky."

THE END

www.ingramcontent.com/pod-product-compliance
Lightning Source LLC
Chambersburg PA
CBHW072229170626
46813CB00003B/1141